PRAISE FOR GUNS ANL

"This book takes the vibe and emotion of *Jesus' Son* and *The Things They Carried*, and shakes it up, telling a unique war-torn, medical thriller story infused with drugs, capers, and layers of trauma. It's Hunter S. Thompson via Usman T. Malik with a dash of Irvine Welsh."

—Richard Thomas, Thriller Award finalist

"Mustafa Marwan is coming out of the gate strong—*Guns and Almond Milk* is an incredible debut, with a gripping voice, enthralling action, and a unique take on geopolitics that introduces you to an often-forgotten part of the world while never forgetting to uncover the depths of humanity to be found there."

—Rob Hart, author of *The Paradox Hotel*

"Tense, fast-paced and propulsive, this novel takes you on an adrenaline-fueled journey into war-torn Yemen where all bets are off. Packed with action and suspense, this book will have you at the edge of your seat as you race through it, devouring every last page. Marwan has truly arrived."

—Awais Khan, award-winning author of *No Honour* and
In the Company of Strangers

"Absolutely amazing. I picked it up and literally couldn't put it down. Darkly comic and beautifully written with many plot twists. *Guns and Almond Milk* has all the elements of a fantastic story of love, grit, thrill, murder, everything. A winner!"

—Pamela Paterson, Amazon bestselling author

"This un-put-downable thriller weaves together two stories: one among high-end thieves in London and another among mercenaries and aid workers in Yemen. The two stories come together through the narration of a sarcastic, sharp-eyed doctor who can see the world clearly—except when it comes to his own emotions."

—Marcia Lynx Qualey, editor-in-chief of *ArabLit*

"*Guns and Almond Milk* is a thrilling odyssey that explores themes of identity, redemption, and the price of one's choices. Marwan's masterful storytelling, rich with cultural and psychological insights, is set against the vibrant backdrops of London and the tumultuous regions of the Middle East, where we follow Luke, a man caught in the crosshairs of his own conflicted existence."

—Ahmed Naji, author of *Rotten Evidence*

"If you can imagine being unconscious in an operating theater somewhere in Yemen while a hideous war without rules is raging around the bedraggled hospital and then suddenly coming awake on the metal table just long enough to glimpse two bloodstained surgeons working away furiously over you who greatly resemble Raymond Chandler and Thom Jones, then you will start to grasp the beautiful monstrosity that is *Guns and Almond Milk*, the brilliant noir debut of Mustafa Marwan both traditional and unheard of, and one worth celebrating darkly. Trust me when I say this book goes places you've never been."

—Lee Durkee , author of *The Last Taxi Driver*

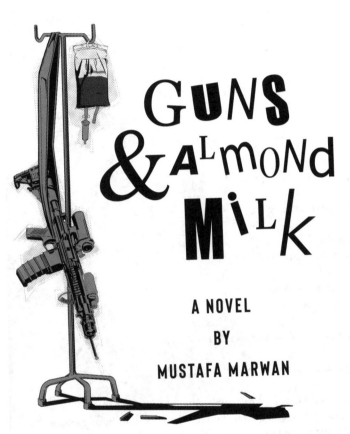

GUNS & ALMOND MILK

A NOVEL
BY
MUSTAFA MARWAN

Interlink Books

An imprint of Interlink Publishing Group, Inc.
Northampton, Massachusetts

For Petal and Peanut

First published in 2024 by

Interlink Books
An imprint of Interlink Publishing Group, Inc.
46 Crosby Street
Northampton, Massachusetts 01060
www.interlinkbooks.com

Library of Congress Cataloging-in-Publication Data available.
ISBN 978-1-62371-105-4

Printed and bound in the United States of America

"I guess I kind of got a foot on both fences, Johnnie.
I planted 'em there early and now they've taken root,
and I can't move either way and I can't jump.
All I can do is wait until I split. Right down the middle."
—Jim Thompson, *The Killer Inside Me*

CHAPTER 1

Present Day, Thursday, 10:13

The road snakes through caramel desert, from the rustic harbor to Aden's only functioning hospital. The sun is yellow and white, shades of my headache.

Seatbelt-free, the driver pushes the three-ton 4x4 beast over 120 kph, challenging the second Land Cruiser with the rest of our medical team to keep up. Next to him is our welcoming committee: Yehia, a young Yemeni nurse with a fixer's attitude. Michael, our team leader, clutches the grab handle above him and nervously peers at the speedometer. The driver glances at him in the rearview mirror and grins.

I'm gazing at the scattered sand outside my window when the car slows as it approaches a stone arch at the entrance to the city. A young, suntanned soldier is waving for us to stop.

He checks our papers as I take in the checkpoint's walls studded with bullet holes like galaxies of black stars. Other soldiers are checking outgoing cars; one is smoking atop a pickup truck with a mounted heavy machine gun, while another is motionless behind a bulletproof barrier, waiting for the one moment in a million when his presence might be useful.

I inhale. The air is bitter, laced with diesel fumes and gunpowder. I wonder what the soldier behind the bulletproof barrier might be thinking of: home, money, love …

"… Metallica!"

The first soldier is speaking to me.

"Excuse me?"

"You like Metallica? Music ... heavy metal?" He's pointing at me as though I were covered in tats, singing "Nothing Else Matters" with a black electric guitar and a mane of hair that would do the eighties proud. Somehow, I feel closer to a lobotomized sloth.

I follow the trajectory of the soldier's pointing finger. Duh. My Metallica T-shirt—the only clean one left after I packed two days ago in London. So much for my situational awareness. I'm tired after our long connections and the boat trip from Djibouti. My two morning oxycodone haven't kicked in yet against the throbbing pain in my head and my fuzzy peripheral vision.

"Ah, yeah. Metallica. They're cool," I say, struggling to remember the last time I listened to them.

"Yes, the best! "Unforgiven" and "Devil's Dance" ... *Black Album* rocks, man."

"Indeed, indeed." I nod sagely, with the wisdom of a Buddhist monk.

"So, you're doctors, huh? Doctors who love Metallica." He chuckles, pleased with his own wittiness.

Michael laughs more than the situation deserves. I purse my lips and shrug as if to say, "guilty as charged." A small trail of cars is forming behind us. Good luck guessing the reason for the delay.

"You look Arab," the soldier says.

"Yes, I'm originally from Egypt."

He scrutinizes the name on my British passport: Luke Archer. "But your name is Western!"

I smile. "It's a long story."

He returns our passports and steps away from the window, a bit disappointed, probably assuming they'd lost another one to the other side. "OK, OK. You go now."

Yehia tells the soldier that the next car is part of our convoy. He nods. Our white Land Cruiser stops about a hundred meters ahead, indicators flashing, waiting for its twin sister.

When the second car makes it through the checkpoint, we merge back onto the road. We haven't yet picked up speed when the explosion hits.

The shockwave slams the seat against my back hard enough to empty my lungs. A deafening roar and a gust of hot wind, peppered with dust, envelops the car and rattles the windows.

I look back. The checkpoint is engulfed in a giant jellyfish cloud of gray smoke, drifting into the sky.

Michael whispers, almost inaudibly, "Sweet Jesus."

The driver stops. He frowns at the flames devouring the checkpoint and the skeletons of the less-fortunate cars and shakes his head. Then puts the car back in gear and moves forward.

"Shouldn't we … shouldn't we go back?" I ask.

"We can't go back," Yehia says. "Those human bombs usually double tap. We'll beat the injured to the hospital anyway." He notices Michael's paper-white face. "Don't worry, suicide attacks are common these days. We call them appetizers."

"I'm sure those soldiers no longer do," I mutter.

Yehia catches my eye in the rear-view mirror. "Welcome to Yemen!"

My pager sits on the instrument tray, the triage code blinking. I ignore it. I'm busy fishing a 7.62 round from the stomach of a sixteen-year-old. The CT scanner is down again, but as far as I can tell, the bullet has not perforated his intestine, which would cause a nasty infection and a slow death. Basically, his chances of survival are either excellent or nonexistent. I don't tell him that. Instead, I finish bandaging him and award him his bullet trophy. They love keeping those things.

He asks, in Arabic, "So, what do I have?"

"A dangerous obsession with a blood sport," I reply with my broken but functional Arabic.

"Huh?"

"You're good for now. Tonight, someone will bring you to do some scans."

"I won't be here tonight," the kid says, trying to sit up.

"Whoa. What are you doing? You need to rest for at least a week."

"I have to go now."

"Your call." At least he will free up a bed, and his mom can take care of him at home. "But make sure that you come back tonight for the scans. Who's coming to get you?"

"No one. I can go back on my own."

I furrow my brow. "Go back where?"

He mirrors my puzzlement. "How do you think I got this hole in my stomach? From eating too much *fahsa*?"

Something is very wrong with the youth in this country. They shove themselves in harm's way as though they've never heard of death—or life. Most of them have the faces of the too young, and the eyes of the too old.

I put my hand on his shoulder. "You can't be serious? You can't go back to the fight in this condition."

He looks at my hand as if he's about to bite it. "Yes, I can. You said I'm OK. Where is my Klash?"

I take my hand off his shoulder. "What I meant was—"

"Where is my Klash?" Panic seeps into his anemic face as he searches under the bed.

Klash is how Arabs affectionately refer to Kalashnikovs, or AK-47s—the assault rifle that's killed more people than any other weapon, including the atomic bomb.

"One of your friends took it. The one who brought you here."

He relaxes. He's still looking under the bed, but this time for his sandals. I try to remember what I was like at his age. My biggest worry was probably an algebra exam.

"Listen, son," I say, in the firmest tone I can muster. "This is not a game. I just stitched your femoral artery. If your wound opens again—which could easily happen if you strain taking a shit—you'll die within five minutes."

The kid fixes me with glassy eyes. He seems to be thinking for a change, then he abruptly lies back in bed and relaxes. "OK, if that's the case, get me some juice. I'm thirsty."

I look at him, thanking God that fatherhood is something I'm not planning on experiencing anytime soon. Then I notice Anne beckoning me to join her in the busy corridor.

Anne is our head nurse and the de facto coordinator of our small trauma team, which includes Michael, Rachel, Emmanuel, and me. I might disagree with her on many things, but she's bloody good at her job and in helping us to do ours. I grab my pager and follow her.

"What's all that about? Femoral injury in an abdomen wound? You lied to him," she says.

I forgot that she understands basic Arabic, as well as a half dozen other languages, gleaned from her decades in the field.

If she had met me five years ago, I would have told her that she was right, that I felt obliged to do something to stop the kid from killing himself. I would probably have apologized, but the oxytocin drip in my brain busted long ago. So I say instead, "Would you prefer him to be dead?"

The pager bleeps, urging me to the triage tent. Pagers have been one of our main additions to the hospital system. Over here, there is more individual ingenuity, patching together solutions with meager resources. But automating operations is a Western specialty.

"That's not your call." Hands on her hips, Anne locks eyes with me.

I head toward the stairs. "I've got to go. And it *is* my call if the kid doesn't know what's good for him. It's called meritocracy."

The triage tent is in the hospital yard that also doubles as the parking lot. I like being here more than in operating theaters. Things are much simpler in triage.

We humans are masters at complicating things. Cats and dogs, for example, can see only a few colors, instead of the explosions of rainbows we register every second. The same is true in Accident & Emergency back in London. Normal people see a mess of blood and pain, contorted lips, and agonizing screams. Patients shout in your ear about how they got stabbed, hit by a car, or shoved the remote control up their asses one lonely weekend. Relatives warn you about the patient's allergy to strawberries or their gluten sensitivity. But you don't see or hear any of that. Whether in London or Aden, you see only the most straightforward of checklists: ABC—Airways, Breathing, and Circulation. This blessing of simplicity is why I like triage.

The tent is busy as usual, but at least there are not many Vascular Sniper cases, which is our nickname for the pattern of injuries we've noticed recently. With a lot of time on their hands, snipers become creative. Head shots are no longer the measure of a savvy sniper, nor even best practice. Snipers now compete to hit major blood vessels. Most famously, the femoral artery in the thigh. This kills two birds with one bullet. First, the wounded soldier drops out of battle, with the Grim Reaper sucking at his soul like water down a plughole. Second, valuable human and logistical resources will be depleted to evacuate and treat the wounded, as opposed to the mere old blanket and rectangular hole needed to deal with dead ones. What a beautiful world we live in.

My first case is raving incomprehensibly. His eyes are glazed and unfocused.

"Hush. It's OK. You're home now," I whisper to him. Then to the nurse, "Get him some morphine."

There's nothing to be done to bring him back. Double tap, two gunshots to the chest. He's in shock, having lost a lot of blood.

Even with the blood spattered on his face and beard, I can see he's in his early thirties. I think of asking his name, but I don't. He's just another case, that's all I need to know. In triage, apathy is good. If I got his name, I'd think of the tragedy that is life and death. I would think of his unfulfilled dreams and crushed hopes. I would think of his mom waiting for him back home. I would think of him as an individual. All while other *cases* are relying on me to save their lives.

The nurse hurries back with the morphine. I shake my head. "*Khalas*. Save it. He's gone."

He has stopped talking and twitching. He stares at the ceiling as if gazing through an invisible hole at whatever comes after this world. I close his eyes for the last time and draw a black mark on his forehead. Here, we sort cases by color. Black: deceased or will be soon. Red: immediate. Yellow: can wait. Blue: minor.

The second case is a young man howling with pain like a wolf in a bear trap. One thing they teach you in triage is to pay close attention to the silent ones, because the ones who scream at least have the strength to make noise. They were right. He has a superficial wound on his left triceps. The bullet went through clean. I feel the phantom limb of a severed emotion inside me, but I ignore it. I tell him to stop shouting, he'll live. I strike a blue line on his forehead.

My third case looks different. A bulky man in his fifties with salt-and-pepper hair and a week's worth of stubble. The reporter badge on his chest declares him to be Karim Helmy, journalist. He's grunting under his ceramic plate. He must have convinced the Golden Belt troops, who control the city, to let him tag along to the frontline, less than twenty kilometers from where he's lying now. It seems that when he got shot, they dropped him off at the hospital entrance and went to catch the second half of today's war game.

I remove the heavy ceramic plate from his chest and Yehia helps with the rest of his clothes, checking for hidden injuries. He wheezes heavily and the bluish hue gradually fades from his face.

"Better, Karim?"

He nods.

I assess his injury. Blood weeps from a bullet wound that pierced his right side, stopping God knows how close to his heart.

The kind of wound that could reach your soul and turn off the lights if you looked at it funny. Tough luck, considering he was wearing protection. He also has head trauma, with disorientation that screams concussion.

"Take any photos that are worth your life out there?" I'm looking at his bloodied camera that he protectively keeps within reach. I'm not usually chatty, but I have to keep him from going into shock.

"I got the son of a dog who shot me. What do you think, doctor?"

"You're going to make it."

"No, I mean the photos. I can't check my camera. I have double vision."

It is incredible how much blood a human has. You get used to it with time, navigating slippery red floors while firefighting death. Karim has lost a lot of blood, and his pulse is worryingly slow and weak. When you lose blood, your heart rate increases to compensate for the oxygen shortage. Having a slow pulse means that the heart is ready for its own coma. Yehia tells me his hemoglobin level is seven, which is almost half what it should be. I stop the bleeding and order him enough IV fluids to fill the Nile Basin.

I finally turn on the camera. The last few photos are blurry and show a surreal mix of sky, sand, khaki pants, and brown sandals. He must have taken them while running for his life. These will go straight to the bin.

"Great shots, Karim. Pulitzer quality." I turn the camera off and give it to him, trying not to look him in the eye.

"Good. I need to be evacuated. We all do. The rebels are coming."

"You're safe here, Karim. You've earned a few months of vacation. I'm sure you're missing the missus."

He snorts with his eyes closed. "I'm out here to get away from her."

I'm about to tag him when his wheezing turns into gurgling. He's drowning, or at least his lungs are. Chest injuries commonly cause hemothorax—the second leading cause of preventable battle-field death—where the lung is squashed with each breath, as blood and air fill its pleural space. The solution is needle decompression, where you pierce the injured side of the chest to allow the trapped air to escape. I take a chest tube and get ready.

"Listen, Karim, you'll feel a bit of pain now. It's because I'm trying to save your life. Don't move."

As I slide the needle between his second and third ribs, he curses and shouts as if I were extracting his soul with rusty pliers. When I'm done, he finally relaxes and breathes normally. I put a red mark on his forehead and gesture to Yehia to take him to surgery.

If you're not bogged down in the triage tent or sticking your hand wrist-deep into the belly of a patient in the operating theaters, you can relax with a hot cup of coffee and watch the dirty gray clouds of smoke ascending from the gunfights and mutual shelling in the distance. You can find solace that some people in this world are dumber than you or that none of the artillery shells flying around have pierced you yet. Otherwise, you can enjoy the humble internet connection in the foreigners' room on the second floor, previously known as the deputy director's office. Last we heard, the deputy director was in a migrant boat traveling anywhere that took him away from Yemen.

I head to the foreigners' room. Emmanuel, or Manu as he likes to be called, winks at me as I enter, like we're old buddies. He's a French surgeon. Anne and Michael are Yanks. I do my best not to hold it against them.

There are two types of humanitarians, I realized early in this job: those who are running away from something, and those who are running toward something. Manu is the first type, a chronic travel addict. Not because of love of other cultures or philanthropy, but because he's constantly fleeing anything permanent: a job, a relationship, a home. He's probably addicted to short-term, long-distance relationships, with an Isabella or a Pierre.

Manu is the youngest on our team, which causes him a lot of trouble in cultures where age is synonymous with authority. Also, he's a strong advocate for teamwork, especially when he screws up. In the past few weeks, he has paged me repeatedly when things went south on him. His standard assessment when I arrived was: "*Zis eez a verry irregularr case!*" as if apologizing in advance. The only irregular thing was, usually, his patients' double strokes of bad luck. First for needing hospitalization, and second for having Manu as their doctor. Still, he activates some paternal instinct in me whenever he does that. If only he knew I have less experience than him as a surgeon, and that I'm no longer allowed to practice in the UK.

I go to my locker and slip a couple of Vicodin in a pack of Tim Tams I pretend to be fetching.

On the wall behind the desk where Manu is sitting, a rectangular shadow of pale paint pays homage to where the portrait of Ali Saleh, the former president, had been for more than two decades. After he was ousted, the country turned from total authoritarianism to total chaos, like a Crohn's disease patient going from constipation to diarrhea. The old clashes erupted again between the Shiite rebels of the north, supported by Iran, and the local Sunni government in the south, supported by Saudi Arabia and the UAE—who later turned against each other and supported different factions. Then you have sponsors of the supporters. The good old slow dance of the American eagle and the Russian bear. A new cold war with new banners for the new millennium. Proxy wars. Preemptive wars. #Responsibility2Protect.

One thing everyone will miss though, with proxy wars, is the fancy titles the good old-fashioned military interventions get. If it were up to me, I would call Yemen's invasion Operation Free the Flamingo. Yes, Yemen is one of the few countries that still have flamingos. Nothing beats a good title. It's what remains when humans become numbers, or at best cameos, and get lost in the fine print. You're welcome, CENTCOM.

I tell Manu that Anne needs him for an amputation.

"Ah, *oui*, I was already on my way." He leaps up from the shared desktop computer, grabs his white coat, and heads out.

I check my emails, waiting for a reply that never comes from a father I never had. I'm about to shut down the computer when—damn! My memory stick is still there from this morning. Shit. I check the recent files. The video is there. Manu must have watched it. I sigh and play it, although I know its content too well.

The camera is in the top corner of the room. The casual setting and the poor quality betray its homemade nature. The woman is lying on her back and the man is plowing her, as if drilling a well in Somalia. Her features become clearer when she straddles him. She's now in control, planting herself on him and rubbing herself against his crotch while looking up, as though receiving revelations. Her expression is of pain and transcendence. Both of them are very intense, with zero tenderness. They are not making love. They are fucking. Blind lust. Stones clashing to produce fire.

I can't watch any more. I close the video and shut down the computer. The black screen stares back at me for a while, until the daily afternoon parade of shelling calls me back to reality. As I leave the room, I whirl back and snatch my memory stick out of the computer, this time not forgetting.

Rachel grits her teeth, one hand squeezing the knee of her faded jeans. Her position is precarious. Any false move will ruin her. She is our Swiss emergency doctor. She grew up in a quiet village near Nyon, but humans can adapt to anything, and her focus is unperturbed by the distant explosions and gunfights that have become like the hum of a fan.

She looks at Manu, who can't contain his winning grin. "I offer you a truce. I can make it worth your while," she says with gritted teeth.

Manu shrugs. "Truces are for those who benefit from them. I don't."

They lock eyes. Not even blinking. Michael and I hold our breath. Rachel pushes the rest of her forces forward across the Austrian front.

"Huh. You've got balls, I give you that," Michael says, assessing the consequences for his nearby troops.

We're on the roof at the residence playing Rhoda, a board game based on medieval European wars. We're sitting next to the kids' rubber pool, inherited from the previous occupants. They were from an international NGO that came for a three-month water project, which was actually implemented by a national NGO. The cost of the expats' salary, per diem, travel, and accommodations were more than double the expenses of the project itself. Not to mention HQ costs, from fundraising to toilet paper. But at least they felt good about themselves and could tell stories at parties back home about how they did their share in saving the kids in Africa, even if Yemen is in Asia.

Anne has long since retired to her room. She doesn't seem like your typical humanitarian worker. In a strange country among strange people, humanitarians usually transform into social Dr. Jekyll, becoming artists in how to massacre time.

Luck does not favor the courageous. Manu's French army sweeps through Rachel's Austrian forces. Her chestnut eyes appeal fiercely to me, but I don't move my British forces to the rescue. She would drag me down with her. Five minutes later, the game finishes with Manu's victory.

The sun explodes when it hits the horizon. A cool breeze is blowing, and life seems worth living. Manu plucks a few beers out of the ice bucket. I don't drink with them. Earlier, I also didn't roast my body under the sun with them. With my olive skin, I never understood the fuss about tanning.

Manu starts one of his "When I was in …" stories. Oh, that's one thing about Manu, he loves telling his war stories. This time, it's about Uganda, where he had a short mission with MSF a few years ago. A small country that, if commercially farmed, could apparently feed the whole of Africa. Manu met a UN consultant there who came to evaluate a mosquito net distribution project for malaria that cost hundreds of thousands of dollars, only to discover that most of the nets were being sold as material for wedding dresses. He laughs as he finishes his story, but I feel I'm missing the punch line.

I gaze out at the sleepy horizon. Our residence is a three-story house in a town of mostly two-story buildings. So much for being low profile. I can see the hospital only a few hundred meters away. If I were to take over the city, these two buildings would be the first I would occupy. Great vantage points and useful back alleys to funnel supplies. We could give Pavlov's house a run for its money—during World War II, a few Russian soldiers managed to hole up there for sixty days against a German offensive.

The intertwined streets wrap around buildings made of black lava rock with multicolored ornamental windows. Some buildings have been touched by the continuous shelling, like a beautiful face with acne scars. The city is chaotic, yet it gives me a sense of space. A stark contrast to London, where everything is organized to look the same. Where nature is tamed and love is calculated.

I heard a few things about Yemen before I arrived. The usual stereotypes. A time capsule of ancient land surrounded by forgotten mountains. A land where the political system is an endless game of musical chairs. Reasons for fighting are abundant, and war is the only pastime for people who are excited to kill and not afraid to die. Besides, it pays more, with fewer working hours, than selling khat in the souk.

Yemen is a democracy in only one respect: any ragtag group

with Kalashnikovs can invent a name and a banner proclaiming themselves "Supporters of" or "Martyrs of" any big concept for which people have died throughout history, like religion or freedom. Then they fight everyone else until they catch the eye of a foreign country, which sponsors them. It's like a continuous "Yemeni Got Guns" talent show.

These days, control over Aden is maintained by the Golden Belt Brigade, headed by General Rahimi, a hardcore militant, and supported by Gulf countries. However, Aden's walls are crumbling under the advances of the northern rebels.

As I work the grill, children are playing a game on the roof of the building next to us, chasing bees and trying to swat them head-on with their palms. They are quite successful. I have never seen anything like it. In every place I've been to so far, people tend to keep a safe distance from bees, not chase and kill them with their bare hands. Cries of joy erupt with each fallen bee. One kid runs in circles, raising his hands and shouting "Allahu Akbar" at the top of his lungs after scoring a hat-trick.

Another group of older kids is having a wrestling competition nearby that's something like a freestyle underage WWE tournament. All this seems normal to the few adults scattered on the other side of the roof, sitting on the ground chewing khat and drinking excessive amounts of jam-sweet black tea.

"I wish I could sail here," Michael says dreamily, interrupting my thoughts. "'Did you know that the flag of the British colony of Aden had a sailboat on it?"

"You know how to sail?" I'm not interested in the discussion, but I'm not interested in awkward silences, either.

"Of course. It's my favorite activity. I only feel alive while sailing or when I'm in the field. Leaving the civilized world and connecting with people on a basic level. Unsung heroes who make a difference. You ever get that feeling?" Michael is on his humanitarian missionary soapbox, sipping an ice-cold Corona with a slice of lime floating in its froth.

"Get off your cross, Michael, we need the wood," I say, putting the meat on the grill. "Only people like Henry Dunant are allowed to say shit like this. The real basic life is when we go back home and do our own laundry and pay rent again."

Michael moves his mouth soundlessly, like a fish out of water. A few seconds pass before he realizes that it's still open and closes it. Manu's whole body is shaking. He's doing that kind of suppressed mute laugh that makes you wonder whether a person is giggling or crying. Rachel only smiles.

"You're being too harsh. I didn't know you hated aid work that much," Michael finally manages to say.

"I don't hate aid work. I'm not even asking for fewer privileges. If we didn't accept how things are, we'd quickly be replaced with others who would. Life is a big prisoner's dilemma," I say, realizing my submission to food-chain philosophy.

After what happened in London, I'd become another selfish pragmatist who can sleep at night by blaming the system. I flip the meat on the grill. "Unlike you, though, I'm no hero. I like it here because I enjoy the fresh honey. Where I come from, honey is full of sugar and preservatives."

Michael turns to Rachel for support. "What about you Rachel, why are you here?"

Rachel sucks her teeth and says, "Maybe because I respect Captain Nemo."

Michael's eyes light up. "Ah. The fish?"

I intervene. "Captain Nemo is a character created by Jules Verne in *Twenty Thousand Leagues Under the Sea*. He's an Indian prince who loses his faith in the world, so he builds a submarine and goes to live in the ocean."

Rachel gives me the pleased expression moms give their children when they finish their meals.

Her face isn't one you would start a war for, which is fine.

Wars have erupted over stray dogs and wild pigs.[1] She has a face that you want to keep looking at. And the more you look, the calmer you get. Her warm, light-brown eyes are different from Tina's icy blue ones. Both their eyes ask thousands of questions. But unlike Tina, the questions in Rachel's eyes are childish ones, like "Do fish get thirsty?" or "What does Santa get up to the rest of the year?" You can keep your sanity with such questions, even if they go unanswered.

Michael squints. "I see. But Nemo the fish did something similar, right?"

She puckers her lips and nods as if thinking. "I guess you're right, Michael. I think they had similar life trajectories."

"These politics are too much for me," Michael says, shaking his head. "I'm here trying to do good. Is that a bad thing now?"

I fix myself a burger. "No. As long as you're not—at best—paint on rust, and—at worst—toothpaste to knocked-out teeth."

I turn to Manu. "Do you want to save the world too, Manu?"

Manu is already tucking into his burger. "*Mon pote*, I don't want to save the world, because I know the world doesn't want to be saved."

I open the door to my room and turn on the fluorescent light, which blinks a couple of times before waking up. The room has white walls with cracked paint and patchy spots that look like yellowish gray vomit.

Mezcal, the house cat, is on a plastic chair salvaged from the

....

1   The stray dog war took place between Greece and Bulgaria in 1925, when a Greek soldier was shot after crossing the border in pursuit of his dog. As a result of the war, Greece occupied many villages in Bulgaria and over 50 people were killed. The pig war of 1859, between the US and Great Britain erupted when an American farmer gunned down a British-owned black boar that had been eating from his field. After weekslong standoff between the two nations, a deal was struck for joint military occupation of the island in question.

rubble of a neighboring physical rehabilitation center. He closes his eyes and emits some lovely vibrating purrs when I rub his head. I smile at him. We accept each other for who we are, which is more than I could say for most humans.

Social activities are tools to avoid the feeling I have now. I take an Ambien and lie on the bed waiting for oblivion, staring at a water stain on the ceiling in the shape of Australia.

The howling wakes me with a start.

Footsteps hurry toward the screams in the room next to mine—Anne's room. It's not the first time she's had nightmares, and I don't feel the slightest inclination to move an inch from under the sheets.

Mezcal retreats to the wall and gives me a scared, quizzical look. I can't blame him. Anne's screams are two decibels away from being heard only by dogs. A few moments later, movement slows down until silence reigns again.

This is going to be a long mission.

CHAPTER 2

Present Day, Wednesday, 10:14

I get dressed at the window, watching the summer rain wash across Aden. Contrary to what you might expect, Yemen is quite fertile, thanks to adequate rainfall, mainly due to its elevation. Maybe that's why Arabs and Greeks called it "Happy Yemen." Who said the universe doesn't have a wicked sense of humor?

I pull on my boot in a hurry, as I'm late again for the hospital. At least compared to world standards—Yemeni mornings start any time after 10:30.

Through the car window, I watch the streets of the tired old city as my meds kick in. Some people see life as a straight line, others see it as a point. Some crackheads see it as a circle. I see it as a wave. Nations go through hills and valleys all the time. Yemen has been stuck in one of those valleys for a while.

Before I came here, I read about its high points, which came when every other nation was down. In Sabaa's time, a woman known in the Bible as the Queen of Sheba, Yemen built its first dam—almost 1,000 years BCE. Apparently, the lack of water in neighboring regions was the main thing that dissuaded Sabaa from controlling the whole Arabian Peninsula. More recently, it was a man-made obstacle that prevented Yemen from controlling the Arabian Peninsula—the British Empire. British money and airplanes supported Al Saud, after whom the Kingdom of Saudi Arabia is named, stopping Yemenis from defeating him almost a century ago.

No empire ever managed to get ahold of all of Yemen. When they managed to conquer a small piece, they were forced to drop it as though it were a piece of burning coal. One Ottoman general described his soldiers vanishing in Yemen the way salt dissolves in water.

Yemen still has rain from the skies, but its neighbors have oil from the earth. This great civilization, which had many woman rulers millennia before women got the right to vote in the UK and the US, is now in such disarray that even its traffic is Mad Max on khat.[2] Nowadays, 70 percent of Yemenis suffer from malnutrition. They lack bread and oil but are awash with bullets and khat. In short, Yemen is no longer happy.

As we arrive at the hospital, I notice the security guard. Instead of his usual bare feet on a chair and cheery "*Hayak Allah*" (May God greet you) to me or "halllooo" to my colleagues, he's standing upright with a pistol instead of his hand-held metal detector tucked into his waistband, smoking with a Golden Belt soldier. Ambulances and pickups are wailing through the gates and vomiting casualties. The fighting has started early. The tent must be a shitshow by now.

In the corridor, staff are congregating and talking passionately, and this is not the usual morning chitchat that Rachel usually shares with them. I'm no longer bothered about being sociable, but at least I know its importance, unlike Michael and Anne, who roll their eyes at how Rachel engages with our Yemeni colleagues. They haven't yet understood that in war zones, when it comes to getting

....

2   Khat is a leaf that people chew and then tuck in their cheeks for hours. It is a stimulant, similar to amphetamines. Westerners might find it weird to see a Yemeni father and a son chewing khat together, but a Yemeni would have the same reaction at the sight of a father and a son drinking alcohol together. Anyway, the city traffic laws are based on a rule that seems to be taken from the Mad Max platinum rulebook: whoever tips the front of his car farther into the intersection wins. This rule in Arabic is called "*Booze* base," with *booze* meaning the tip or front of something. An English equivalent would be something like "winning by a nose."

things done, morning pleasantries are more effective than the four Geneva conventions combined.

The word *garad* is repeated around me, and I'm surprised that even locusts—*garad* in Arabic—are attacking the city. Then I realize they mean another form of destruction. "Grad" is also the name used for Katyusha rockets. The rebels have acquired some and are putting them on display around the city.

On the old television in the reception, Anne is standing watching Al Jazeera, biting halfway through to her knuckles. The rebels are attacking Aden from three different directions. The photo of the Golden Belt Brigade commander, General Mansour Rahimi, flashes on the screen. He's a short middle-aged man with a white beard. He has that glint in his eyes that says, "What I see are nails, and what I have is a hammer." The news clip swiftly transitions to Putin's arrival in Stockholm for a conference on Yemen peace talks. She snaps at me to go help in the operating theaters.

There are so many patients flowing in that Michael, Manu, and the Yemeni doctors are operating in the corridor. I instinctively move toward Manu, who is wrestling, forceps in hand, to remove a bullet from a young man's neck. Yehia, forever stoic, is doing his best to stem the blood spurting from the wound.

Manu wipes away his sweat, muttering, "This is very irr—WAIT!" His shout is for Yehia, who has casually reached in and wiggled the bullet free. He holds it in his hand, smiling calmly at us.

I grin. "Now *that* is what I call irregular."

Present Day, Wednesday, 21:49

The news keeps coming. The rebels are tightening the circle around the city, and General Rahimi's brigade is in disarray.

We're in the basement checking on supplies for the expected surge when Anne screams. She drops the pyramid of gauze she's carrying and jerkily runs to the door.

I search for the scorpion that doubtlessly bit her ass, but all I find is a malnourished gray rat scurrying away. Jamal, the hospital director, lifts his foot and cracks the rat's head when it gets within reach, then deftly flicks it toward the nearest wall. He then goes back to his business, muttering and shaking his head.

The first time Jamal and Anne met was akin to a meeting between E.T. and earthlings. It was three weeks ago, on our first day in Aden, when she interrupted his briefing to ask where she could buy almond milk. Luckily, I had just flooded the opioid receptors in my brain in honor of an expected boring briefing, which allowed me to follow the almond milk discussion with the serenity of a sacred cow. I had to give it to Jamal for his self-restraint, especially when she clarified that she had no allergies to normal milk. I should try his deep breathing technique one day. Michael finally intervened, offering to go on an almond milk-hunting expedition over the weekend. Incredibly, they found some in one of the shops that catered to expats. Who said aid workers weren't good for local economies?

Anne tries to compose herself. Cautiously, she comes back to collect the gauze.

Jamal volunteers. "You can go up if you want, Nurse Anne. This is a man's job. We can do it."

"Excuse me?" she says.

"I mean, you know, this requires a man with considerable strength," he says, choosing his words with care.

"I don't accept the insinuation, Dr. Jamal."

"Which one? That you're not as strong as a man, or that you are not a man?" he replies, confused.

A few minutes later, and with enough tension to achieve Tesla's dream of electricity from the air, Jamal excuses himself and leaves. Anne quickly follows suit.

Michael raises his eyebrows and sighs. "Sorry for that."

I nod in understanding. "Don't worry about it. Not everyone is easy to live with."

Michael freezes. "You know we're married, right?"

Damn it. I'm going to kill Manu for failing to mention this.

We continue our inventory in uncomfortable silence before Michael bites his lower lip and shakes his head. "Shit, man. This situation is getting serious. Maybe I should have kept my condom job."

"What? You worked in condoms?"

"You bet," he says enthusiastically. "I interned with a condom company[3] during my gap year."

"What did you do there? Test them?"

"No, I mean ... well, yes, but not in the way you're thinking. I worked in the Regulations Department."

"How did you get from condoms to medicine?"

"I got fired. Some of the condoms got holes in them, which led to a lot of unwanted pregnancies—and a lot of unwanted lawsuits. We interns were some of the scapegoats."

Intrigued, I ask, "How did the holes come about?"

"In the beginning, we all thought it was nature's usual way of fucking things up. Then we realized that some anarchists in the QA team pricked them just for fun—and they did it after the electricity tests."

"Electricity tests?"

"How else would you test a condom? In a brothel? Condoms are tested with electric currents. If the condom is intact, it won't let them through, get it?"

I blink. "Beats me. Why not use water?"

"A single condom can hold more than a gallon of water. That's neither cost effective nor practical." He sighs. "Anyway, we just need to be careful."

"I don't use condoms much anyway."

"I was talking about getting out of here alive."

....

3   He mentions the name of the company, but I don't want them to sue my ass.

Present Day, Thursday, 07:37

When there's a balance of power, the most vicious of animals can walk civilly past each other, almost nodding in respect. But when there's a power imbalance, either problems or opportunities arise, depending on which level of the food chain you're on. Peace is the exception in this world, not the rule.

In the current conflict, the balance has clearly tipped. Now that they've realized that the pack of hyenas has become much stronger than the old lion, rebels are getting bolder.

Watching out for that imbalance in the streets should be common sense. But common sense is not very common, especially for people like General Rahimi, the precious puppet of foreign powers, who has never walked the streets of Aden, but only observed them from the balconies of his big estate or through the bulletproof glass of his armored car.

We usually commute the few hundred meters back to the residence every day, but we spent last night in the hospital to reduce unnecessary movement. This morning, we decide to go to the residence to get essentials.

"How long are we going to live in the hospital?" Anne asks in the car.

Michael exhales. "I don't know, Anne. All I know is that with these clashes around the city, the hospital is our best shelter until we manage to find a way out, or the situation stabilizes."

"Just for the record," Rachel says, "I think maybe not all of us should go, considering the circumstances."

"You can stay here if you want, Rachel," Michael says, impatiently. "Tell us what you need, and we'll get it."

"No, it's fine. I'm coming," she says, not wanting to argue.

We start our journey, tension saturating the air. Most shops are closed. The few people in the street are hurrying home for cover. Rachel might be right. Even this quick trip might be too risky—maybe only the driver and I should have gone. Would this be too cautious—or not cautious enough? Either way, unlike Rachel, Anne probably wouldn't have entrusted the collection of her panties or stash of Swiss chocolate to anyone else.

The car stops in front of the residence. Michael reminds the driver to park nose out for emergency departure and to keep the engine running, then turns to the four of us crammed in the back. "Make sure to get all your essentials. We have only ten minutes, starting now," he says, in his most *Mission Impossible* tone.

"Ten minutes?' Anne glares at him. "You must be kidding. That's how much time I'm about to spend in the toilet."

I exchange a quick glance with Rachel. She rolls her eyes. Next to her, Manu is yawning.

"Fine, departure is in fifteen, then, but you can take maximum two bags. That's final," Michael says.

"OK, OK. No need to get all macho about it."

We get out of the car. Rachel gestures at Michael to go through the front door first, as though to say, "Go ahead and take the lead, Indiana Jones."

He hesitates for a second before heading toward the door, brandishing the keys like a weapon.

My muscles tense when I see the door ajar. Some wood splinters and paint are gone from around the lock, betraying signs of forced entry.

Michael loses his cool at the sight. He retreats backward to the car, whispering, "Let's go."

"No, wait," I say. "You guys stay in the car. I'll go in."

"What? No," he hisses.

I make up my mind. "I'll only be a minute. I'll get Mezcal." I slip inside before any more protests.

I hate myself for doing this. I'm neither worried about gunmen nor Mezcal. I'm worried about my stash of narcotics.

I have always wondered if I would do and say the same things if I weren't on drugs. People think I'm either brave or reckless. I'm neither; I'm just high.

The thing with these drugs is that they don't just take away your brain-splitting headaches and bad memories. They also take away your fear. Certainty replaces doubt. But without fear and doubt, life can be dangerous.

The living room looks like a herd of rhinos has just passed through. Someone was greedy, but also in a hurry. I head to my room. Mezcal jumps out from under the bed to greet me. His fur is standing on end, as though he had stuck his paw in the socket. I cradle him against my chest. His purring cushions the blow of finding my travel bags gone, along with all their contents.

A couple of old T-shirts and a pair of old jeans are on the bed. One of the T-shirts is the Metallica one I wore on my first day here. Here is our first clue—our robbers are not bloody metalheads.

I'm in my en suite bathroom when a loud whistle fills the air. Then the shelling starts, and I almost dive for cover. The whistling sound tells you how close it is. It's earlier than usual, too.

I unroll the toilet paper holder. A few strips of tablets bound by an elastic band fall into my hand, and I remember to breathe again.

Present Day, Thursday, 08:02

Not a word is spoken on our way back to the hospital. The shelling is getting heavier. We can hear it hitting the parallel streets and see the buildings shake. The rockets don't differentiate between the modest Soviet-style apartment complexes and the bourgeois British colonial-style houses. Even the righteous sun is hiding behind a foreboding cloud, refusing to bear witness.

The driver glances at me as I sat next to him this time. I know what he's thinking. It's not safe to be in the street, but at the same time, there's no way to turn back to the residence.

If a shell were to hit the car and kill them while I kept them waiting, I wonder what that would make me.

The driver holds the radio to communicate with the hospital. "Heavy shelling. Passing Tahrir Street. Tango Alpha Honey Rambo India Rambo." He glances at Anne in the mirror to see if she's going to remind him, as usual, about memorizing the official radio alphabet, but she doesn't even seem to have heard him.

A white car stops a hundred meters in front of us. The car is beaten up and in need of a wash. In desert countries, white is supposedly the preferred car color because it shows less visible dust, although, looking at this one, it seems quite the opposite.

As we draw closer, two heads become clearer inside the car. The driver's door opens, and a young man emerges, raising his head to the skies as if checking the weather. A ball of fire flashes between his legs. He disappears into the cloud of a red and white explosion.

Our driver slams the brakes, and my head hits the dashboard. Someone screams, but I hardly register it.

Rachel is the first to speak. "Is there another road to the hospital?"

"All roads are the same," the driver replies, looking expectantly at Michael and then me.

We're repeating the same mistake of indecisiveness. I shout, "Keep moving. Stop next to them."

Manu sputters, "No, are you crazy? Let's take cover."

"Lightning never strikes twice. Move."

As we move slowly ahead, the passenger door of the white car swings open, but no one gets out. We stop behind it, and I get out with the driver. The passenger screams as we ease him out of the car. His face is paper-white, polka-dotted with tiny red cuts from the blast, and his long curly hair is sticky with blood but not dripping. I check him for other wounds. He has shrapnel in his left buttock. How on earth it got there, I have no idea.

We try to figure out how to lay him down in the back seat of our car in a way that doesn't worsen his wound. He ends up flat on his stomach across the legs of those sitting in back, his face resting on Michael's crotch until we reach the hospital.

We pass the gate with a feeling of dread. It's going to be a long while before we get out again.

CHAPTER 3

"We need to leave immediately," Michael says. "I'm in contact with HQ for evacuation."

He's just finished a series of phone calls. I picture the bosses taking his calls in yet another hotel conference room, surrounded by other white men and women in their fifties, debating about "triple nexus," "localization," and the quality of the hotel's spa services.

"I'm trying to arrange a flight or a boat with UNHAS or IOM out of here." His face is flushed, and he's sweating profusely despite the air-conditioning.

He turns to me. "I'm obliged to report what you did when we get back. I'm the team leader, and what you did put us all at risk."

"I can't argue with that."

"I'm serious, Luke."

"Me too, Michael. I admit it. I'm sorry."

"OK, OK. By the way, did they take everything?'

I nod. 'Yeah, they swept the place."

Anne is smoking and staring at the carpet as if she wants to burn a hole in it. I've never seen her smoke before. Manu is silent, rewinding his mental tape of what just happened.

Rachel stands. "Is there anything else? If not, let's get on with attending to the patients."

Present Day, Thursday, 10:31

In the foreigners' room, I try to shed the morning's extra adrenaline along with yesterday's clothes in preparation for my morning rounds. I swallow a couple of chill pills to help me find my sense of well-being, then I hear the shouting.

Out the window, I see a doctor's worst nightmare: gunmen in the yard. They are marching some injured men directly to the main building without passing through the triage tent. The guard is giving them VIP treatment. I don't blame him.

Some of them don't look Yemeni. They look Western. Where did they come from? Hopefully, this dog food is on someone else's plate.

The trick to amputating a limb is making sure to leave a circular flap of skin that can be closed around the chopped-off bone and flesh, like the wrapping around the end of a sausage. I enter the recovery room in the government troops' wing and head for the teenager whose left leg Manu amputated yesterday. The kid is thin and malnourished, with stubble that does a miserable job imitating a full-grown beard. He was hit by seventeen bullets, all 0.50 caliber, which they mount here on makeshift pickup trucks. The bone saw is sitting to the side, shiny and contented after its hefty meal.

Jamal is standing by the kid. He beams when he sees me. "Here comes the Egyptian doctor to check on you. Bye for now, *ya batal*. All is worth it for the homeland."

It's interesting to see the shift in Jamal's heart. He was pro-rebel until a few weeks ago, when a random rebel shell destroyed his beloved Nissan Patrol. Now, I wouldn't be surprised if he has a Golden Belt tattoo.

On proud display, on a surgical plate next to the patient, are the half a dozen bullets that tore through his flesh and bones. Pointing at them, I say, "There was a fight over these bullets last night, but we decided that you are the rightful owner."

"Oh, thank you," he says with sudden interest, gathering up the trophies. He looks around before deciding to put them under his pillow.

I smile and sit on the side of his bed. I'm glad he isn't the sentimental type who would ask for a last look at his severed limb. Mainly because I noticed that his late leg is still in a black trash bag beside the door, waiting for incineration. I need to have a serious word with the nursing staff.

"So, what happened?" I ask him.

"The insurgents machine-gunned me on the Wehda front."

"What did you do?"

"I screamed and fell down."

Deep breath. "I mean, why did they shoot you?"

"Ah. Last night, I put my faith in God and went there for reconnaissance." He lowers his gaze, then says, "I couldn't fight back. I only had a knife on me."

I nod slowly. "I see." I don't see anything. I haven't felt this bad for a patient since I accidently set one on fire when a diathermy machine came into contact with his alcohol-soaked skin.

Aristotle said that virtue is a middle ground between two extremes. One of excess and the other of absence. Both extremes would be vices. Here, a courageous *batal* has to be in the middle, between recklessness and cowardice, which is obviously not the case for this kid.

Anne gets me out of my philosophical drift when she hurries into the room. "Dr. Archer, we need you in Surgery 2." Since this morning's trauma, she's no longer making any effort to smooth her American southern drawl. She looks as though she has eaten a rat.

"Couldn't anyone else ..."

"No, it's that ... fella we saw on TV earlier."

I compute this in slow motion. Pretty sure it's not Putin. That leaves us with ... bloody hell. General sodding Rahimi.

"Ah, shit. What's his status?"

"Big-caliber chest wound. He's being prepped now. I need you to work on his companion. Superficial injuries."

They must have been the source of the commotion earlier. "Sure thing, Anne. Be right there."

After she leaves, the kid says, looking at his thigh as the blood inside it detours prematurely to the heart, "*Ya* Doctor. Can you tell them it's OK to give me some khat, please?"

I study his stunted figure. One of the reasons half the Yemeni population is stunted is that khat makes you anorexic. Sometimes, what you think is your salvation is actually your curse. Hmm, this could make a nice Facebook quote with Einstein's name on it. Or a fortune cookie.

"Of course not."

"I'm sacrificing my life for the cause, and you refuse to give me some khat?"

I check the measly amount of pethidine in his IV fluid—we don't have enough to go around—then throw the kid two Vicodins from my pocket. He seems unconvinced. I nod reassuringly on my way out. He earned them. "Hang in there, kid."

Present Day, Thursday, 10:51

Two steroid cases from the latest edition of *Call of Duty* are standing in front of Surgery Room 2 in what we colloquially call the West Wing. We usually put government troops here, while rebel forces go to—yep, you guessed it—the East Wing.

Yehia told me that this separation was at the insistence of previous foreign medical teams, to minimize potential frictions. The separation took place despite the observations of the Yemeni staff, who had regularly watched patients share food, tea, khat, and laughter. Fighters who had spilled each other's blood the day before on the battlefield were fighting in the hospital to give each other the last remaining pack of juice in the canteen. I guess life is not a mathematical problem where one plus one equals two, but a biology lesson where context is everything.

Today's gunmen are foreigners. One black and one white. No insignia or name tags. Fatigues, boots, bandoliers, and M16s with fingers parallel to the trigger, in complete disregard of the "No Guns Allowed" signs. One of them even has aviator sunglasses perched on his head. These people take themselves way too seriously. To be fair, it's not only them. There's something in the rugged landscapes of Middle Eastern countries somehow make expats feel like Marlon Brando or Clint Eastwood wearing brand-new Timberlands and carrying a pack of Marlboros. You are finally the hero in your own life story. Until a stray bullet leaves you watching life trickle out of you, with no rewind button.

The first one scans me from head to toe while the other keeps watch on the opposite side of the corridor. I'm holding my forearms up high, as I've just finished washing them with soap and iodine and am ready for surgery.

"You can put your hands down. We are not going to hurt you," the white one says. His accent is rough, foreign. Maybe Russian.

I roll my eyes.

His Black colleague smirks. "Sorry, doc," he says in a London accent. "They don't see much of *ER* where he comes from."

"Do you mind?" I say glacially to the Russian, who is still blocking my way to the door.

The Russian hesitates for a second before he steps aside, saying, "Make sure they—"

I shut the door before he completes his sentence. Two patients are in the room and a third is on the floor in a body bag. The more serious case is indeed General Rahimi. He looks older and less groomed than on the television. He has fluids running through his veins and a hole in his chest the size of a pear, from which blood is slowly but confidently oozing through the bandages. I could put my fist in there. It must have been from a 14.5 mm anti-aircraft gun.

Injuries from this cannon are not uncommon here, but surviving one is. Lucky bastard. Or maybe unlucky, for getting shot in the first place.

The rest of his chest is soaked with iodine in preparation for surgery. The nurse has already finished prepping the surgical tray next to him. Two giant milky ampules of propofol, a reliable short-acting anesthetic, stand ready for action. Michael Jackson's preferred way of knocking himself out and the cause of his current long nap.

I turn to the other patient. I wouldn't be surprised if he's an Eskimo, completing this Tower of Babel of mixed nationalities. He's on his back, bare-chested and seemingly in a deep sleep. His left shoulder is covered in bloody gauze. He's been lucky. His face is turned toward the wall, but I can see that he's white, tall, and bearded. The same beard that foreigners sport in movies when they want to "blend in" in the Middle East, unaware that they stick out like a polar bear in the desert, no matter what they do. I go for the medicine cabinet and pick out two novocaine vials and a syringe. As I'm filling up the syringe, I glance back at the man, and I freeze.

He's staring directly at me with piercing blue torches. Scary eyes, and yet with their own share of fear. He looks different. His hair looks like he's recently spent too many days on a hike, and his face is as bronzed as if he'd overslept in a tanning salon. But it's him, alright. He moves his hand to grab his gun from his fatigues on the ground. I drop the lidocaine and we do a quick synchronized dance, with me raising my hands and him raising a Glock 43. He still likes that bloody pistol.

"Luke! What the hell are you doing here?"

"Fuck me! I could ask you the same thing, Max."

"Cut the crap, you little prick. Who are you working for?" he says, checking his surroundings and the saline solution running through his veins.

"I work here. I'm an aid worker."

"Yeah, and I'm Mother Teresa."

I cock my head to have a better look. "Max, is that a Popeye tattoo on your forearm?"

"Oh, fuck. Why do you care?" He rolls his eyes. "It's my lucky charm."

"Lucky charms make you lucky. This ... this makes you dorky," I say.

"Rich coming from you."

I pause, then say, "I'm a doctor, Max. I never told you that before." I shake my head in embarrassment before adding in a hushed tone, "Technically, an ex-doctor, as I got sacked before we met, but they don't worry much about that here."

"You aren't going to operate on me, pal. Not in a million years."

"I'm happy to be as far away from you as possible. But you wouldn't want to swap me for the surgeon who'll operate on your friend here, even to cut your nails. They call him the butcher."

He looks at the General and weighs his options. "Are you trying to convince me this is a fuckin' coincidence?"

"I'm not trying to convince you of anything. You think I ever wanted to see you again, after you left me in a pool of my own blood?"

"I saved your life, you ungrateful little shit." He pauses, then pouts determinedly. "I choose the butcher."

"For God's sake, Max, this is not the Mayo Clinic. Your wound is superficial, but you lost a lot of blood. Let me help you."

I hold his gaze as Michael, a Yemeni doctor called Tawfiq, and two nurses enter the room to work on the General. Max finally relaxes and gives me his arm.

Silently, I patch him up. When I finish, Max sits up and grabs me, pointing toward the General. "You want me out of your hair, don't let this man die."

"Don't worry. He has our best doctor."

CHAPTER 4

London, September 2000

With a flourish, Dennis unveiled seven bottles of ice-cold lager from a cooler he had stashed under his older brother's camping gear. Six bottles were quickly snatched and one remained. All eyes were on me. I wished there were just one other person, it didn't matter who, to share my lonesome choice.

My parents had warned me this day would come. It was the last weekend of school break when Dennis, one of my on-and-off friends, had invited me over.

"Um, I'll pass. Thanks," I mumbled, pretending to focus on the Catan board in front of me.

Dennis tried to get the spotlight off me by explaining how alcohol was a big no-no in Islam. "As bad as, I dunno, believing that Jesus is coming back," he said.

I should've held my tongue because everyone was even more confused when I explained that Muslims actually believe that Jesus *is* coming back.

This made it harder for me to say no when an immaculately wrapped spliff materialized moments later. All I wanted was to fit in, but at that moment some of the girls were looking at me like I had just landed from Al Rub' Al Khali desert on the back of a flying camel.

I took two careful tokes, swallowing the rich smoke and trying not to cough. I passed the joint to the next eager hand and lay back, watching the cities unfold in the board game a hundred miles away.

For a few seconds, nothing happened. But then I felt like I was being sucked inside my soul. Vibrations curled around my spine and sprang through me like ripples in a lake. My body hummed like a fridge. After two more hits, my brain turned into a big fluffy cloud. Noticing my heavy tongue, I kept my slowed speech to a minimum. I ended up dead last in the game, having built a wild maze of tracks, with no home and no destination.

Ricky Martin was playing in the background, never tiring of repeating his "Livin' la Vida Loca" for the zillionth time that year. One of the girls invited me to dance. I don't remember her name, but she was blonde with cute freckles all over her face.

"Um, maybe in a bit?" I felt dizzy sitting, let alone dancing.

"Come on. Don't be shy." She smiled. Her body was swaying with the tunes like a cobra responding to a street performer's flute.

Dennis laughed. "Shy? Him? This bloke does mad things you wouldn't believe. You should have seen him jump off that twenty-meter cliff in Cornwall last summer. We dared him, and he did it. Balls of steel, but a brain made of marshmallows."

If they only knew that I took that dare just for moments like these. To feel like a valued member of the group. Unlike them, I felt I had something to prove.

"He's a regular James Bond. Luke isn't even his real name," Dennis said, turning a suppressed cough into a hiccup.

Dennis, you wanker.

"Wait, what? You changed your name?" asked Freckles.

"Really? What's your real name?" someone else asked.

There I was. Fifteen years old, trying to explain the most taken-for-granted feature any other kid had. No wonder I hated both my names.

My biological parents named me Adam Elraey. I was born less than a year after they migrated from Egypt to the UK.

My dad, not seeing any blonde cheerleaders rolling out the red carpet and hugging the tired masses yearning to breathe freedom when he landed at Heathrow, became a construction worker. Back home, he was an engineer; in the UK, what he found was minimum wage and a shoebox in Ladbroke Grove ghetto.

The problem with immigration is that only the few good stories float to the surface, the Magdi Yaqubs or Mo Salahs, atop the mortal heaps choking unnoticed beneath them.

My parents also quickly realized that the West's diversity coin had the words "which means you become like us" written on its flip side. Dad purposely chose the name Adam, common in both the Arabic and the English-speaking worlds, to show that we're all the same and all that jazz. My father was a Muslim, you see. He believed Muslims had a lot in common with Christians and could integrate easily into their cultures. After all, both religions thought that Jesus was the Word of God. What a man my dad was. What ended up happening was that I was an Arab with the English, and English with the Arabs.

Freckles smiled after I told her my real name. "Adam is nice. I like it better than Luke."

I shrugged. "Sorry for that."

"You never told us why you did it, though? Were the same people after you?" Dennis asked, the weed either fucking with his brain, or giving him an excuse to bring up a topic he knew I didn't like to discuss.

"What same people?" Freckles' eyes were wide with excitement. Sea blue with corrugated rivers of blood red.

Dennis hissed in Freckles' ear, in a whisper that everyone heard, "Some skinheads offed his dad."

Her eyebrows arched and she put a hand to her mouth.

That much was true. This was even before 9/11 further clarified that the enemy of the new era was the religion with the most diverse followers on earth.[4] A few months after my mom died of

---

4   Arabs comprise only about 14 percent of the world's Muslims.

breast cancer, my father got into a fight with some skinheads who called him a "dirty Arab Muslim" as he returned home from work in Kilburn. Things escalated, and he was shanked seven times, twice in the heart. Apparently, the same gang had beaten up a Sikh wearing a turban a few weeks earlier, calling him the same names and completely unaware that he was neither Arab nor Muslim. Maybe it was the force of conviction that time with my dad. There were two measly arrests, and they got manslaughter charges, not even murder. Neighborhoods like Kilburn and Ladbroke Grove are not the ones with police patrols, or even regular garbage pickup.

I was seven at the time, sitting at home with our neighbors' fourteen-year-old daughter, who had been watching me after school since Mom died. A female cop came and leaned down to my level, telling me that my dad was in the hospital, and it would be a while before I saw him again. Did I have any relatives nearby? No? Was I OK? What kind of stupid question was that? I didn't even ask about my dad right away. I only asked if I could hold the walkie-talkie dangling from her hip.

Sometimes I wondered, Did my dad know how he was killed? Why was he created? Where he'd gone?

I'll spare you the details of your life changing in a second, at an age when you still literally piss your pants, so I can spare myself any fake sympathy. I don't believe people can understand, anyway.

"I don't get it. Why did you change your name?" Freckles asked.

I fidgeted. Her eyes on me were high-watt interrogation spotlights. "I took my adoptive family's name."

After spending six months in the Lonesome Orphans' Orphanage—no kidding—in the East End, I was adopted by Mike and Ruth Archer and continued moving clockwise, this time south of the river. They were an English couple in their fifties who had converted to Islam; white baby boomers clinging to the mirage of better times. They collected old stamps, still cut out newspaper clippings, and went for Sunday walks in the park. Neither of them knew how to use computers and they didn't believe in gluten sensitivity.

My new mom never liked my first name, so it became Luke. Not after the *Star Wars* character, mind you—she wasn't that progressive—but after Lucky Luke, her childhood comics hero. Anyway, it changed most of the time to Loki, the mischievous Swedish—or whatever Scandinavian country's—god, depending on how *naughty* I was. She said the music of my new name made me sound friendly and successful. Like tax lawyers and football players. Maybe she meant friendly *or* successful. But I kept my thoughts to myself.

Dennis stood on wobbly feet. "You guys want more beer?"

"Sure," came the almost unanimous reply.

He turned to me, embarrassed. "Um, Luke, you want a Coke?"

"I'm fine," I said. "I'm going to get some air."

Outside, the moon was cold and brittle. Like old hopes. Casting shadows I couldn't reach. It followed me until I got home.

I felt less like myself that night and decided that weed was no good for me. Little did I know that, less than three years from that night, the shit I'd be consuming on a regular basis just to keep afloat, would make weed seem like herbal tea.

London, October 2001

Someone once said that you have three personalities. One is what you think you are. The second is what other people think you are. And the third is what you really are.

My new name was my alter ego—what I thought I was. The old me, Adam, was a clear outsider to the others. And between Adam and Luke, the real me had gotten lost. This rebranding wasn't enough, not for a world that loves simple answers. A world of resumés, not achievements; cute noses, not kind hearts; words, not actions.

I spent my Lambeth school days like a turtle without a shell. Fragile. Different. And with no place to hide. Things were tolerable until my skin color and 9/11 jointly conspired against me. It took only a few days for the New World Order to start taking shape, after a bunch of morons—who could fly planes but not land them—went through those buildings. 9/11 was a radio signal that broadcast on all wavelengths. The compassion wavelength, the hatred wavelength, the solidarity wavelength, and the fear wavelength. Everyone reacted according to their heart's own frequency.

I asked my adoptive father, Mike, about 9/11 and the people who did it. An amateur gardener, he talked about flowers and thorns. He said he never understood why people were attracted to the thorns instead of the flowers, when it came to religious teachings. In morphology, he explained, thorns are extensions of leaves and have one function: deterring animals from eating the flower.

What happened next is what you would expect for cannibalistic societies, witch covens, or high schools. The spotlights persisted despite all my efforts to blend into the shadows. The school bully, Dave Banks, stopped me with his pack of hyena friends.

"What's the difference between a jihadi and a virgin?" he asked, then answered, "A jihadi is trying to die, but a virgin is dying to try." When I didn't laugh, he took offense and started a fight.

From that day on, Dave Banks made it his mission in life to turn everyone in the school against the Middle Eastern terrorist boy, and unfortunately, Dave was extremely popular—for reasons beyond my comprehension. He was your classic handsome-dumb jock. "Camel Jockey" became my official nickname. One thing I never managed to absorb was how some people have the incredible ability to flip their position from perpetrator to victim. You see it everywhere around you, and the majority buy the lie. No wonder science fiction is more popular than science.

I began working out, as well as dipping into boxing and martial arts. Since my first fight with Dave, not a day has passed without at least fifty push-ups. Yet I knew I wasn't in a cheesy coming-of-age movie, and that I couldn't face off with Dave and his gang, Spider-Man style, and get away with it. The best I could do was ignore them, and if that didn't work, stand up to them, even if that meant a bloody nose every once in a while, until they decided to pick on someone weaker. My tongue didn't help much though. Throughout my life, there was a shortcut that bypassed any brain filters, allowing it to utter things guaranteed to get my ass kicked.

Mike and Ruth never knew about the bullying, and for that I was proud. It was my own problem to take care of or live with. Besides, Mike's attitude in life was perfectly reflected in the stoic motto on his desk: "Relax. Nothing is under control." Meanwhile, Ruth was bedridden from multiple sclerosis and withering day by day in front of our helpless eyes. Thank God they never heard the stories about how I'd changed my name because I was a jihadi spy, or how I was waiting for the right moment when I would come to school with fireworks around my belt. It's ironic given that jihad actually means to exert effort to better oneself.

When I scored high marks in chemistry, a kid I'd never spoken to before told me, "Nice work in chemistry. When will the bomb be ready?" Out of the corner of my eye, I saw him high-five Dave. But the snickers of the passersby were what cut through me.

Are teenage years evidence that humans are worse than animals? Some animals are natural predators because they need food, but they don't prey on each other like humans do. When was the last time a lion systematically made it his mission to make another lion miserable, just for kicks?

London, January 2002

Omar took me aside on my way home. I didn't know much about him except that nobody messed with him and that he was a part-time drug dealer (and two years later, my drug dealer). He told me he knew about the pickle I was in at school and offered to "take care of things" for me if I joined his "team." I refused. I wanted revenge, but I wasn't ready to be in his pocket or go to jail. He laughed at me and told me how dangerous it was to be on my own in this world, and to get back to him if I decided to grow some balls.

Less than a week later, after Friday prayers in Finsbury Park Mosque, Noor came up to talk to me. He told me that my situation was God's way of offering me a road back to religion, that once I joined his religious studies group with Abu Qatada, grew my beard, and stopped talking to foreign girls, God would put angels on either side of me and no one would be able to touch me. He said he could teach me some *dua'a* that would make me invincible and put fear in the hearts of the Daves of the world. I thanked him for his advice. He shook his head and told me that the more I was alone in this godless world, the more danger I would be in, and asked me to come back when I grew a heart.

I knew I had problems, but I didn't want to solve them by becoming one. On Fridays, I kept praying in the same mosque as Noor and living on the same street as Omar, but I didn't take either of them up on their offers. I kept a stiff upper lip, studied doubly hard, and walked a tightrope.

CHAPTER 5

Present Day, Thursday, 12:15

In new settings, you can surprise yourself by how quickly you pick up new habits. Like becoming addicted to the shoe polish called instant coffee, in a country that, until the mid-18th century, was the sole producer of the beans of this most respectable addiction.

I'm in the canteen, halfway through my second pint of shoe polish and wondering how Max's reappearance in my world might affect me. I have not seen him in five years and yet here he is, in the least likely place possible. It seems like another lifetime when we last met. I feel the same embarrassment you get when Facebook reminds you of the clumsy status updates you posted when you first signed up. Except these posts had consequences. A dusty attic has opened in my head. Darkness and memories are spilling out, and the weight of the past is crashing down on my shoulders.

Yehia and another male nurse are chewing khat at the table next to mine, under a sign that says it's strictly forbidden in the hospital. They tuck the wads between their cheeks and teeth, and the leaves slowly ooze juice.

"I'll give you the Klash for a dozen cartons," Yehia says.

"No way. Unless your Klash is gold-plated!"

"Ten then."

"Not even four," the other nurse scoffed.

"Nine."

"Are you joking? I can get two Klashes for that."

"What about my 9 mm? That's a rare commodity these days."

"Klashes are better than pistols," the other nurse says in an unconvincing tone.

"The market is flooded with machine guns. It's supply and demand. Besides, pistols are easier to conceal."

"OK, six cartons of imported Marlboros for the pistol."

"Done." Yehia bangs on the table.

I receive a bleep for a case on the second floor. Yehia follows me, asking to have a word outside. We go to the hospital yard as he smokes a cigarette. We stand next to the small makeshift museum of rocket shells, a collection of all the near misses that have fallen on or near the hospital since the beginning of the conflict.

I try to ignore the bulge in his cheek, but I can't. "You chew khat every single day?"

He shrugs. "How else can we work for less than a dollar a day and still come back the next morning?"

Good point. Not that I have the moral high ground. The only thing that puzzles me is the timing of their khat consumption. Most government offices close at 2 PM in Yemen, and people start chewing around the same time or a bit earlier, but always after midday. This simply means that your average Yemeni worker will be wide awake and energetic at night and sleepy and lethargic during the workday. Go figure.

Yehia inhales deeper than usual, his hand trembling slightly. "How are you?" he asks.

I nod, distracted. Then I realize he's genuinely waiting for an answer. "Not as bad as many people around us."

"Speaking of which, I hear he's stabilized," he says.

"Huh? Who?"

"Who else? General Rahimi."

"Oh, yeah. He's a lucky bugger."

"He's going to affect us more than a mere bug. Him being here with the rebels closing in is nothing but trouble for us."

"You think I don't know that?" I sigh. Max and General Rahimi, my double jeopardy. "What do you think is going to happen next?"

"Akrami won't stop until he finishes the job." He says "Akrami" like a devout Tory would say "Margaret Thatcher."

"Who's Akrami?"

"He's the head of the elite rebel force that ambushed Rahimi's convoy today. Last month, when Akrami took over Dar Saad, he made a video next to the bodies of Rahimi's soldiers, telling him that he's next."

"Shit."

"It's getting worse. More of Rahimi's men have entered the hospital, and now they're occupying the roof. I hope he gets dick cancer and dies before it's too late."

"Dick cancer is very rare."

"Balls cancer. Ass cancer. Any type of cancer."

My pager bleeps again. I leave Yehia with his cancer-inducing cigarettes.

The patient is in his mid-twenties with long hair and a fierce gaze, as if sizing everyone up for a fight.

"Who is this?" I ask Anne.

She looks at me like I spat in her coffee. "He just got transferred from the tent. He was screaming his lungs out. Doctor Malone is asking you to be ready for appendicitis once blood results are in."

She's still pissed at my reckless stunt at the residence. I ignore her formality and look at the patient. "He's not screaming now."

She shrugs. "I'm not his mother and he doesn't speak English."

"He seems to understand us." I cock my head at him. "Isn't that right, my friend?"

His Adam's apple shifts with an involuntary nervous swallow. He fidgets slightly, focusing his wide unblinking eyes on me. I would bet my left kidney that he understands English. I move toward him, putting my hand on his abdomen. "You have appendicitis, right? Is it continuous or intermittent pain?" I ask.

He shuts his eyes as if remembering to feel the pain and grunts, "*Mabahky inglizy.*"

I move my hand to the left side, under his rib cage, and ask, "More pain here, right?"

His eyes are still shut and his grunting increases. Dr. Ismail, a British-Egyptian doctor and one of my medical mentors at King's College, taught me that, as a rule of thumb, when in severe abdominal pain, patients don't shut their eyes but rather open them widely, monitoring every one of the doctor's hand movements.

"I'm sorry, I don't speak Arabic. But I think you'll be well enough to get out of here very soon."

Anne throws me a look that translates, in any language, to "You lying bastard."

"*Kos okhtak,*" the boy whispers.

I pretend I don't understand the most insulting curse in Arabic: "your sister's pussy." A curse that perfectly illustrates the patriarchy of Middle Eastern societies, targeting the female members of a man's family as if they were his Achilles' heel. It doesn't even mention what might be wrong with the sister's reproductive organ. The mere mention of it is enough to cause shame and invite myriad creative images of dishonor.

I whisper to Anne on my way out, "Don't prioritize his tests. It will come back negative anyway, and when it does, throw him out."

"How come, Sherlock? You didn't even speak his language."

"Elementary, my dear Watson. Otherwise, I'll go down in history as the first doctor to discover a left-side appendix."

Present Day, Thursday, 13:01

I put my plastic meds bag on the toilet tank after dry swallowing two Vicodins, then I meticulously spread tissues on the toilet seat. I make a mental note to find a suitable hideout for my meds bag after Manu almost found it while preparing our new sleeping spots.

The toilet paper is soaking wet from the seat, so I delay number two and pee standing. The glory of a standing pee. One of the rare benefits that no progressive age can take away from men.

Shouts come from the hospital yard. Still peeing, I crane my neck to look through the small bathroom window. Seven or eight armed men are storming through the gate, everyone scrambling away from them. Michael emerges from the triage tent to see what's going on and freezes. The boss seems to be the one with the largest beard, in the middle. He sports a Klash strapped to his shoulder, with an extra banana clip taped to the original one for ease of reload.

Are these reinforcements to secure the General's temporary residence, or rebels with a cause? The answer comes quickly. They are strolling rather casually and chatting, as if there weren't the slightest possibility of being observed. As if what you can't see can't hurt you. They are halfway through the courtyard when the boss signals for the group to disperse with a wave of his hand.

Then a single shot hits the boss smack in the middle of his forehead, and he drops as if his bones had turned into rubber.

I flinch. In high school, I'd read in *Keen Jugs* magazine that stopping mid-pee can improve pelvic muscles and hence help with premature ejaculation, an obsession of my dying-to-please teenage years. I don't remember the last time I practiced this before other obsessions took hold, but I have certainly turned off the tap now.

I imagine Max holding his breath to steady his shot. He must have aimed a bit lower than the head, as from this range, any sniper rifle would drift higher.

Everything fast tracks. The armed men run in different directions, taking refuge behind cars and the walls of the main building. One idiot enters the triage tent in confusion, sees how flimsy it is, and exits—only to be met with a barrage of bullets. His Kevlar deflects them, so he shoots in all directions before a round hits him in the nose.

Michael is scrambling on his knees to hide behind the rear of one of the ambulances. The engine side would offer more protection—not the trunk side, you moron.

Max and his men have the vantage point on the roof. The shooting continues. More rebels come through the gate. One ducks behind Michael's ambulance, who quickly raises his hands to show that he doesn't have a gun.

Shit. I start connecting the dots. This timing is not random. I run to the second floor, fly unzipped.

When I get there, the man with the left-side appendix has already finished off the first of the General's two Yemeni soldiers, who had replaced Max's team on guard duty. The second is shooting frantically, and he has the assassin pinned behind the cement handrail of the opposite stairs.

I quickly duck from the corridor into the makeshift rooms and move through the curtains toward the General. Max promised to leave if the General made it.

I reach the General's room through the side curtain. My hands are already up when the second soldier directs his gun at me from his place by the door. He whirls back to the corridor when something rolls across the ground toward him.

A grenade.

He moves quickly, leaning down to pick it up and send it back. I throw myself flat on the ground next to the General's trolley, open my mouth so the shockwave wouldn't rupture my lungs, and cover my head with my hands.

He's about to touch it when it goes off. The soldier flies back and falls headfirst. It wasn't much of an explosion—not the kind you see in the movies. Just a lot of sparks and smoke. Throwing myself on the ground instead of running probably saved my life.

The smoke is heavy. Had this been the plan all along—to

distract the General's elite team with an outside battle while the appendix assassin worked his magic?

What now? The second soldier is shredded on the floor, his Klash a foot away from me. Should I pick it up and defend the General? Why would I do that? I owe Max one, but not to the extent that I'd kill for him.

I decide to backtrack, but the appendix assassin leaps through the smoke and into the room with admirable gusto. It's done.

I freeze, hoping he doesn't notice the conspicuous Klash next to me or remember how smug I was with him. He points his gun at me, and I nearly let loose the pee I interrupted earlier.

An abrupt full stop of a gunshot.

The bullet hits the assassin in the solar plexus. He staggers for a moment, gasping as if trying to breathe underwater, before falling into the small fire in the corridor.

I look at the General, my ears still ringing. He's conscious. Oxygen mask on his face, drips running into his veins, and ... a gun in his hand. I put my hands up. He raises his, slowly, the muzzle pointing upward, his finger off the trigger. It is impossible to breathe from the smoke, and the heat of the room would rival a sauna with a broken thermostat.

The ringing in my ears recedes, overtaken by the patients' screams. I unplug the General's drip and take him out of the burning room through the side curtains, where two patients cower under their beds, wrapped in a confused pile of sheets.

Max is running down the corridor with the English bloke, guns drawn. They stop when they see us. Max stretches out a hand, motioning to his comrade to lower his gun.

I glare at him. "We're even. Now get the hell out of my hospital."

Present day, Thursday, 14:37

The dust settles, leaving a lingering cloud of shock. Although we're in the middle of a war zone, a hospital usually provides a layer of insulation. This layer has now been ruptured with a bang.

Max and his men confirm our fears. They don't intend to leave the hospital anytime soon. Instead, they barricade the hospital gate with their armored Humvee and gather in the canteen, now their makeshift command center.

Our expat team and a few local staff who couldn't leave during the shootout are asked to stay in the basement until further notice. Two of Max's men finish searching the hospital for any more rebels. One of them is the Russian, whom I heard Max call Piotr. He looks like the kind of offspring a couple would have if they had consummated while a wrestling match was on the television and metal music blared from the radio. The second one looks like a bull, if bulls had crew cuts, constant red Viagra faces, and spoke American English.

"Where were you?" Michael asks when I enter the basement.

"I was in the toilet," I say with a tired smile.

"Why are you smiling?"

I'm thinking of an Egyptian play I saw many years ago. The actor was playing a Middle Eastern dictator. When he was asked, "Why did they rise up against the government?" he answered, "I don't know. I was in the toilet when it happened."

Something crucial is missing in my communication with other people. The worst thing about being lonely is that you don't share inside jokes with anyone. Instead, I need to pantomime through a thick glass wall to be understood. I relate to Edgar Allan Poe, who said, "And all I lov'd, *I* lov'd alone."

"I'm trying to stay positive," I say.

He shakes his head.

Rachel, ever the practical one, asks, "What's the plan?"

"Shall we call the police to secure the area around the hospital?" Anne asks.

"What police? The police are gone. The whole military is gone," I say.

"We're safe here. This is a hospital, for God's sake. We're doctors. Civilians!" Michael says.

"How many civilians do you see shot every day in this war?" Rachel asks.

Michael shrugs helplessly. "We're between a rock and a hard place. We can't stay here if those mercenaries are taking over the hospital, and we can't go out to the rebels. For all we know, they might be the same group who beheaded that American contractor on camera last month."

I look around. Paint has flaked off the naked walls, and a faint, sweet, putrid smell permeates the basement. Cobwebs decorate every corner. Two rusty wheelchairs are next to a big autoclave from the Age of Dinosaurs, along with loads of dust-coated supplies, mainly cotton and different shapes of gauze. A small, high window faces the front yard. It's covered by old, yellowed pages from a newspaper, from the time of the Arab Spring uprisings. I can't help but notice a headline: "THE YOUTH AWAKENS." Below the headline is a photo of smiling youths cleaning the streets around Tahrir Square, where the peaceful sit-ins that toppled the regime took place. In that fleeting moment, their faces held hope that would soon be smashed into tiny, jagged pieces.

Just one week ago, the only way to navigate through the basement was by swimming. It was full to the ceiling with mountains of donated, half-expired medications from different parts of the globe. Shipments were dumped on the hospital without even an inventory list, leaving the gigantic task of sorting it to the already overstretched staff. Who would donate near-expired piles of statins to a country in the middle of a famine? Manu and I volunteered to help, but after one day we realized the amount of work needed and we bailed, leaving the local staff to their fates. Now I see they did an excellent job.

Yehia walks in, carrying the television from reception. Is he serious?

"What's that for? You don't want to miss an episode of *Dihbash*?"[5] I say.

Anne intervenes. "I told him to bring it. We need to follow the ceasefire talks. Who knows how long we'll be stuck here."

Rachel rummages through her backpack. "Speaking of which, we need to pool our food resources."

"Whoa." Michael raises placating hands. "Let's not jump to the worst-case scenario already."

Rachel looks up at him and asks, matter-of-factly, "What are you unsure about? That humans need food or that we're trapped in a war zone in the middle of a famine?"

"Still, that's an invasion of privacy," Anne says, frowning.

Rachel glares at her, but before she can respond, we hear footsteps at the door and Max enters. He's still pale from blood loss, but his shoulder injury doesn't seem to be limiting his movements. He looks like he's in his element. Unlike the civilian clothes he wore back in the multicolored world, which were too tight for his soul, fatigues fit him perfectly. He strides to the center of the room. Silence falls. He would have made an excellent primary-school teacher.

"We're sorry for this inconvenience. You will all remain here under lockdown until we receive reinforcements or until evacuation. This is for your own protection."

We exchange looks, but nobody speaks.

"How many of you are here, um, *doctor*?" he asks me, cocking his head at "doctor," with a shadow of a smile.

....

5   A famous, borderline racist Yemeni TV show about Northern Yemenis. Basically, a "dihbashi" is more or less the Yemini equivalent of a chav or a redneck.

He might be a good soldier and potentially an excellent school-teacher, but as an actor, he makes Arnold Schwarzenegger look like an Oscar winner in comparison.

I look pointedly at Michael to take the lead, but he studiously ignores my gaze. He seems about to have a heart attack. I finally say, "If you're talking about the foreigners, we're a medical team of five."

"Nationalities?"

"Two Americans, one Swiss, one French, and one Brit. But I'm not sure how many of the local staff—"

"OK," Max says, interrupting. "Locals and patients who can leave are free to go. The foreign medical team stays. My men will help you arrange these sandbags more strategically."

I notice for the first time the sandbags poking out from behind the autoclave. "You can't bunker here," I find myself saying, my voice higher than intended. I sodding hate bullies.

Everyone stares at me.

"Is that so, Doctor ... what was it again, Loki?"

I swallow my tongue.

Rachel comes to the rescue. "We are not part of your war. Hospitals are protected under international humanitarian law as—"

"May I interrupt you there, Ms. ...?" Max says, amused.

"My name is *Doctor Kessler*," she responds, ice-cold.

He matches her tone. "Doctor Kessler, please don't mistake this for a criminal court hearing. This is not a democracy, and I'm not here to argue." He shakes his head in fake disappointment. "I was actually expecting gratitude. Those people out there would happily sell you to ISIS slave markets. You're in better hands than your poor planning could ever have managed." He lets his words sink in. "On the other hand, evacuation will come more quickly if we all stay together. You can't leave us here to get slaughtered. That isn't very humane now, is it?" Another pause. "Are you the boss around here?" he asks Rachel.

Michael says, as though there's a cork in his mouth, "Um, I am ...."

"Great. You and your team will continue taking care of the remaining patients here in the basement. Of course, we're expecting you to take care of any of our injured soldiers as well." He flashes a barracuda smile at Rachel. "I'm sure there's something in your international human rights about that."

Manu corrects him. "International Humanitarian Law—IHL." His face reddens under the weight of everyone's stare.

Max turns to Rachel and shakes his head in the direction of Manu. "That too. Now, how much food have you got?"

"None. We don't have any stocks," Rachel answers in a rush, with an unblinking stare.

Max looks back at her, tired of arguing. He inhales. "OK. We'll include you in our food rations. But don't expect fresh veggies and almond milk." His gaze lands on Anne. How did he know, or does she just look the type?

He meets the eyes of the expats again, totally ignoring our Yemeni colleagues, whom he hasn't addressed. "That will be all, everyone. And remember, you can't explain your international rights to bullets."

Anne musters up her courage and says, "I need to call the American embassy." She says this tight-lipped, emphasizing "American."

"Of course. Give them a sat phone." Max signals to Piotr.

We look surprised.

"We have one," Michael admits.

"Then use it. What are you waiting for? We need to get out of here more than you do," Max says.

"American forces won't take you," Anne says, with remembered pride.

"Oh yeah, why not?" Max asks, wincing as he moves his injured shoulder.

"You're mercenaries or military contractors or whatever you're called these days," she snaps back.

"Terrorists?" Yehia chips in his two cents.

I admire his courage.

Max regards Yehia with an accordioned forehead before he chuckles and addresses Anne. "I'm pretty sure they would be happy to evacuate me. After all, they're the ones who hired me. They pay my salary the same way they're probably paying yours."

CHAPTER 6

London, October 2004

This is how life changes—or not.

These moments were the best life had to offer. As I shot along the M40, in my red Shoei helmet with tinted face shield and black leather jacket, I was larger than life. My eighteen-year-old mind was drunk on adrenaline and my newly acquired driver's license.

My Suzuki GSX wove through the meek commuters squeezed into their energy-efficient cars. Their eyes followed me, full of wingless dreams. No wonder women like bikers. Later in life, I would see motorcyclists as weekend dipshits with small dicks, begging for attention. Maybe some things change after all.

I loved my foster parents. They loved me back. They were eager to learn Arabic, but we never managed to speak the same language in English or Arabic. We tried to build bridges through our triangle but failed, and I have no doubt that each of us only blames ourselves. Maybe each of us is right.

I had no real friends. Whenever I came close to forming a friendship, I had to give up parts of myself to conform. It took a lot of effort, so I gave up. I became a loner. And what do loners do? They run away from everyone else. So, I asked Ruth and Mike for a motorcycle for my eighteenth birthday. The happiness it brought me was matched only by the destruction it caused.

Out there, with the wind racing through your whole body, the line blurs between what's real and what's imaginary. You become more powerful and free on that endless, seamless blacktop that leads to nothing but the journey itself.

That night on the M40, I revved up the engine and veered left to overtake a black Range Rover in the middle lane, only to face a red Cherokee that was at a standstill after hitting a truck . I knew I couldn't slam right into the Range Rover, which was less than a meter from me, nor left to smear my brain onto the highway's stone separator. As I hit the brakes, a voice in my head said, "I'm not ready to die ..."

The front wheel bit into the asphalt with a screech, and the back wheel lifted from the ground. The Cherokee approached at an incredible speed, then hit me. A child's panicked face in the passenger seat is the last vivid memory I have.

My body flew, paying all due respect to Sir Isaac Newton, at the same speed and in the same direction, waiting to be acted upon by a balancing force. It doesn't matter if you are talking about apples falling from trees or human bones crushed against hot steel. My head traveled first, as I smashed through the rear glass and into the car. Something crashed into my helmet, and all I saw was white void.

I was suspended in the air. I pushed myself forward and found myself flying. I felt the serenity of a bodiless soul. Not for long, though—flying became crawling as my body weight returned and I grew exponentially heavier with each movement. As I struggled forward, I found myself back at the first time I rode a bicycle, when I was nine. I had wobbled only fifty meters before realizing it had no brakes. To my left, cars flashed past on Green Lanes. To my right, a sea of pedestrians on the sidewalk. In front of me, a middle-aged man walked earnestly. In real life, I clamped my eyes shut and waited for the inevitable. That time, though, I tried to warn my victim or fall off the bicycle. I finally managed to let out a muffled scream, a moment before I woke up to another type of white. A hospital room.

I had concussion, a crescent gash on the right side of my face, a darkly bruised torso the color of chocolate, a couple of broken ribs and a broken shin.

Ruth and Mike hugged me and told me how lucky I was. They didn't look me in the eye though, when mentioning the driver whose head I smashed with my helmet, right in front of his son. I realized that was the impact I'd experienced before blacking out. Another human's head cracking like a watermelon against my helmet.

You would think that a near-death experience would change you forever. It doesn't. Almost dying doesn't change anything. Only in *The Lion King* can one suddenly change and go on to lead a life of wisdom and depth. But me? I still had the same bicycle nightmares. Still acted like the average teenager I'd been. Except for one thing: the bloody headaches.

I started having headaches that drilled into my head until I squirmed and cried. Red hot kebab skewer wedged into the right ventricle of my skull and into my brain. Pain that made me know the fragility of my existence. Doctors were useless. Nobody had invented a definition for my case yet, let alone a cure. Many of them referred to it as being of "psychological" origin, whatever the hell that meant, as if my scar were a bloody tattoo, not a sign of a physical injury. I was in limbo until I met my life's true friends: opioid painkillers. I made strong ties with all of them: Oxycontin, Vicodin, tramadol—the whole lot. Weirdly, of all the black spots that peppered my heart, taking narcotics didn't feel like one of them.

That was how my life changed after the accident. Headaches that stretched out time and stopped life, and drugs that did the opposite.

London, May 2006

Erkhart explained everything to me.

"Your fate is determined by your character, and your character is written in a map you carry everywhere," he said in a hypnotic, late-night DJ voice.

How I came to be sitting with this guy in his piss-off cul-de-sac villa in Hampstead was through an emergency ambulance crew program that I had volunteered in with St John Ambulance in the dark ages after high school, before growing a pair and deciding what I wanted to do with my life.

"I knew you were coming for me," Erkhart said, relaxing in a throne-like armchair that must have belonged to one of the King Louises—whatever number.

It was a rainy Saturday night, and I was covering for an EMT who'd stubbed his toe on a table leg and broke it (his toe, not the table). On our first call-out, we found a man on the ground in his Hampstead villa, convulsing and choking on his own vomit, froth coming out of his mouth. An Iranian carpet had soaked up a caramel-colored liquid that spilled from a cup next to him.

I could feel his shallow breathing despite the froth, half of which he must have swallowed between the convulsions and the periodic loss of consciousness. Well, we could worry about the vomit in his lungs later, after it had formed healthy bacterial colonies.

He extended his hand out to me. "May I read your palm?"

"I don't know, can I read your first love letter?" I neither wanted to know my future nor go through my past.

"It will help you know yourself."

Who said I wanted to know myself? To know how I'd live and die? I didn't want to be another Cassandra. In the end, curiosity killed the cat.

Near his semi-conscious, convulsing body was a broken chalice on the carpet. I smelled the caramel-colored liquid. Ayahuasca. I had seen it only once, when I joined a camping trip in Wales. I chose to be the trip

*sitter while they went on their "spiritual journeys." He was probably
seeing me with Mickey Mouse ears right then, or himself in a dark cave
under the ocean, jerking off with penguins.*

"The heart line shows your emotional energy."

Holding my reluctant right hand, he pointed to the thick line cutting across my palm. "Yours is chained and complete. Commitment is your highest fear. You are likely to fail in love many times."

I didn't need a palm reader to know that, but I endured. I had saved the man's life, which put me in his debt somehow.

"Your long-term partner will have the same heart line as you."

His villa hadn't changed since that emergency call over a year ago. A museum of antiques and paintings. The real kind. The kind that defies time. I looked around while he inspected my hand. We were on the second floor, in a vast study that smelled of leather and stillness. It had two red doors and floor-to-ceiling wooden bookshelves covered most of the walls. We were seated next to a massive mahogany desk, with lamps providing indirect lighting.

"The head line shows your mental energy." That was the horizontal one, which ran below the heart line. "You have suffered many traumas in your life."

No shit. Any barista could figure this out from my facial scar and my extra shot of cynicism.

*Ayahuasca poisoning meant he had serotonin syndrome and needed a
muscle relaxant, a serotonin antagonist, and some oxygen. We had to
get him to the hospital.*

*His hand clawed at my shoulder when he heard the word 'ambu-
lance'. He shook his head and rasped about the meds in his bathroom
cabinet, his voice hoarse and husky. Sir David Attenborough after two
days without water.*

*I don't know why I complied, against my colleague's and my better
judgement and against established procedures. What would life be*

without breaking a few rules from time to time? Don't all breakthroughs break the rules?

"The lifeline shows physical energy and passion for life," he said, adjusting his low-frame glasses.

I pictured a lonely white owl in the woods at night, hooting warnings of what was to come but with no one taking heed. This line began on the thumb side of the palm, under the index finger, and arced down toward the wrist. It's the dotted line you would slice if you were a cannibal who fancied hand drumsticks. Passion for life? I was surprised the line even existed on my hand.

"It is connecting with the head and heart lines in a way that shows a cautious attitude and great stamina."

Great stamina? Now he was talking.

"You have a lot of worry lines crossing your lifeline. You worry about things that never happen. You'll likely have stress-related health issues if you are not careful."

In the medicine cabinet, I found a box labeled "OD" in thick red marker. What an organized junkie. I put two ampules of cyproheptadine and levetiracetam in a syringe and injected him. I could get kicked out of the service or even go to jail for this, but in the heat of the moment, it felt like the only reasonable thing to do.

And my fate line? The "sense of purpose" line that ran vertically down the middle of the palm, from the wrist toward the middle finger?

"It's alarmingly short," he said.

Good. I don't want to be like you, my friend. Old, lonely, and dead before I die.

"It fades out in the middle, which shows you had a purpose but might drift aimlessly for a while before regaining it."

I said nothing.

He studied my thumb and fingers. "Your fingerprint is a whorl pattern, which means you are individualistic and independent. You have a line between your third and fourth fingers that shows you have inherited, or will inherit, a fortune."

Bollocks. The only things I inherited from my two sets of parents were hands-on frugality lessons. Apart from them, the only living relative I was aware of was my grandmother back in Cairo, who only had her husband's pension, a cat, and three photo albums.

Almost a year later, a bloke from Men in Black *with douchebag mirrored shades appeared on my doorstep and handed me a phone. Erkhart had hired a PI to track me down, and he'd managed to find me, even though I left EMT work shortly after that incident to start med school.*

"Do you like chess?" Erkhart's voice echoed through the phone. "I saw you many times in my dreams. We were playing chess."

Of course, you did, I thought. In your trips, you could have seen Cleopatra herself fucking Mark Antony, cowgirl style.

And that was how I met Erkhart. I visited him often after that. We would play chess or cards, exchanging views on life, mostly his. He was retired, having spent most of his life in the States, working as a venture capitalist. Since being mugged five years previously, he was entirely housebound. They smashed him on the head and he went into a coma. When he woke up, he was a different person. A social anxiety form of OCD, apparently. His main companions were his psychedelics, which would probably kill him one day.

"Does it say how I'll die?" I finally asked.

"No. Even if it did, I wouldn't tell you." He looked up from my palms and studied my face for a moment. "Reading the last page of a new book can either make you bored or utterly satisfied with each word you read. I'm not sure yet which type you are."

As I was stretching my limbs after reclaiming my hand, I noticed what was different in the room. For the first time, the drapes on the far wall had been opened, revealing a mesmerizing array of paintings as well as a closed steel door that separated the two sections of the library. A hidden room? My curiosity cat clawed at me to feed her. Yet I wasn't going to ask. I wasn't Bluebeard's wife. Hell, I wasn't a wife, full stop. My gaze lingered on a particular painting next to the hidden room.

"You like it?" he asked.

"I'm not sure why." I scrutinized it, trying to understand what was so special about it. It depicted a medieval city facing the sea, with farmers and ships going about their daily business.

"It's an oil painting called *Landscape with the Fall of Icarus*," he explained. "Icarus, in Greek mythology, flew too close to the sun despite the warnings of his father, Daedalus. His wings were made of feathers and beeswax, and would melt if he flew too close. As in any self-respecting tragedy, the worst happened, and Icarus fell to his demise in the sea."

Yet the painting didn't focus on this. Instead, a plowman plowed, ships sailed for trade, a farmer checked the weather for his crops, a fisherman cast his line. Near the bottom right corner of the painting, I finally spotted the legs. Icarus flailing in the sea as he drowned, the world moving on around him, indifferent to his ordeal.

"The painting was *acquired* from the Royal Museum in Belgium," Erkhart said. "I bought it off the black market, as I did many other antiques. Do you know how much this painting is worth?"

"If I found it in car boot sale, I might offer a tenner, but now that it's in your house, I would say half a million."

He paused. "The last offer I received for it was thirty-three million. However, its open market value is ten times more. It's fair to say it is the most valuable piece I own."

I stared at him, not sure if he was joking. I turned back to the painting, searching for what I'd missed.

"I see the price tag intrigues you more than the painting itself." He drew closer.

"I would say rather it disgusts me," I scoffed, squinting at

Icarus's drowning figure.

He went back to his chair and relaxed. "It took me a fortune and a lot of risks to acquire it. It was an obsession."

"Right. And ...?"

"And what?"

"Now that it's finally here?"

He looked up at the ceiling. "I know it's hard to understand. In my childhood, pictures fascinated me. My family smiled all the time in my childhood photos. Or rather, smiled with no time. Time doesn't exist in the dimension of pictures. They are the closest thing our human brain can use to relate to the Garden of Eden. My interest extended from photos to paintings, which have the advantage of not only freezing time but also shaping the world to our liking. They became my addiction."

He looked back at Icarus. "Other collectors have different reasons, of course." He pursed his lips. "Most are addicts, too. Not to the artefact itself, but to the sense of accomplishment. They cling to these expensive toys the same way a child would cling to a teddy bear. It gives them a sense of worth. They are so terrified of death that the only way to fight it is to collect the continuity of life. To be part of something bigger than themselves."

Wise words from a glorified stockbroker. I scowled at the plowman, farmer, and fisherman, wondering about Icarus's last thoughts.

London, June 2007

Whomp!

Neither the thick judo mat nor the cheers of the small crowd muffled the sound of my body hitting the ground. I was glad I had told Mike not to come. He wouldn't have liked seeing his son's ass literally kicked.

I hadn't practiced much for this local tournament. Meeting

last year's champion in my first match wasn't helping, either. I had stopped exercising six months ago, after Ruth died from multiple sclerosis. The death of a loved one hits hard, even if you watched them dissolving from the inside in front of you, day after day.

Another reason for my bad performance was that judo wasn't the only sport I nibbled at. I dabbled in jujitsu, aikido, and boxing on the side as well. Over time, it became clear this only led me to get worse in each. What kept me going was my high tolerance for pain, even without drugs. Take boxing, for example. Any matches I won were usually because I was the last man standing, not because I was any better than my opponent. Any other pain was tolerable when compared to my headaches, or my accident at the moment of impact.

As I was lifted in the air by my opponent, my heart sank, not because of the fear of impact but because my brain remembered the moment of flying off the bike and colliding with that car. The moment of crushing another man's life.

I was in my second year of medicine. After my stint as an EMT, I decided that I wanted to be a surgeon. Don't get me wrong, I hated medicine. My college years were horrible. But the first time I held a scalpel made it all worthwhile. Surgery was the only thing I liked. I liked the reminder, every time I saw a body on the operating table, that we don't own our bodies. We just rent them.

I also liked that a surgeon lives in the moment. In the blink of an eye, you could rupture a blood hose or pierce an organ, and the miracle of life would hiss out of the body like air from a tire. It was living free from the world of what will I, why did I ...

Speaking of which, being a doctor also guaranteed me access to my beloved narcotics. Redemption, you ask? Sorry, mate. I didn't believe in it. The dead will be always dead. I was doing it for myself. At least I was honest about it.

Anyway, after having my ass delivered to me on a plate, I was in no mood to stay for the rest of the matches, so I headed home. It was the first night of summer, but the weather hadn't received the memo yet: the sky was bleeding its heart out. I remember this because that night, I came back to find Mike dead.

Since he'd retired from his job as a tax accountant, Mike had been spending a lot of time in his garden tending to his plants. I found him there on the ground, a rake still in his hand, his half-opened eyes telling me all I needed to know. I ran to check his pulse, but there was none. I called 999 and then sank to the ground, sobbing. Seconds, minutes, or hours later, an ambulance arrived.

It was a heart attack. He had told me several times, in passing, that he had sudden increases in his heart rate. This should have rung alarm bells, but instead only lead to banter about how he needed to do more exercise. The things we'd be willing to give for more time with loved ones. Or to change small things that could have saved them.

He went to meet Ruth at the sharp edge of eternal life, where the stars go to die or are reborn as diamond dust. I wanted to ask them for a final hug. Apologize for all the times they wanted to have a talk, but I was too busy dealing with headaches or bouts of loneliness. Apologize for not being able to convey what I felt for them in words and actions. That I loved them just as much as I loved my biological parents. That it was my ultimate plan to take them for pilgrimage, to spend the rest of my life giving back a fraction of what they gave me. All these words I'd thought I would have time to say to them weathered and rotted inside me, unsaid. Corrosive words eating at a rusty consciousness.

I became "cut from a tree," as the Egyptian proverb goes. This translates to something like "alone as fuck." The next day, Mike didn't check on me when I overslept, didn't make me morning coffee in his old Italian coffee machine, and didn't chat with me when silence grew thick in the house. I knew then that I couldn't continue living there without him, so I moved to a rented flat on Talgarth Road.

Maybe I was cursed; I'd lost two sets of parents and I wasn't yet twenty-one. Maybe their deaths cursed me, spraying gray gloom into my world before they left.

CHAPTER 7

Present Day, Thursday, 15:18

"I don't want your thoughts and prayers. I want your guns." Michael bristles in the corridor, resisting the urge to pace to maintain the satellite phone signal.

Everyone is waiting for their turn to call loved ones, if they have any, or their embassies if they don't.

I decide to busy myself by changing the dressings of the handful of remaining patients, one of which is the young man we picked up on our way back from the residence.

He must still be in shock, otherwise he would be howling in pain. We no longer have any morphine. He has not spoken much since he arrived, and I don't dare to ask him about the person in the driver's seat.

As if to prove me wrong, he says, "God delivered you to me in time."

"It was a 1988 Land Cruiser that delivered us, but no matter."

"Are you Muslim?"

"Yes," I say, throwing the old dressing into a makeshift rubbish bin.

He looks up at the ceiling. "If God can hear the footsteps of an ant on a thick rock on a dark night, then he must have heard that shell coming for us. Why did he make it land at the same spot where my brother stopped? And on his side, not mine?"

Doctors and soldiers have seen too many prayers go

unanswered when people needed God the most. Thank God the reason why I'm a believer is not because I need a superpower to watch over me. For me, faith is mindfulness plus direction.

"I don't know. You're lucky, I guess," I say.

When he flicks his gaze at me, his smile is sad but serene, his pupils shrinking to pinpoints. "You don't understand. I'm the unlucky one."

I hold his gaze, not knowing what to say. This guy is on something, and it isn't khat. A memory flashes through my mind—consoling Dennis for losing his brother to cancer. I did it the Arab way, saying stuff like, "Life is not worth it, mate." He pushed back and kept repeating, "Life is great. It's all we have, and my brother got the best out of it."

I have since learned my lesson. Anyway, I'm not one to argue if either of these perspectives helps Dennis or this man sleep at night.

Rachel comes in from the corridor. "Luke, if you have someone to call, this is the time to use the sat phone. All mobile networks are down."

"Yeah, sure," I say. I'm not at all sure who to call.

Michael is telling Anne that the Americans are doing their best to negotiate a ceasefire, so they can evacuate all foreign nationals. I cringe when I see that Yehia, who insisted to stay with us, is listening.

In the corridor, Manu is talking to someone in what seems to be fluent Spanish. Or maybe it's Italian. I have no clue. He finishes his call and hands me the phone. I hold it for a moment, thinking. I open my wallet and get out a small, wrinkled piece of paper and dial.

My foster parents often asked if I wanted to visit any relatives in Egypt, even offering to fly me over to see them, but I always refused. I dreaded going there. It was a place that kept dragging me down like a dead weight, even though I had never seen it.

"Hello?" her old, cracked voice vibrates through the line.

"Hi Grandma," I say in Arabic. "It's me ... Adam." I lower my voice when I say my name.

"Who?"

"Adam, *Teta*. Your grandson."

"Adam *danaya*. How are you, *ya habibi*?"

"I'm good, Grandma. How are you?"

"I'm well, thanks be to God. *Habibi*, how are you?"

"Yeah, good. How is your health?"

"*Alhamdullelah*. I'm angry with you. You never call. How are you?"

Greetings could go on forever. The truth is, I don't know this sweet old woman. We have nothing to say to each other.

"Well, *Teta*, I'm good. Listen, *Teta*, I have to go now. Um … it's nice hearing your voice. Will call you back."

I stare at the phone for a moment after I hang up. This is partly why I'm really in Yemen now and why I followed Tina all the way in the past. When you don't have an anchor, it's easy to drift.

I have always wondered how things would have been if my parents had stayed in Egypt. Would I be a normal "sociable" person? Would I still have all these struggles over who I am and what defines me? Culture, religion, relationships. Am I afraid of visiting Egypt because it might answer these questions?

You know you're reaching rock bottom when your main wish is to find hot water. I smell like a pig, and I don't have any deodorant to smother the smell with. I have four different colognes back home, but I consciously decided not to bring any with me.

Our makeshift mass casualty center in the basement is rapidly taking shape. The remaining patients have been haphazardly transferred here, and we've collected all we can of pressure dressings, IV fluids, airway openers, and a stretcher. The air is throbbing with the humid smell of sweat, dirt, iodine, and fear. You can still hear the clashes in nearby streets, getting closer and slower.

I'm busy moving four oxygen canisters to a safer location, in the corner of the basement. We don't want any surprises to trigger these bombs and incinerate us. The irony would probably kill us before the flames. I'm on my way to retrieve the last canister when I find Rachel standing in front of me, her big honey-colored eyes bright with accusation.

"Who are these people, exactly?" she asks calmly, so Anne won't hear us.

"Isn't it obvious, Rachel? Mercenaries. They said they work for the American government."

"Sure. And how exactly do you know these people, Doctor *Loki*?"

I freeze and then remember Max calling me that in front of everyone. "I don't know what you're talking about, Rachel. The bugger was trying to be friendly and earn my trust."

She cocks her head. "So you haven't met him before?"

"Of course not," I say, with the same indignant tone and expression that I used when Ruth accused me, correctly, of smoking when I was fourteen.

Rachel just looks at me.

"Come on now, Rachel. This isn't a good time to be paranoid. Are you going to help me with this or not?" I point to the oxygen canister.

She moves around and her arm brushes mine. Instinctively, I draw back, feeling micro vibrations through my body. She puts her hands on the other side of the canister, and as we move, she doesn't take her eyes off me.

I liked Rachel's no-nonsense attitude from the day I met her and the rest of the team in Geneva, before we traveled to Yemen.

The lady at the registration table had a plastic smile and an automated demeanor that made me think she was the missing link between humans and *Ex Machina*.

"*Bonjour, comment puis-je vous aider?*" she said, in a voice steamy enough to melt the North Pole. Maybe she had a soul after all.

"Um... hi. We're guests here at the conference," Michael fumbled.

"*Bien sûr*. May I have your names please."

The banner next to the registration table proclaimed in bright letters, big enough for starving kids in Somalia to see, "ACCOUNTABILITY IN THE AID SECTOR." The table was festooned with name tags with grandiose titles: Country Director for Yemen, Regional Operations Manager for Asia, Relief Coordinator for Iraq. Supposedly busy and important, these people's main job seemed to be jerking each other off using big words and recycled reports that articulated the obvious.

Here I was in Geneva, the mecca of humanitarian virtue signaling and inflated salaries, from my previous posting in Somalia. The director of my new NGO, Groupe d'Aide Internationale (GAI), was attending this OCHA-organized event along with half of the Paris HQ, so he'd asked us to come over to Geneva for a briefing before travelling to Yemen the next day. International conferences, trainings and meetings are senior humanitarians' bread and butter. They attend these gatherings like lawyers attend court.

I had met Michael only an hour earlier, at a relaxed late breakfast. I was busy eating my fill for the day. I'd been hungry when I arrived late the night before, so I'd crunched two Kit Kats from the minibar. In the morning, I realized they were more than a king's ransom. Michael was sitting at the table next to mine, wearing a suit without a tie and glasses that kept slipping down his nose. He kept glancing at me before asking, "Hey, we came on the same flight. Turkish Airlines, right?"

"Yeah," I said. "Last night."

"Did you manage to get your mileage? They refused to add mine at the counter. Those pinhead bureaucrats."

"I didn't ask ..."

"My name is Michael Malone. I'm a surgeon from the States." After a quick handshake, he continued. "Are you with GAI? Jean-Frederic's replacement?"

"I don't know who Jean-Frederic is, but yes, I'm starting with GAI as a surgeon joining the Yemen trauma team—"

"Great. Me too. I'm the team leader. Doctor Michael Malone."

"Yes, Michael. You just told me," I said with a smile.

When he moved to my table, I prayed he didn't start discussing his favorite frequent-flyer program. My prayers were answered when he put on his team-leader face and asked me about my previous experience.

From one peek inside the conference room, I knew I wasn't going in. Everyone was either half asleep or playing *Candy Crush* while the presenter at the podium spoke in a hypnotizing monotone. Behind him, the screen showed a PowerPoint with more words than I could count. A few people were writing things in notebooks that they would never read again, unless they were calculating how many starving kids in Africa their per diem can feed.

"I'm not going in, Michael. I'll go to the bar and have some coffee. When you find the boss, bring him over."

"OK," Michael said, resigned to my will. "Can you get Rachel to come then? Room 227."

I called the room from the lobby but only got a busy signal. So I went up and knocked on the door.

"*Pas de service de chambre, merci.*"

I don't speak French. I knocked again.

"*Merci de ne pas déranger.*"

I didn't get that one either. "Hello. Michael sent me."

"*Putain de merde,*" the voice muttered.

This one I knew.

The sound of footsteps came closer to the door. The bolt winced, and something told me to run and hide. Too late. The door had already cracked ajar. Warm air breathed in my face as I took in the sleepy stranger in front of me. Curly auburn hair almost covering hazel eyes below thick eyebrows. Carved pink lips of the type that didn't need makeup. She probably wasn't wearing anything, as I could see her bare left shoulder in the narrow opening. Verdict: good-looking for the average person, exceptional for a doctor.

"Yes?"

"In your defense, Michael mentioned it was a long flight."

She squinted. I tilted my head to match hers and gave her a smile.

"What time is it?"

No French accent that made me want to bang my head on the nearest wall or agree to whatever they were saying just to make them stop talking.

"Ten past ten."

"And you are?"

"Luke. New team member."

"You're Jean-Frederic's replacement?" she asked, suppressing a yawn.

"That's what everyone keeps telling me."

She looked me over appraisingly. "You don't look like his replacement."

"He must have been a piece of work, just like you."

She gave me a deadpan expression. She probably had two master's degrees and spoke five languages and already had her will sorted out. Yet there was something childish about her.

"What do you sell again?"

"Michael is reminding you of the briefing at ten."

She rolled her eyes, which I came to know as one of her trademarks. "Yeah, well, tell them I'm missing, presumed dead. That's what I would be anyway if I met those HQ creeps again."

"Fair enough." I moved toward the elevator.

I didn't hear the door close. I glanced back. She was still looking at me with puffy eyes, as if surprised I'd given up so easily.

She caught herself. "Don't get your hopes up," she said, and shut the door.

Thirty minutes later, I had managed to drown the imposter syndrome brought on by all those humanitarian warriors around me with three cups of coffee and a hundred milligrams of tramadol. Eventually, Michael showed up. With him was a seri-ous-looking, self-inflated man in his fifties who looked like the ugly brother of that French choreographer in *Black Swan*. His name was Thierry something. We shook hands and he sat down, ordered a double espresso, and began complaining about the *jus de chaussette* American coffee served during the conference breaks.

I wondered why they kept organizing these events if nobody was happy with them. Whenever I had to endure attending one, things seemed upside down; aid was the goal and beneficiaries were the means. A wise old humanitarian once told me that real humanitarians used to be the majority, but they were replaced by adventure seekers searching for some sun and a chance to recreate themselves. I only doubted the first part of his statement. Thierry launched the "briefing" in a business-like French accent.

"So, what questions do you have for me?"

I immediately understood why Rachel couldn't care less about this meeting. Not that I expected earth-shattering insights. "Um, I was under the impression that this was a briefing."

"Sure, sure. You are going to Yemen. Aden, to be precise," he said, chuckling. "We dried up some resources in stagnant conflicts and relocated our focus. Yemen is the new Syria; donations are coming in and we need to keep up. We will start with a core group to test the waters. You will be ... what is the word in English... ah yes, you will be the ... trailblazers for the other teams to come."

Michael smiled and nodded humbly, as if accepting a great honor, forgetting that the trailblazer for space discovery was a monkey.

Thierry received a phone call and spoke in French for some time while I drifted off, thinking about how French sounds as slippery as soap to my ears. One small pronunciation mistake and you're screwed. If languages were diseases, French would be diarrhea. By the time he finished, Dominique, GAI's Head of HR, had arrived. She was a thin, tall woman in her fifties who moved quickly and aggressively. The kind of woman whose best friend was probably a vibrator. I baptized her Iron Lady.

"Will we be able to give any salaries for the local teams there? I asked. "I understand that most of them have been working voluntarily after the near collapse of the public sector, and many have left the country already."

Black Swan villain and Iron Lady exchanged a meaningful glance. The money for her Gucci bag and his Rolex watch could probably retain the hospital staff for another year.

"Doctor Archer, this is not your first humanitarian mission, correct?" Iron Lady asked.

One look at her long, polished nails and his trim, manicured ones betrayed that they only knew the meaning of "hardship mission" from Webster's dictionary.

"No, it's not," I replied with a smirk. Two could play the game of ball busting.

She put on the fakest possible smile. "Then you must be aware that we cannot pay government staff salaries. That would be colonialist."

"And paying *our* salaries, and sending us over there, isn't?"

"That's different," she said, with the disdain of a vegan eyeing a piece of sausage.

"Just do your job. Don't look for any problems and things will run smoothly," Thierry advised condescendingly.

I shrugged. "What if problems look for us?"

"I'm sure you will figure something out."

Present Day, Thursday, 16:18

"This is so humiliating. Now we're at the mercy of a bunch of thugs," Anne moans to Manu as Rachel and I wrestle the oxygen canister past her. She's changing General Rahimi's catheter under a dim yellow light.

Manu says, "You know, in my first mission in Darfur, I had to sleep for a whole week in a sleeping bag that smelled of vomit, in fifty-degree heat in a Janjaweed-controlled area. So I would say we haven't reached rock bottom yet."

Anne mutters under her breath, "At least they are American."

Rachel rolls her eyes and shakes her head.

Yehia comes from outside, passing a familiar plastic bag to Anne. "Look what I found in one of the bathrooms. Mostly tablets, so only for post-op patients. I distributed some of them already."

Cold sweat washes over my body. Fuck! Fuck-fuck-fuck! Now I know what the unlucky brother was on. My bloody emergency stash.

"Ration them. We don't know how long we'll be here," Anne says.

Rachel stops Yehia. "Yehia, are you sure you want to stay? If help comes, they won't take you with us."

He gives a knowing nod. He's seen this too many times in American movies. "I know you can't take me, but I can't leave you here alone. I'm staying until I make sure all of you are safe."

I would have been floored by his dignity, if I weren't already floored by my sudden lack of meds. What am I going to do without my pills? What about the patients who need them? Is it time to face my inner demons and quit? I have always known I needed to do it before the inevitable day comes. The day when I fully succumb to its siren call. When I would be like the patient I once saw who pimped out his wife for a fix. He knifed himself in the abdomen after the customer who shagged his wife paid him less than the price of a bag of heroin. All he cared about in the ER was to finally get a shot of narcotics. After all, addiction comes from the word *addictus*—a citizen of ancient Rome who, unable to pay his debts, became a slave to his creditors.

The only one with enough brains to put me and that bag in one sentence is Rachel. A week ago, she made a seemingly innocent remark about my needle-head pupils—that was the opiates saying hello through my eyes.

"I'm grand," I said with raised eyebrows, in case the mockery in my voice wasn't obvious. "I use Visine. Allergic reaction."

"You also scratch your skin a lot. Any other allergies we should know about?"

The opiates again, through my skin this time. "No, I just like touching myself."

Who would believe my headaches? Addicts make up a deluge of excuses to score, leaving no place for the odd real need.

The Bull enters the basement with a Yemeni soldier as I'm fighting the tidal waves of my dark thoughts. "Howdy, ladies. We just need to take the General with us. Don't forget to come and check on him from time to time," he says.

We turn to look at the General, who stares back at us silently from his trolley, most of his face covered by the oxygen mask. For all I know, he's holding a gun under the sheets right now.

Rachel aims a cold smile at the General. "I hope you're enjoying our hospitality."

He doesn't blink. For a second, I fear he might shoot her in the face.

The Bull says, "We need the doctor to come with us."

"I'll go," Rachel says.

"No." He stops her with a raised left hand that's missing a pinkie but is still as big as her head. Then he points a thick finger at me. "Him."

From the window, the sky is getting darker, with shades of blue and red. The canteen is packed with adrenaline and enough lead to start an industrial revolution. Some soldiers are sifting through ammo, others huddle over maps. Piles of explosives are in one corner, some military grade. From movies, I recognize the distinctive shape of Claymore mines. More explosives are in big pots like the ones you find in any kitchen.

No more reinforcements have arrived beyond the handful of Yemeni soldiers who remained from a force of almost two thousand that was fully ready just a couple of days ago.

Pointing at me as if I'm the pizza they ordered, the Bull asks Max, "Are you sure you want *this* one?"

Max looks at him blankly, holding his radio. "Yeah, why?"

"Nothing. I thought you'd want one of the expats, is all."

Max grimaces. "TJ ..." He waves his hand in the air. "Find some bombs to work on, would ya?"

Aha, so the Bull has a name.

"Don't mind him," Max tells me. "His red neck didn't leave Oklahoma until he joined the army. He would've gotten culture shock in Miami. A charmer with ordnance though."

I couldn't mind him even if I tried. The fact that TJ is double my weight and a head taller makes sure of that. I open my mouth to say something, but Max raises a hand to speak into the radio. It's OK because I don't know what I was going to say.

"Echo One, this is Bravo. Send sitrep."

"Bravo, this is Echo One. The .50 cal is up and running. Over." I recognize Piotr's voice.

"Maintain a critical terrain outside the range of their AKs. Out."

I'm sure they feel cocky saying these words, which may work on a movie set but in real life sound very pretentious.

"Nice boots, Luke," Max says.

I look at him, expressionless. I'm familiar with his off-topic remarks. Still, I'm happy that he didn't ask everyone's usual question about why I wear boots in the summer.

Instead, Max proceeds with the radio calls. "Echo Two, this is Bravo, sitrep."

"M240 ready, over."

"Standby," Max says.

If I'm right, Echo One is the armored Humvee that the General and Max arrived in, which is now outside the hospital gate to protect the western flank—a narrow dirt road with buildings on either side. It's the only flank that Max and his men don't have a clear line of sight on from the roof. The Humvee is the front-line defense, with its .50 cal machine gun mounted on its roof. It also has good control over the northern side, which is an empty piece of land used as a garbage dump. Echo Two protects the green fields to the west and south of the hospital through the soldiers on the roof.

"What the hell are you planning to do?" I ask.

All eyes turn to me, giving me a "Who is this fuckwit?" look.

Max arches an eyebrow. "For a war-zone humanitarian, your context analysis isn't exactly up to date, Loki. The fight for the city is almost over, and they're headed in our direction. We just heard news that nearby residents are leaving."

He continues throwing instructions to his team. "TJ, I need those charges ready, stat."

I sigh. "That's the plan then? Stay here and use the patients as human shields?"

"You're safe in the basement, and we're safe on the roof. Their crappy 109 rocket launchers can't go that high or that low."

I shake my head, unconvinced.

"Why the hell are you here, anyway? What brought you to this shithole?"

I wince and say sullenly, "I'm trying to find my place in the world, Max."

"Wasn't that the problem in the first place? I thought you'd had enough of being reckless."

"Please, tell me more about recklessness. It's enlightening, coming from a gun for hire."

"OK, OK. Jeez, you're more serious than I remember, Luke."

"Maybe you're the one who lost your sense of humor after killing so much."

"Whatever. So, you and your team of white saviors were already living here in the hospital?"

"We bunkered here just yesterday. We used to live on Istiklal Street. You know the tall building there?"

"Yeah, I know it. Everyone does. The one with the crazy Friday parties."

I roll my eyes. Maybe Rachel is rubbing off on me more than I realize. "What? No. That must've been the previous occupants."

He waves his hand dismissively. "You'll probably be safer here anyway. Your house is in the middle of a death trap. We call it the traffic light street."

I squeeze my memory. I'd swear the street didn't have a single traffic light. So I play along. "Alright. How come?"

"Cause gunmen had the habit of stopping people at intersections and robbing them of their belongings," Max says with a smile.

I blink to remove the mental image of our home invasion. Then I lower my voice. "Why are you still holding the flag? This is not your war. Let things take their natural course."

He shakes his head and grits his teeth. "I wish I could. That fat fuck there," he says, glancing at the General's trolley, "is backed by Gulf countries who contracted me to train them though the CIA. They promised to pay double what I get with the Americans, but I haven't gotten paid yet. Besides, it's a matter of reputation."

I give him a "cut the crap" look." Pride is preventing him from admitting that he feels stupid for believing the CIA. He didn't realize that a bunch of malnourished flipflop fighters had better intel than all those suit-wearing Washington wankers.

He shifts uncomfortably. "OK, here's the thing. It's not like we have a chance to fight our way out on our own, Luke. We stand out like shit in snow. Once active fighting is over, it will be open season on any foreigner. Being dragged by a rope behind a pickup truck through the city wouldn't be the worst-case scenario."

He reaches for his bag and pulls out a plastic zipper bag of baby carrots. He takes one and munches. I watch him blankly until I feel the overwhelming need for a cigarette. I grab one from a pack of Camels on a nearby table and light it.

I finally say in resignation, "Listen, people are starting to ask how I know you. You need to be subtle and keep in mind that Michael is the one in charge here, not me."

He nods, distracted, and keeps crunching on his carrots. I keep puffing smoke. I haven't smoked in years, but losing my stash freaks me out more than this shitty situation. The first few drags are alien and short. But then my lungs' memory activates, and years of abstinence are blown to the wind with the drags that follow.

"How is ... Erkhart?"

He gives me a sideways look. "No idea. He went underground after the shitstorm you caused."

Guilt sweeps through my brain the same way bile rises in your throat when you feel sick. I'm sure he forgave and forgot. This makes me feel less guilty, but then I feel guilty for not feeling guilty.

"What about your girl? Are you still together?" he asks.

"We broke up long ago. She's the one who got me into this crazy business."

"Oh, look at you, all innocent and pure."

I redden. "Money wasn't the issue if that's what you think."

"You didn't want to lose her, huh?"

"Maybe."

That wasn't much of an answer. But I'm human, and humans talk about everything except what's really on their minds. What I'm really thinking is that I mustn't have loved her, so much as I hated being alone again. A stranger in a strange land. Tina gave me some assurance that I wasn't a total freak.

Max takes me by the arm, pulling me toward a corner. His radio crackles. "Bravo, this is Echo Two, we just lost four out of the seven Yemeni reinforcements that came this morning. Only three of the General's blood-relatives are left. Over."

"Copy. Put those three on guard duty at the building entrance. Over." And then to me, "I wonder what took them so long. Blue helmets would have skipped much earlier."

"Can we make it?"

"We're in hostile territory, and we have no idea when help will arrive, if ever."

"I take it that's a no, then."

"Our CIA handlers say there are ceasefire talks going on now in Stockholm. They say it's difficult to do an aerial evacuation without that agreement. Hopefully, it's a matter of hours. Anyway, the Red Sox are finally on their way to the playoffs. If they can do it, maybe we can, too."

I search for signs of sarcasm in his face, but there are none.

"Luke." He puts his radio down, gives me an intense look that I've never seen from him before. He lowers his voice. "'If I don't make it, I'll need a farewell favor."

"Geeks are never good at farewells, Max."

He ignores my comment. "Can I trust you to give my ring back to my family if something happens to me?"

"Family? Oh, Max. I didn't take you for the type." I quickly continue, "Well, I guess if I get out of here alive, that would be the least I could do for you, mate."

He sighs with relief. "Good, good."

He glances around the canteen before extracting a big shiny ring from his khaki pants and slipping it into my hand. He writes an address in Boston on a piece of paper and tells me to tear it up after memorizing it.

I stare at the ring. "Who the bloody hell brings a diamond ring to war?"

"Shhh. It's not diamond, it's my mom," he hisses.

"What are you doing with your mom's ring?"

"No, the ring *is* my mom. Her cremated ashes made into glass. It doesn't have any monetary value, but it means the world to me. Give it to my daughters, would ya?"

I put the ring and the piece of paper in my pocket and nod.

"Now get the fuck out of here," he says.

CHAPTER 8

East Yorkshire, August 2013

Out of the thirty thousand days the average person lives, only a few define a life. Meeting Tina during that group hike in Spurn Point Nature Reserve was one of those days. I can connect all my life's subsequent turbulence to it.

It was the end of the summer, and we were camping near a beautiful, deserted shore. I woke up late, groggy and with a splitting headache, so I chased a cocktail of Lyrica and tramadol with half a liter of water. I hadn't had more than two hours of continuous sleep in the last week of long shifts at the hospital. I was hoping that the hike would change something—I didn't know what—and help me sleep better.

I decided to explore the beach. Spurn Point is a sand spit stretching five kilometers into coastal waters, like a giant lizard's tongue, as narrow as fifty meters in some places.

I swam in the still waters and then floated, my brain drowning in endorphins. The world pulsed orange and red behind my eyelids, a million small stars. Being carried gently by water on that summer day—half my body shivering in the cold water and the other burning in the unusually hot sun—was a metaphor for my life. I felt my body spin. Gradually at first, then speeding up. Time stood still. I didn't know if the spinning was real or imagined. And I didn't want to open my eyes to find out. I didn't want it to stop.

After an eternity, I got out of the water, swaying and unable to keep a steady pace. That was when I first saw Tina Zielinski.

We were the only people on the beach. She had claimed a spot close to mine while I was swimming. She was lying on her stomach when I wobbled to the shore. Even from thirty meters away, with drugs fucking with your vision, you could tell she was a looker. From five meters away, you could see that her blue eyes could drown a man. She was 4K resolution when the world was still a decade away from HD.

I sat on my towel. I hadn't noticed her during the hike, and I wasn't sure whether she was part of my group or a different one.

There was nothing dreamy or cute in Tina's beauty. She was all sharp angles and magazine gloss, from her strong jawline and high cheekbones to her tall, lean figure. Her blonde hair sprang through the back of her cap in a ponytail that grazed a black T-shirt with *Guts or Glory* written in white. Thank God I was self-sustaining on drugs. Her self-sustenance seemed to consist of earphones, a book, and a lazy bottle of beer next to a black Gucci bag.

After a while, she took off her T-shirt, revealing more of her creamy skin. She rubbed sunscreen over her shoulders. I was happy she was on my left. My scar is on my right.

She asked if I could rub her back. As if anyone would say no.

I knew her kind. They wanted to lure you close, only to enjoy the sound of your crushed hopes as they slammed the door in your face. I wasn't planning to give her the pleasure. I kept a double buffer between beautiful girls and me. They made me feel clumsy and inferior. If I had learned anything from boxing, it was not to punch above my weight.

I silently spread the cream, Banana Boat Ultra Protect SPF 50, on her artistically freckled skin as she held up her ponytail. I rubbed her slightly burnt back in circles, but then I realized I would never finish like that, so I rubbed from bottom to top and went back down again. Her black G-string did nothing to conceal a tattoo on one of the two rounded parentheses of her cheeks: a snake eating its tail. Probably everyone she slept with told her how much they liked it. Not me.

"Can I ask you something?" The dopamine flooding my brain was making me bold.

"Yes," she said in a bored tone. She was expecting me to flirt.

"Did you try laser treatment for those freckles?"

"Excuse me?" She looked up from her phone.

"I'm a doctor. I assure you the results are guaranteed."

"You don't like my freckles?" Her tone was like the one you would use if someone said they didn't like water.

"I've seen better, but don't worry, nobody's perfect."

She turned her head and half her body toward me. I stopped rubbing. "Have you now?" Her frosty blue eyes gazed into my soul.

"Have I what?" The sparkle in her eyes was too intense. My gaze met the sun before it went back to hers.

"Seen better."

I wondered if we were still talking about the freckles. "There's always better," I said, expressionless.

She flipped back onto her stomach, and I smeared the last bits of sun cream on her back. That would teach her a lesson about asking a stranger for a back rub. I returned to my spot, and she went for a swim or a walk or whatever people do on beaches when they're not enjoying a blessed-with-opioids meditation.

Sometime after she came back, she turned to me. "Are you high?"

I gazed back at the sea. "Yeah, I guess."

"You have a spare joint?"

"Oh, no, I don't smoke weed. I have chronic pain. I take pain-killers and enjoy the side effects."

"Right." Then, after a short pause, "How is that working out for you?"

"What?"

"The side effects."

"I don't know. Less guilty, I guess."

I saw her a few more times in the remaining days of the hike. She was part of a different group that had arrived a day earlier but with the same organizers, so we all camped in the same spot. I tried to avoid her as much as I could. As the Arabic expression goes, no point building sandcastles. She had the kind of beauty that would open any door in life, yet she would probably fall only for her testosterone equivalent: someone dumb and athletic, who treats her like shit because he thinks the world owes him something. Karma, I guess.

On the last night, she came to my sleeping spot. "Hey, listen, I have a sore back and a long drive tomorrow. Would you mind fixing me up?"

Her eyes, impatient seas of gray, gave two quick blinks. The other day, I was almost sure they were blue.

"Sure." I opened my rucksack and gave her some Vicodins.

"Are you here on your own?" she asked, swallowing one.

"Yep."

It made sense for someone like me to be alone, but why on earth would someone like her? "What about you?" I asked as nonchalantly as possible.

"Same. My cat just died." She shrugged, as if that explained it.

"Oh. Condolences."

"Yeah, yeah, yeah. Hey, you play 6 Nimmt?" She pointed to the card game that had fallen from my rucksack.

My face lit up. "You know it?"

"Of course. One of my favorites. Want a quick round?"

"Prepare for your demise."

"So where are you traveling home to?" I asked once the game was underway.

"I live in North London. St. Jude Street."

I smiled and shook my head.

"What is it?"

"That's near to where I live, but that's not the irony. Do you know what Saint Jude is known for?"

"No idea, mate."

"He's the patron saint of lost causes."

She smiled. "Very clever. Are you Catholic?"

"No, I'm Muslim."

"Ah, OK. But what gave him this gloomy honor?"

"His name—because it's similar to Judas Iscariot's. Nobody prayed to Saint Jude, because people thought he and Judas were the same person. So he was eager to help anyone with a desperate case."

"Nice. They teach you Catholicism in the schools where you came from?"

"I *came from* the dark depths of London. And believe it or not, Bible stories are part of my religion, too."

We played a few more rounds before we noticed that most of the hikers had already gone to sleep.

"Ever had sex in the open?" she suddenly asked, after some star gazing. Her eyes were fixed on the woods nearby.

"Um ... not yet!"

In high school, the students around me liked to brag that they "fucked like rabbits," but I kept my distance from forbidden territories. I tried to stick to my identity as a practicing Muslim. Sometimes I wanted that mysterious experience everyone around me had had, and sometimes I wanted to be above everyone else, depending on which had more blood at the moment of contemplation: my brain or my loins.

"Would you like to try?" Tina's eyes met mine. Her tone was very pragmatic, as if she were talking about ordering Chinese, but her eyes twinkled.

I don't know what I would have said if I were off meds. A soft and desperate voice inside my head whispered, "Do not say yes."

"Yes. It'd be good to cross it off my bucket list," I said, realizing how easy it was for the express train to forbidden territories, fueled by the blue fire of her eyes, to test my virtue. "The weakest of all things is a virtue that has not been tested by fire." Who said that?

"I'm sure you'll tick more than one item off that list in just a few moments." She winked at me, and my face and loins tingled with heat.

We went to the woods, a hundred meters away from the camp. When we stopped walking, before she put her blanket down, she looked straight at me. I could see emeralds in her eyes, even in that dim light. I later realized that her eyes changed color: blue, green, gray, irrespective of the light.

She said, "To be clear, no Romeo crap with me. This is just sex."

I gave her the Scouts' honor sign, trying to act cool. No matter that I've never been a Scout or even had sex, for that matter. "Of course!"

She reached for my face and kissed me. I kissed her back fiercely, and her lips tasted of sweet bitterness, like lemon juice. I held her waist and slowly moved my hands down her body. Her skin was warm against the cold night and smelled of vanilla and jasmine. I asked her later what perfume she had on that night. "Dior Addict," she said. And who said the universe doesn't send signs?

I slid my hand into her panties. She was hot and wet. The next second, we were on the blanket.

When she finished riding me like a Dakar Rally pro, we lay on the blanket, facing the stars, panting and full of heat despite the cold weather. We smoked cigarettes under the full moon's light.

I cared about her pleasure more than my own. The tremors in her thighs, the pained expression on her face. Her silent gasps and her hand squeezing her left breast, the tell-tale sign I grew to know, which marked her genuine satisfaction.

I had no point of reference, but I guessed it was safe to say that I owed my opioids for a not too-shabby performance for a first-timer.

The next day, when everybody was readying to return to civilization, she casually said, "Maybe I should take your number." She wasn't asking.

These were the kinds of orders I was happy to abide by.

I waited a whole week until she called. It was the most stressful week of my life, followed by months where my world was full of colors, because we were together.

I met Tina because of grief. Grief and loss, handing over to love and attachment, in an infinite "lazy eight" cycle of life. I saw clear signs that I was in love. I struggled to see the same signs reflected back at me. She kept me at arm's length, no matter how hard I tried. It didn't help that I couldn't spend as much time with her as I wanted because of my long residency hours as a junior doctor, with most of my shifts being the graveyard ones. I would often crash at her place after work. We would get high on drugs—*cocktails*, as she liked to call them—watch films, and have sex. But I never managed to reach her heart through her pussy or her brain.

Tina was an artist. She had worked for Christie's auction house in New York before she came back to the UK to manage a Soho art gallery that she'd inherited from her dad.

I had this unresolved religious conflict over being with Tina outside of marriage, itching at my soul since day one. So I pretended we were married. The main condition for marriage in Islam is *ishhar*—publicly announcing the relationship. That's why I was very happy when, one autumn day, she took me to visit her mom, who lived in a care home in Chelsea.

Tina's mom was thin and old, but they had the same eyes—pale blue-gray eyes that froze or melted, depending on whether you were in their good or bad books.

Tina told me her mom was from Liverpool and used to work as an immigration barrister, which was how she met Tina's Polish dad, her third husband.

"Where are you from?" her mom asked, not for the first time. She had a giant red shawl over her shoulders that she kept adjusting with thin restless hands full of blue veins.

Tina had warned me about her early signs of Alzheimer's, so I didn't feel like arguing the existential question of whether I was from the UK or Egypt. Or neither.

"London," I said.

"Where did you two meet?"

"On a hiking trip. Enough about us, Mom—"

"What do you like about each other?" she asked.

"We like hanging out together," Tina said.

"We love each other," I replied in the same breath.

Tina raised an eyebrow at me.

"That's not the same thing now, is it?" her mom said, cocking her head.

"Mom!"

Damn, she could be a Stasi officer with those eyes. I felt I was in an interrogation room and Tina was my lawyer.

"Just keep the same open mind you used to enter this relationship, and you'll see if it will work out. I'm not being mean; I'm just trying to save your precious youth."

"Enough about us, Mom," Tina repeated with a sigh. "How are you doing? Are they taking good care of you here?"

She waved a veiny hand dismissively and turned to the window. After a pause, she said, "How's the gallery? Are you managing with all those debts your dad left you?"

It was the first I was hearing about any debts.

Tina glared at her mom and tugged on her earlobe, then said, with a borrowed smile, "Everything is fine, Mom. Nothing to worry about." She followed her gaze to the window. "It's a beautiful day, isn't it?"

"Can't complain. We're doing better than those twenty people a trapeze artist with diarrhea shat on last week in Paris."

"Mom, I told you before that was a hoax."

"What are you talking about? I only just heard of it the other day, from Nurse Williams. You don't have a monopoly on the truth."

"Fine, Mom. Anyway, we have to leave now. Very soon, we'll be able to move to the States for good. Remember how I was telling you about the care homes with golf courses there?"

I cringed at the mention of moving to the US. What made things worse was that I wasn't even sure if *I* was included in the *we*. In Arabic, nouns take on a special form for duos, different from proper plural. Until that moment, I had never thought it was of any real use.

Tina had always dismissed any long-term plans together. "This makes us happier," she would say. She had a free spirit, and the only things that kept the chains of reality weighing on her wings were her mom and the gallery. After all, her all-time favorite movie quote was from *Heat*, when Robert De Niro tells Al Pacino, "Don't let yourself get attached to anything you aren't willing to walk out on in thirty seconds flat if you feel the heat around the corner."

London, February 2014

Here's a little advice in case you're planning on trying to fight a physical illness with sheer willpower: it doesn't work.

The headaches after my accident ten years ago taught me that if the pain went unquenched for too long, my brain would misfire like an old car. The sharp jolts of pain eventually turned into convulsions, near-blindness, and blackouts.

The nearest I've gotten to the finish line of life was on a Monday afternoon at Tina's place in St. Jude's. A penalty for trying to go off the meds cold turkey. A penalty for trying to be normal.

On the third day of annoying but tolerable headaches, the jolts of pain hit like lightning. I fell to the floor, gasping, curled into a ball. A blanket of cold covered my body, squeezing me mercilessly. Losing consciousness would have been a welcome relief, but the remaining dim light inside me continued spinning uselessly, like a car stuck in sand. Convulsions came in waves and kept coming faster and faster. My mind was barely functioning. I had a first aid kit for such emergencies, but the bathroom was galaxies away.

I tried to stand and walk. Crawl and move. Open my mouth and shout. I failed. I even failed to prevent drool dripping from my mouth and urine from my bladder. After God knows how long, I started to welcome death and urge it to take control of my faulty existence. That was when Tina came back and saved my life.

I recall fragments of her warm hands on my face and the sound of her words, before she rushed for the emergency kit. When she injected me with the mix of morphine and a muscle relaxant, I didn't even feel the needle.

My body started to relax. Breathing no longer felt like a form of exorcism.

My name is Luke Elraey. Or is it? The question melted in my mind without leaving my lips, as the light in my head finally shut off.

When I woke up, Tina was next to me in her bed. The curtains were closed, and the bedside table light reflected on her face. I had no idea what time it was, and I didn't care. She kissed me and smiled. Her vanilla and jasmine scent brought more colors to the cozy room with its retro wooden floorboards and dreamlike wall paintings. That night, I felt less like an orphan.

A big glass of water materialized in my hands, ice cubes swimming idly in it. "You must be dehydrated. You slept for fourteen hours," she said softly.

I drank the whole glass. I even chewed on one of the ice cubes.

"I thought I would lose you. How do you feel?"

"Better. You saved my life."

She winked. "You better remember that the next time I want you to go shopping with me." She ran her fingers through my hair and then along my scar. "Are you sure doctors can't help? We can try again."

"Trust me, I'm a doctor," I rasped.

"You know, I asked my psychiatrist about it. He told me you could be suffering from unconscious guilt from, you know, that old accident."

"Psychiatrists don't know shit."

"So, you don't feel any remorse?"

I shifted in the bed. "I killed a human being in front of his son, Tina. Of course I feel remorse. It's just that's not the cause of my headaches."

After a momentary silence, she asked, "Have you ever tried to meet the surviving son?"

Now I was sitting fully erect in bed, not at ease with where this conversation was heading. "What? No. Bloody hell, no. Even reading about it in the papers made me feel sick. Thank God the funeral wasn't in London. It was in Glasgow. Or Belfast? I don't remember."

She kissed away my discomfort and I was back at home. She could be very tender when she wanted to. I tried to tongue kiss her, but she didn't extend hers. "Not now, it's three AM and I have a meeting at eight for this weekend's exhibition," she said, resting her head on the pillow.

As I remember it, something was weighing on her mind as she spoke. Although whether that was my hindsight's sharp vision or what I felt in the moment is impossible to tell.

"And don't forget to take your cocktails from now on," she said, closing her eyes.

Since that day, I haven't tried to break loose from opioids. I'm what you would call a reluctant addict.

CHAPTER 9

Yehia comes hurrying to the basement. "Cars approaching."

"Everyone on the ground." I shout. "Get behind the sandbags, now."

In position, we lay still. The shouting and the sound of revved-up engines grow louder by the second, much like the heartbeat thudding in my ears. Max said that the insurgents' 109 cannons mounted on pickup trucks can't reach us here, but RPGs, from the right angle, definitely can.

A few bullets hit the building. Then bursts of machine gunfire kick off the symphony. *Da-da-da-da-da-da-da*, with the occasional *crank ... crank ... crank* whine when the bullets hit metal objects.

Both parties flex their iron muscles. I hear and feel the roar of the 14.5 mm anti-aircraft machine guns and their little brother, the 12.7 mm DShK, affectionately known in Russian as Dushka—a dear or beloved person. Both were designed as anti-aircraft weapons, but in Yemen they point at humans.

Dududuf ... duduf ... dududuf ... duduf .... dududuf ... duduf. If they continue at this rate, I won't be surprised if the whole building crumbles on top of us.

Apart from a few wails from Anne, no one speaks. We've been working near active fighting for years, but this is the first time we're in it. It's like the difference between watching a play versus being on stage without having read the script.

Most of us are covering our ears and curling instinctively into fetal positions behind the sandbags. Manu closes his eyes and tries some deep breathing technique he must have learned in Nepal or some other hippie haven. From what I can see, it only makes him hyperventilate, increasing his panic.

I wonder if Max and his team feel the same, or if repetition has blunted their responses. I salute those sons of Ares. Facing death and still being able to function is real-men cool. Playing snooker and smoking cigars is real-twats cool. Then I notice Yehia, who doesn't seem scared. His head rests on a sandbag and he's smoking a cigarette, knowing that this time, Anne will not stop him. He has been living through this all his life. Even death doesn't seem like a big deal to him.

Is there a threshold here? Is the earth demanding a set number of bodies so it can be reborn? Or maybe we have passed the point of no return. People have been killing each other until their hearts have become harder than black stones.

The exchange of fire is growing more discernible—generous incoming fire and pragmatic fire in return. Max has probably picked out every gun already. The drumming of the M240 carries a different rhythm than the screams of the .50 cal, which sounds like a chainsaw tearing through ceramic. Not to mention the clear distinctions between M16s and Kalashnikovs, which every civilian here can distinguish as easily as twitchers identify birdsong. Ugly sounds, but somehow I'm grateful to hear them. At least the battle is going two ways. The beauty of balance.

A few rounds of RPGs hit the walls above us, and a yelp escapes Anne. With each explosion, the air reverberates like a massive Nepalese gong. My ears are blocked, as if I'm in a plane taking a nosedive, and I swallow hard. Shreds of concrete fall from the ceiling. Showers of gray dust fill our noses and disturb our vision. Who was it that said dust is made of dead skin?

Anne crawls toward me on her hands and knees. She crosses

over Rachel as if she doesn't even see her and asks, "Should we trust that Max fella?"

"He's a killer. But I think he's a decent man."

"What will happen to us if we're taken hostage?"

Her eyes widen, insanity floating at the edges. Get this woman away from me.

"I don't know, Anne. I hope we—"

"Are they going to use us as sex slaves?"

I look at Yehia for help.

He says helpfully, "Don't worry, Anne. They will either kill you on the spot or sell you to Al Qaeda."

The remaining blood drains from her face. She looks as if she's seeing the future.

"Can you get off me now, please?" Rachel says from under her.

Anne snaps out of her dark thoughts and crawls back to her spot. I remember one of Manu's "when I was in ..." stories, when he talked about an aid worker who was kidnapped in Kabul, only to be dropped a few hundred meters later because his kidnappers discovered he was Moroccan. They wanted a *foreigner* from a wealthy country for ransom. Maybe I should destroy my passport and let the color of my skin do the talking. What would my team think of me? What would Rachel do in my position?

I can't stay with my dark thoughts any longer. If I'm going to die, I want to at least see how. I head to the door, but Michael stops me. I can barely hear his voice over the war symphony.

"Where the hell are you going?"

"I'll be right back," I say, although I doubt he can hear me.

Two of the three relatives-of-the-General soldiers are guarding the hospital door, as instructed by Max. They swing their guns in my direction as I dash up the basement stairs, but when they see it's me, they quickly revert to nervously peering out a small window facing the front gate.

I continue up the stairs to the roof, hunching forward to take up as little space possible. But apart from a sniper trying to nail me while I'm crossing in front of the second-floor window, I arrive safely.

The view from the roof is hardly real. It's more absurd than an action flick. I move cautiously, as I'm aware that dying from friendly fire is much more likely than dying from enemy fire. Thankfully, I spot Max. He's wearing full fatigues and carrying double his weight in ammo. I wave at him to let him know it's me. He scowls like a father interrupted by a child in the middle of a business call. I crawl over to him.

"What's up, Luke? Is your team OK?" He pauses from firing his big-ass machine gun through a hole in the parapet. He turns to the English mercenary I met earlier, who's holding a sniper rifle. "Shut down those heavy calibers on the pickups, Ray."

"Yeah, all good," I say, wiping my brow. "I couldn't stay down there. How are you holding up?"

"Not the time for a sitrep now, Luke. Let's just say they've killed a lot of concrete so far."

He then asks for sitrep from Echo One, and I notice the .50 chainsaw is no longer joining in. The Humvee is exposing its thick armored skin to a barrage of bullets that come from the road leading to the main gate, with no return fire.

The radio crackles with a thick familiar voice: "Bravo, this is Echo One. We can't move the vehicle. The engine is dead and the .50 is jammed—over."

"Of course, it is, you fuckin' idiot. You were going cyclical like you were hosing a fuckin' garden. Fix it—over!"

"Can't un-jam the feed tray without exposing my butt crack for everyone to aim at. Over."

"Copy. We will provide cover fire when ready. Fix it from the left side and Echo Two and Bravo will cover you. How copy?"

Silence from the radio, then Piotr's resigned voice comes, "Shit, copy. Wait for my fucking signal. It's still overheating. Over."

Moments later, his shout into the radio makes me flinch. "Now!"

The whole team immediately provides covering fire. My eardrums shriek. Max's machine gun runs through the belt like a hungry dragon. Spent shell casings tumble clanking and dancing to the ground with snake tails of smoke.

I risk a brief glimpse down off the roof. Piotr goes up the turret to unjam the ammo belt of the big-dick gun. A few bullets hit the metal shield in front of him before he finishes and gets back inside the vehicle. The Humvee's windows are spiderwebs, but none are broken.

Max stops the covering fire, with only few stray bullets here and there, and a short silence ensues.

Along comes Piotr's voice, "I'm hit. My left hand."

"Can you fight?" Max asks.

Silence.

"I repeat, Echo One, can you fight? Over."

"*Khonya etavsio*. Yes, I can. Out," he says grudgingly.

I say, breathing again, "Shit, now I know why you like this guy. He's not as bad as his haircut."

Max laughs cheerfully. "Piotr? Yeah. I love him more than my chihuahua."

I try to peek again from the roof, but Max's heavy hand pushes my head down.

"They're retreating. They tried to rush in zombie-style in the beginning, but after heavy casualties, they pulled back. They are mostly on rooftops now, with snipers."

A few minutes later, I risk another peek. None of the attackers would be teaching anytime soon in Sandhurst military academy, but the enthusiasm was great. Two pickup vehicles are burning, and several bodies in the traditional *thobs* with suit jackets over them are scattered around them, some scorched.

"They look like ocean waves," Max murmurs, as if to himself.

One of the rebels is still alive, stuck halfway out of one of the burning pickups that tried to flank the Humvee from the eastern side.

Noticing the direction of my gaze, Max says, "I wonder what your humanitarian laws say about him? Apparently, we're not supposed to put him out of his misery."

I sit, my back to the parapet, hands shaking and eyes wide. I should go and save that man, right? Would the snipers shoot me? Would he do the same for me? Does it matter?

I gulp a mouthful of air before looking back. The rebel's body is still, his head and arms lying at impossible angles. Thank God this test is canceled.

It is 19:47 on my watch. Except for the snipers' crosshairs peering down at us, I think we're in a "to be continued" moment.

"Break time, fellas. Echo One, don't get out of the Humvee. Snipers are everywhere. We will find a way to bring you food and ammo, over."

"Roger that, waiting for the fucking Big Mac, out," Piotr says.

"We need to leave," Yehia says in a low voice when I come back to the basement. He makes sure no one is listening except our team.

"Yeah, and I need a massage and a sun bath," Rachel says, closing her eyes and resting her head on the wall behind her.

"No, I mean I have a plan." He continues in a more hushed tone. "There's a way out of here. A tunnel."

"What tunnel?" Michael asks.

"Hush," Yehia hisses. "There's an old utility tunnel that connects this building and the abandoned rehab center next door. It used to be part of the hospital. We can use it to leave."

"And then what?" I ask.

"The center is in no-man's land between the main concentration of the rebels to the west and the hospital. We can sneak out of there through the backstreets until we reach the harbor and take a boat out of here. Worst-case scenario, we can hide in my house until this is all over."

After a short pause, Anne says, "I can't do that. I'm not part of this war."

"Yes, that's why we're running away from it," Yehia says.

"I can't do it," Anne repeats, more to herself than anyone else.

"What about you, Michael?" I ask, warming to the idea.

"We can't go. That's final," he says quickly, evading my eyes.

"Whoa, why not?" Rachel asks.

"I'm the team leader. I'm responsible for your safety."

I adopt Rachel's Socratic method in asking him questions until he realizes the flaws in his logic. "Alright team leader, can you guarantee our safety here?"

"We have to do things by the book," Michael says, "Otherwise—"

My short fuse burns out. To hell with Socrates. "Wake up, Michael. Your *by-the-book* bureaucracy will not work here. We have the right to decide for ourselves."

His face reddens. "Then I decide to stay with Anne."

I turn to Manu. "Are you coming?"

"No way, man. Too risky," he says, biting his nails.

I meet Rachel's eyes. She says, "I'm coming with you."

Anne looks at her with disbelief verging on horror.

"If it's safe, why don't we tell Max and his team to use it and get the hell away from us?" Manu asks.

Yehia says, "They are foreigners with guns, but Luke passes for a local, and Rachel can wear one of the nurses' hijabs. We can blend in until we reach my house."

"When shall we—" Rachel cuts herself short as we hear footsteps coming down the stairs outside.

Max and TJ enter the basement. The former is carrying several army-issue Meals, Ready-to-Eat, or MREs, that look like brown plastic bricks.

"How're you all doing?" Max asks with a grin, in a voice loud enough to wake those he just killed.

Nobody answers.

That does not affect his big smile. "Anyone hungry?"

He puts the MREs on the ground and we all hover around sheepishly, suddenly aware of our stomachs growling.

"Only half an MRE each though, until we figure out a food distribution plan," he says.

Anne can't resist. "This morning we were human shields, and now you bring us food?"

Max seems confused. "You were never human shields. Do I look like the bad guy here?"

His question is met with glares all around.

CHAPTER 10

"What now?" Michael rasps, as though sand were in his throat.

"We managed to repel the attack. As I said, you're safe here." Max opens the food packages and adds water, producing an obnoxious smell as the contents mysteriously warm up.

"What about rescue teams?" Anne asks impatiently.

Max studies her for a second before saying, "Extraction teams are on the way. We just need to keep it together for a little longer." He gives her a substitute-teacher smile.

She nods and looks at me as if to say, "See? All we need to do is sit here and wait." I pretend to be helping Yehia put newspaper on the ground for the food.

"What about the injured fighters?" Rachel asks. "Luke saw many of them around the hospital perimeter."

"Well, Doctor Kessler, if you want to go and pick them up, be my guest."

Silence.

Rachel breaks it. "Fine, I'm ready to go."

Michael turns his whole body to her. "Ready to go where?"

"Get the injured. I'll wear a lab coat and carry a white flag if need be. These are their men, after all, and we're trying to help them."

"Or take them hostage." Manu shrugs. "Depending on how they see it."

"He's right," Michael says. "They might shoot you. Our first principle is do no harm, and that means to ourselves as well."

"I think you're confusing do no harm with do nothing," Rachel says.

"It's too late anyway," Max says, ending the discussion. "By now, the injured have either crawled back or bled to death."

I exchange a look with Yehia and Rachel that tells me nothing has changed in our escape plan. They didn't buy Max's tranquilizer line about evacuation either.

I share an MRE with Yehia. It turns out to be egg noodles. The same thing I had with Tina after we had first-time sex in the woods in a faraway galaxy.

Anne looks at her meatballs—half in horror, half in disgust—and says, "I don't eat meat."

"We have a noodle one here we can trade with you," Yehia volunteers eagerly.

"No need. I assumed that not all of you are carnivores. There are tuna and bean ones there," Max says.

Yehia seems disappointed. "I thought vegetarians don't eat fish," he murmurs.

"I'm pescatarian," Anne replies proudly, carefully sniffing a tuna ration.

"What's that, a new religion?" TJ asks with a smirk.

This guy is no doubt another finalist in the Premier League of alpha male dicks, same as Dave Banks. Unfortunately, bullies are always bigger than everyone else. I'm sure he was a quarterback or a catcher or whatever the hell Yanks play in high school. I wonder how many teeth will be left in my mouth if I ask him whether his initials stand for Total Jerk.

Anne doesn't dignify his question with a response. Meanwhile, after a careful bite from our egg noodles, Yehia retrieves an impressive number of small packets from his bag and generously adorns our plate with a mix of cheerfully colored condiments: red, yellow, brown, and white.

Satisfied with the surreal mess, he says, "With this, there's nothing I can't eat." He spreads the remaining packets in front of me. "Put as much as you like."

I stare at the mess on the plate. "Thank you very much."

The mix tastes like reality TV, but I don't have the luxury of a hundred-channel remote control.

Meanwhile, Manu notices TJ's missing pinkie and asks, with a conversational smile, "What happened to your finger?"

"I left it in the mouth of a terrorist in Northern Syria," TJ says, not taking his eyes off his food. "After I blew his head off."

We eat in silence after this, except for Max, sitting to my right, who shares Anne's discarded meatballs with Rachel.

"Consider this the last supper," he whispers dramatically in my ear. The food turns into acid in my stomach, and I wonder if he overheard our escape plan.

"Why?" I ask with a mouth full of preservatives.

He seems genuinely confused. "So you can enjoy it more!"

Max and the two Yemeni soldiers linger after the food, drinking tea. One of the soldiers turns out to be the General's nephew and the other is one of his cousins. The third soldier in the Humvee with Piotr is also a blood relative.

Rachel and Anne retreat to one of the corners, clearly not interested in testing the potential for Stockholm syndrome. Anne clings to her bottle of water for dear life. I notice her biting off a piece of a granola bar hidden in her palm, even though we were all supposed to pool our goods and ration them. What happened to all the "sorries" and "pardon me's" she used to say whenever our hands accidentally met at a dish back at the residence?

"So, why are you here, Michael?" Max asks, breaking the awkward silence around the slurps of tea.

Michael shrugs. "To heal my fellow man who's suffering."

Max gives him a stare.

Michael gives a nervous cough. "What about you?"

Max smiles. "To kill my fellow man who's causing the suffering. Plus," he says after a slurp of tea, "I hate to pay taxes."

Michael puckers his lips and nods. "So, are you guys Blackwater?"

"There's more to this profession than Blackwater."

"I didn't know it was a growing business."

"Growing business?" Max's smile widens. "Man, this is the second-oldest job. It's older than the fuckin' pharaohs."

The call for *Isha* prayer, the last of the five daily prayers, echoes outside the hospital. I make quick ablutions and join Yehia for the prayer. Cousin and Nephew excuse themselves to continue their "watch duty" as Max and my team pretend not to watch us.

After the prayer, we hear chants in Arabic in the distance: "Death to America, death to Israel," in a repeated chorus.

Max says, as he stands to leave, "Someone seems to have a broken compass." Then to us, he adds, "Don't worry about those cheerleaders. They're still licking their wounds. There probably won't be any more attacks tonight."

Present Day, Friday, 00:11

I can't find Mezcal to say goodbye. I wouldn't blame him if he had already fled this death trap. "Has anyone seen the cat?" I ask.

"Who cares about the stupid cat now?" Yehia asks, getting antsy waiting for me and Rachel.

"Why do you hate Mezcal?" I ask.

"I don't hate it. I'm indifferent to it." He steals a peek through the door that stands ajar, making sure that Cousin and Nephew are still asleep by the front entrance. Then he says, "I already get all the love I want from my family."

"Don't worry, I'll look for him," Anne says. "We won't leave him behind."

"I knew it," Yehia hisses in my ear as Rachel ties her shoes.

"Westerners care about animals of all nationalities, but only humans with matching passports."

Yehia, Rachel and I sneak into the generator room. The utility tunnel's hatch screeches open, sending our hearts into freefall. It's pitch black down there.

Yehia descends first and turns on his flashlight. A few rats scurry away. Good thing Anne decided to stay behind. At least the tunnel is dry.

"What if they've occupied the rehab center?" Rachel whispers after we're all in the tunnel.

"Then we'll run back to Daddy Max," I say, carefully closing the hatch behind us.

About a hundred meters in, we see the rusty rungs leading to the rehab center hatch. Yehia climbs up, turns to us with his finger on his lips, and then turns off his flashlight. The hatch opens with a muffled thump and showers him with a storm of dust. He pops his head up, then climbs out.

We wait to hear shouts, screams, or gunshots, but nothing happens. He turns his flashlight back on and motions for us to come up.

The center is empty. It smells of rust and stale sweat. Dust is everywhere. A few exercise mats are scattered across the hall along with stacks of old wooden boxes. My eyes adjust, and I recognize the boxes for what they are: crates for guns and ammo. This place is now the rebels' bloody ammunition warehouse.

We go out to the main hall and peer through the windows to the side street. It flickers with giant dancing shadows from a burning car. A group of rebels huddle around the fire, shivering in the late-night coastal wind. Under the cover of the night, they have managed to sneak much closer than anyone thought they could.

"We need to warn Max," I whisper.

"We can't go back," Yehia says. "Besides, shouldn't humanitarians be neutral or something?"

He moves toward the back door. We sneak out and find

ourselves in a back alley. I breathe the fresh night air. We're out. We made it.

A scabby yellow dog stands at attention next to a pile of garbage. He gazes at us with curiosity. Yehia crosses the street first, then Rachel, and then me. As I pass, the dog growls, showing remarkably white fangs, even in the dim light.

We hear distant chatter in the street we're about to slide into. People are coming toward us. The dog barks at the smell of the adrenaline-perfumed intruders. Rachel and I freeze, but Yehia moves to the nearest house and motions for us to follow him.

The door is open, as if there were no thieves in this city or, more realistically, as if they had already come and gone. It's dark inside and we can hardly see.

Yehia cautiously peers out the window as two rebels pass in front of the house.

"We need to go out through the back door once the coast is clear. From there, it's five hundred meters to my house," he whispers.

Rachel and I aren't listening. We're watching a man who has just stood up from the couch, sporting a Kalashnikov. We can only see his silhouette in the dim light. The gunman seems as surprised as we are. We raise our hands slowly.

Yehia finally turns back from the window and sees him.

"Don't shoot," Yehia says in Arabic.

Hopefully, he's a startled civilian thinking this is a home invasion. Maybe he can even help us.

The light flickers on. Another man, in military khakis, comes out from the toilet with an open zipper and a pistol pointed straight at me.

Now this changes the situation a bit.

The man with the pistol comes closer and says in Arabic, "Who are you?"

He's very thin, with oily skin. I smell his sweat, pear-scented from starvation.[6] I would feel a stab of sympathy for him if he weren't pointing a pistol at my heart.

"We were just passing by," I say, trying to calm my erratic heartbeat.

"You're those doctors, are you not? How did you get out of the hospital?" the other one asks. He's wearing a dirty green tank top and gray tracksuit pants. "Where do you think you're going? The whole area is surrounded. There's going to be an attack any moment now." He exchanges a smile with his comrade. "That's why we're here."

Shit. Just as I feared. These aren't civilians, they're Akrami's men.

"We won't get in your way." I point to the khat leaves on the tray next to Tank Top and the candles around the table for the frequent electricity outages. "Please, carry on."

The one with the pistol wiggles it in my face, as if I can't see the massive Magnum that allows him to control the conversation. Sodding Dirty Harry pop culture. "Shut up. Empty your pockets." He spirals to Rachel and Yehia. "All of you."

Tank Top devours Rachel with hungry eyes. Her scarf is on her shoulders now, showing her auburn hair. He grabs her by the arm and holds her as a human shield.

Yehia holds up his hands. "We don't want to get hurt. We will do exactly as you say. Just don't deliver us to Akrami."

"Why not? He would be delighted to see you."

"Will he be also delighted to know that you're hiding from his big battle in abandoned houses?" Yehia asks.

I sense the wheels turning in Tank Top's head. He exchanges a look with Dirty Harry before he says, "You two, get out of here. We will ... take the nurse. We have wounded soldiers."

....

6   With prolonged starvation, the body starts dissolving itself, leading to the formation of ketone bodies, which smell fruity or like nail polish remover.

I exchange a brief look with Yehia. He nods slightly to me, and his right eye narrows and twitches. I'm not sure if it's a nervous tic or a clumsy wink that's part of a coded message I don't understand.

Then the lights flicker and go out. Glory be to houses with no generators. I instinctively duck away from the pistol's line of fire, moving my hand at the same time to push Dirty Harry's arm up. He doesn't even fire, and would have hit the ceiling anyhow. I hear noise and curses from Tank Top—Yehia must have jumped him. I swiftly maneuver to Dirty Harry's right, twisting his forearm above my shoulder. It feels the same as the thousand times I practiced it in aikido class. All I need now is a slight pressure between his wrist and elbow to snap his forearm like a stalk of sugar cane. I take hold of his wrist, which is propped on my shoulder, with both hands and ... *crack*! It all takes less than two seconds.

Dirty Harry drops to the ground. I get on all fours, fumbling for his gun until I find it. I'm sure the punk no longer feels lucky.

I point the cinderblock hand cannon toward the sound of fighting. At the same moment, Rachel turns on her flashlight.

Tank Top is hammering the butt of his Kalashnikov against Yehia's head so he'll let go of the muzzle that he is desperately latched on to. When Tank Top sees the light, he twists the Klash to aim at it. At Rachel.

I fire two shots at his hand. One misses and the other draws a hole through his right cheek to his brain.

The heavy recoil jerks me a step back. My arm hurts up to my shoulder blade. I turn when I hear a sound to my left. Dirty Harry is reaching for his Klash leaning against the wall.

My brain wants to say, "Stop, or I'll shoot," but instead my finger squeezes the trigger, as if it has a will of its own, and a black flower blooms on Dirty Harry's back before going down for the last time.

We run back to the rehab center. We hear people closing in on us from both sides of the street. The bloody dog is in full-automatic bark mode.

Once inside, we burst into the side room where the hatch is and stop short. Two rebels are collecting ammo in a cloth bag next to a big kerosene lamp. One man, thin as a scarecrow, is carrying belts of large-caliber bullets over his shoulders; the other, much older, has a Klash strapped to his back.

The one with the Klash aims it at us and we raise our hands. "Sons of a dog!" he shouts in Arabic.

"Shoot them," commands the other.

Shots ring out, and the head of the rebel with the gun explodes like a fresh egg.

Max pops up from the hatch. "Come on," he snaps at us, and to the other rebel, who drops the ammo belts. "Don't even think about it, Skinny Pete."

"American infidel. Son of a fucked woman." The rebel moves quickly toward Max with fists clenched.

Max, still halfway inside the hatch, overcomes his momentary bafflement from the illogical attack and snaps the butt of his M16 to the side of the man's left knee, which cracks loudly. He holds the gun by the barrel and swiftly swings the butt, like an expert golfer, to meet the man's jaw, sending him crumbling to the floor.

The commotion outside is getting louder. Max's eyes flare at us with rage. "Move!"

We jump in after him and sprint through the tunnel.

TJ is waiting for us on the hospital side, wearing a gas mask. The humming of the generator fills the room. Or is it my heartbeat in my ears?

"To the basement," Max orders us as he puts on the gas mask TJ handed him.

Yehia and Rachel rush downstairs, but I linger at the door to the generator room. Max and TJ now stand on either side of the hatch.

TJ pulls three cylindrical grenades from his bag and looks at Max.

Smoke grenades? They're deadly in such confined spaces. I take a few steps back.

Max is counting inaudibly to TJ as noise from the tunnel grow closer, slightly moving his head with each count. "3 ... 2 ... "

Oh, God.

" ... 1."

TJ throws in the smoke grenades. A barrage of shots comes in reply. TJ slams the lid shut and Max locks a steel rod into its handle. The bullets hit the lid, and my body rattles with each dent. The muffled explosions are followed by faint smoke rising from the hatch like white snakes heading toward the door. Toward me. I shut the door and run to the basement.

I killed two human beings. Intentionally this time. They are no longer here. All they've done, all they could have been, is gone. All because *I* decided so.

My mind is replaying all the different paths I could have taken on a loop. Maybe I shouldn't have agreed to Yehia's plan. Maybe I should've told Max. Maybe I shouldn't have killed the second guy. Maybe I should've warned him first.

Something tells me that I didn't want him to turn back when he reached for his weapon. I didn't want to see his face. I didn't want to see the face of Dave Banks.

Do they have families? Kids? Are their moms waiting for them?

Max's voice thunders from behind a heavy cloud of thoughts, "You fuckin' snake. I shouldn't have trusted you again."

I'm not even looking at him. As the adrenaline rush from playing Liam Neeson subsides, the shockwave of what happened replaces it. I clasp my arms to get my shaking hands under control.

"It was my idea, not his," Yehia says.

"I think it's time your friends here know about your bright past," Max says, ignoring Yehia.

"Who do you think you are?" Rachel says as she faces him, sparks flying from her eyes. "We have every right to escape this death trap. So back the fuck off."

Silence. Even TJ is startled.

"Do whatever you want, Max. But not now," I say. "They're going to attack any minute."

He says, quietly this time, "Oh, yeah? Do you expect me—"

"The rebels told us. And we saw them regrouping in the street," Yehia interrupts.

Max's jaw tightens. "Are you ready, TJ?" he asks.

TJ nods.

Max looks back at me. "I'll deal with you later."

CHAPTER 11

London, March 2014

Every morning I asked myself why she had chosen me. She could've had any man she wanted. Would she wake up one day and realize her mistake? I asked her once, and she talked about how *different* I was. She mentioned something vague about opposites attracting and Marilyn Monroe's marriage to Arthur bloody Miller. I knew I needed to ask myself serious questions regarding the future of our relationship, but if procrastination were an aspirin, I would have given myself a peptic ulcer long ago. The unspoken questions bruised my peace of mind just as Tina's bites marked my shoulders during sex.

The week after my episode at Tina's place, I came to hers for breakfast after an all-nighter at the hospital. She could have stayed at mine, but she never liked it there. She was asleep when I arrived. I took a shower and fixed myself a cold breakfast. Night shift gives you that weird feeling that you've cheated the system. You're out of the meat grinder. Even if that meant you became, pun intended, coarser than everyone around you.

She woke and took a couple of puffs from a fat joint, and then we had lazy morning sex. I enjoyed being near the constellation of freckles on her shoulders and the brown mole above her left nipple, like the polar star. Looking back, I realize I was dealing with stuff I should have gone through ten years earlier. I was entrusted with life-or-death decisions inside the operating theater, but my experience with the other sex was less than that of a teenager with a spiderweb-thin moustache. For example, I thought passionate regular sex was a universal antidote for any couple's problems.

Afterward, she put on some music and we got caught up.

"So how was the exhibition?"

She popped a cotton ball in her mouth, chewed it, and swallowed. A cotton ball diet was zero calories, didn't taste bad, and was bite-size. Think of them as tasteless popcorn. She followed it up with a cigarette. Exhaling the first drag, she replied, "You mean the one you didn't attend? It was alright. Not as many sales as I wanted though."

I never liked attending her showings. A weird mix of rich conservatives and poor liberal artists, both looking for what the other had.

"Sorry to hear that." I sucked my teeth and proceeded with caution. "No offense, darling, but you know what I think of Baldini's work. His paintings are ugly and primitive. Same as Picasso's, minus the fame."

I had asked about the gallery debts her mom had mentioned. She told me that her father had never been good with money. He invested in some independent artists, one of whom was a hippie called Baldini, who ended up being a partner in the gallery.

"None taken. That's exactly why Dad chose him. You know that Picasso painted much better works in his early years? But none sold as much as when he created a different style. Cubism was the new *moda*. People don't care about how good something is, only how different. The world is full of talented painters, but not many Picassos."

I didn't want to argue. These days, there was no definition of good art. Good could be bad and vice versa, based on sheer luck.

"Maybe you should add some disco biscuits to the refreshments until his artistic reincarnation completes," I said.

She gave me the finger, preparing her second cup of coffee in her futuristic espresso machine. I wasn't allowed to touch it, ever since I had messed up her delicate ratio of different beans.

"Speaking of snacks, how many of these do you eat per day?"

I say, pointing to the cotton balls.

"I have to check my logbook," she said, putting a few drops of almond milk in her coffee.

Was she counting them?

I squinted. "Is that a joke?"

"Only if your question is." She popped another cotton ball into her mouth. Her eyes said, "Go ahead. I dare you to question my dietary decisions."

If only she knew that all of these diet recipes were useless for burning fat. Take it from an expert. The best fat liquefier was a head boiling with thoughts. Not to mention that cotton can cause intestinal obstruction.

From the speakers came Leonard Cohen singing "The Future."

"Did you know that Leonard Cohen recently changed this song's lyrics from 'Give me crack and anal sex' to 'Give me crack and careless sex'? I wonder why," I said, trying to lighten the mood.

"Gosh, you guys are such bigots. Leave gays alone."

"Who said I have a problem with gays?"

"You're religious. Sometimes even practicing," she said.

"So?"

"So? You hate gays, of course. You can't live with different people; you want everyone to be like you."

"Actually, if I'm religious, I'm obliged to do the exact opposite."

"Oh, really?"

"The Quran says, 'For each of you We have assigned a legislation and a method. And had Allah willed, He could have made you a single community, but in order to test you through what He has brought you; so race toward good works. To Allah is your return, all of you, then He will inform you regarding whatever you used to differ over.'"

I paused, thinking. "You know what? It's the supposedly open-minded people like you who want everyone to be like them. I should be either a liberal, non-practicing Muslim who enjoys

over-hyped arts, drinks alcohol, and eats kale or I'm a bloody
bin Laden in the making, ready to let rip a corner-shop bomb at
moment's notice. Do you have any idea how frustrating it is to be
the outsider all the time?"

"Would you do it then?"

"What, eat kale?"

"Anal. With a woman I mean."

"What has this got to do with—is that a hypothetical question?"

"Huh, I knew it. In your dreams, mate," she said triumphantly,
heading for the shower and leaving me perplexed over how the
conversation had evolved.

Tina was very open about her sexual fantasies. We tried every
position there is. Well, except anal, which in my dictionary was a
different game. Recently, she dragged me inside the changing room
in Burberry, where we tried the Reverse Houdini, apparently "ideal
for confined spaces." I ended up shooting on an ugly blouse that
she was trying on, with a cramp in my thigh from my acute fear
that someone would wander in and catch us in the act. Maybe I
shouldn't have been so concerned. In my father's generation, an
intruder would have viewed us as a couple of sick creeps, but in
these glorious times, they would feel envious and question what
else in life they were missing out on. Anyway, we paid for the blouse
and dumped it in the first trash bin we saw when we left. To be
honest, though, I wasn't into kinks. Which made me feel there was
something wrong with me.

When she came back from the shower, she said, while drying
her hair, "Something weird happened yesterday. I can't get it out of
my head."

"Someone finally realized that all this artwork is just ego
enhancement?"

She ignored my comment and swallowed a cotton ball. "Have
you heard of the Birch Cent?"

"No. What is it?"

"It's a coin valued at twenty million US."

I whistled. "What for? Was it handmade by one of the founding fathers or something?"

"It's unique, Luke. That's why. Yesterday in the gallery, one of my acquaintances told me between the lines that he has access to the coin, and he's looking for a buyer."

I wondered for a second how a message like this could be conveyed between the lines.

"Get as far away from him as possible. Fencing gets more people in prison than stealing." I paused, then raised a finger and gave her my doctor smile. "Unless you have the right connections. That makes all the difference between Van Gogh, who died piss-poor because he couldn't sell his art, and Picasso, who started as an art-magazine publisher with all the proper connections. Or in this case, the difference between a millionaire and a convict."

I was back to being the teenager jumping off cliffs. Wanting to impress. Wanting to fit in.

I told her that sellers without connections only have two options: either spreading the word to find a buyer, which was by definition indiscreet, or taking the desperate measure of selling it back to its owners. Both methods attracted enough attention that police would drop their donuts and pose as buyers.

I told her several stories, including the one about the drug dealer in the US who couldn't find a buyer for a million-dollar stolen Rembrandt and ended up selling it to an undercover cop for less than twenty-five thousand dollars.

All of what I said was true. It was Erkhart's words echoing through me.

She listened with an amused but surprised expression, her hands under her chin, her lips slightly parted. In moments like these, I doubted that I had ever kissed those lips.

Finally she asked, "And you know all this because ... ?"

I hesitated before uttering the sentence that changed my life,

"Because I know the kind of people who could have made Van Gogh a very rich man."

Now you tell me; if you had been in my shoes, wouldn't you have said the same to the woman of your dreams?

London, April 2014

My headache and I were having a meeting with Dr. Claire Evans, the hospital director, along with the hospital's legal advisor. Never a good sign.

Trying not to lisp because of the recent cut in my tongue, I muttered, "I *wath* tired, *pathed* out for few minutes. Could happen to anyone."

Dr. Evans's office was white. White walls, white window light, white floor, even her fake smile was full of immaculate white teeth. The office was cold and hostile. So was Dr. Evans. She sat behind her desk, hands on the table, clenching a pencil so sharp it could easily pierce a trachea. On any given day, how strongly she pulled her hair back showed how serious she was. That morning, she had it stretched back with the suction force of a black hole.

It was a crisp April day. I remember being cold on the outside and melting on the inside from the heat of my increasing headache. Cold sweat gathered on my forehead. Not from the effect of Dr. Evans, although she could scare the living shit out of anyone, but from my fear of losing control. I felt like a city mayor before a hurricane.

Just after being promoted to Senior House Officer after three years of practicing medicine, I had a quick-onset blackout episode— this time, in the middle of surgery. I had bitten my tongue during the convulsions and it was incredibly annoying. The phrase "pain in the ass" should definitely be replaced by "pain in the tongue."

It all started with the sharp nose of the head nurse, Maggie. I was at the tail end of a night shift from hell, on my feet for twelve hours straight. My dinner languished uneaten in the shared fridge.

I had just finished treating a stab wound when the emergency buzzer sounded. All hands on deck. I dashed across to the OT and found Matt, one of the junior residents, sweating and panicking. He had accidentally cut the renal artery of a bicycle-accident victim. Maggie and I rushed to scrub in.

Standing close to Matt, I caught a whiff of alcohol. Maggie's sharp nose also caught the smell but couldn't tell whether it was from me or Matt. I took over most of the operation—after smelling him, I didn't trust him to operate a vacuum cleaner.

As I sewed the patient back together, my headache pounded in rhythm with my pulse, despite my double dose of Percocet. I could feel my brain throbbing against my skull as if it had a heart of its own. Long story short: my mind unplugged and I passed out.

Maggie, with her good soul, reported smelling alcohol in the operating room. Both Matt and I did the tests. I was normal of course, but dear old Matt tested 0.09, higher than the drink-drive limit. To my surprise, he got off the hook with a verbal warning from Evans and a Condition of Practice rehabilitation and supervised monitoring. Unlike me, the scary legal advisor wasn't even present.

"Dr. Archer, you lost consciousness and started convulsing in the middle of performing a surgery. And if that wasn't enough, we had to open your cupboard because your next of kin wasn't answering. And we found, uh, some controlled drugs there."

She flicked her hand to the strips of Percocet lying in front of her with disdain. There had to be something that said they weren't allowed to open my locker without my permission, even in an emergency. Some shit like, "You didn't have a warrant," like on television.

Ironically, for this particular batch, I had opted for the black-market dealers because I was too embarrassed to ask James, my colleague at the hospital, to sign yet another prescription. He was reluctant last time he did it. This stupid bureaucratic mistake was now putting my career on the line. I wanted to tell her that these pills were probably Indian duds, as the double dose hadn't prevented my episode nor my current headache, but that would probably have made things worse. Dr. Evans was known for her idealism, which refused to shatter despite the recurrent shortages of staff and equipment, long wait times, and the cold misery of dealing with sick human beings as numbers. She was also known for having been spotted having sex with one of the nurses in her office. Yet here she was, talking to me about rules and procedures.

For people of color in the West, default expectations are reversed. We are expected to fuck up until we prove otherwise. And if we do fall, nobody helps us get up again, because that's where we belong.

"I have a medical condition because of an old head trauma," I said, touching the scar on my right temple. "I apologize for not disclosing my use of meds, but it doesn't affect my surgical abilities."

"A medical condition that no doctor can explain, no scanner can detect. I wish the GMC regulations agreed with your self-diagnosis, but they don't." She sighed and leaned away from her desk. "Have you seen a psychiatrist?"

"Yes, plenty. They give me a different diagnosis with each visit."

My brain was being chewed up like a giant wad of bubble gum. I touched the top of my mouth with my injured tongue and felt sandpaper. "Dr. Evans, I'm perfectly capable of performing my tasks as a doctor. To show my commitment, I'm ready to take the night shift for three consecutive weeks. No, five. As well as Easter and New Year's Eve."

She regarded me with what seemed to be empathy. Or amusement. She pursed her lips, which were coated in deep red lipstick. This was the face she made when she was about to deliver bad news to patients' families. I braced for the bunker buster.

"This has nothing to do with your productivity. You are a fine doctor. This is about your pre-existing, um, condition, which affects your abilities to practice medicine, not to mention surgery."

"Can you hear your contradictions?"

She cleared her throat, and leaned across her desk to deliver the knockout. "I have already informed the GMC, and we're happy to accept your resignation today to avoid the ignominy of involving the police in a formal investigation of the unregistered narcotics. You deserve a chance for a fresh start. A few years from now, you will thank me for this opportunity."

Like a leg thanks a body for the opportunity to be amputated. I shook my head, trying in vain to rid myself of her words. "Igno-*bloody*-miny"?

The legal advisor finally spoke. "Dr. Archer, given the circumstances, this is an appropriate solution for all parties involved. The sooner you accept what is happening, the sooner you will find your feet back on the ground."

I looked at him as if he had materialized out of thin air. I held his gaze. I refused to blink, and my eyes started to itch. A blacksmith was driving a hot nail into my head with an iron hammer, sparks flying everywhere. He averted his gaze to Dr. Evans.

"I know you have Paki herit— I mean Pakistani heritage, right? You could try to practice there. Maybe they've different rules," Dr. Evans said.

A bitter drop of sweat entered my right eye and I double-visioned for a second. That was it. No, I didn't throw a chair at her. I only said, "Different rules, huh? Like the rules about having sex in the hospital during working hours?"

Silence fell, and so did any last shred of hope of practicing medicine in this country. The legal advisor raised his eyebrows and cleared his throat. Dr. Evans blinked twice. On the first blink, she looked as though she had swallowed a bad egg. On the second, she gave me a look that would defrost a snowman in mid-January.

"I think we're done here, Dr. Archer," she finally said.

After I was sacked by my profession's sole employer in the country, the NHS, I felt like a speed bump on a desert road. Utterly use-less. I became addicted to things like Tesco's jacket potatoes with cheese and existential questions like how to write zero in Roman numerals, all while trying to figure out how many Oxys I could take without killing myself.

Since I stopped drinking Nitro Cold Brew at Starbucks, no longer am I surrounded by middle-aged women in full makeup on their way to work and yuppies with holier-than-thou attitudes and inflated egos inversely proportional to their IQ. I was out of the big machinery of the system. Out of the predictable *free* world where you can see where you'll be in forty years and know there's nothing you can do about it. Now I was truly free, and that was even more dreadful.

London, July 2014

He was holding his right hand up with pride. In that hand was the skin of his whole body, held high, on display. His face was trium-phant, as if shedding his skin had set him free.

A group of Asian tourists chattered in awe and took turns to freeze the moment on their phones. Most giggled and pointed to his penis, making sure it featured in the photos.

Tina whispered in my ear, as she walked next to me, "If you really can find a buyer for this coin, I'll have a gift for you."

The hot air she blew in my ear reminded me of when she would initiate sex by crawling toward me in bed like a tigress and licking my earlobe.

A woman was stuck with a bow in her hand, aiming for a target she would never reach. Her brain was exposed to the open air. She seemed immensely focused on her task, unaware of my predica-ment. Nothing else in the world would distract her anymore.

I leaned toward Tina and caught her scent. Recently, she had switched to Miss Dior Chérie. "What gift? Your Nintendo?"

"No, silly. Anal." She beamed.

Blood rushed to my loins, but my head kept its fair share. "But I didn't ask for …" I stopped quickly when I saw the tide shift in her eyes. "It's not that I don't want to, Tina. But anal should be the reward for when I beat you in tennis, not for when losing the bet means ten years in prison."

"You won't lose. You can do this, because you have what it takes. You know why you can do this?"

"Didn't you just answer—"

"Because having fewer options leads to more sacrifices. What options do people like you have in life? Even before you got fired, you were treading water and living most of your day as a body mechanic. Whatever straight line you take, twenty-five years later, you still won't earn half this cent. Don't let your ancient beliefs hold you back all your life."

I let it slide. Trying to talk faith and spirituality with Tina was like trying to talk equality to a KKK hood.

Another woman stood in saintly surrender, with palms open and eyes shut, her stomach opened horizontally, exposing a small fetus. Kids around her were laughing and pointing. I wished the meteor headed toward earth would move a bit faster.

The night had started with Tina calling me at home while I was devouring a large anchovy pizza. She was a feverish outdoor extrovert who only went home to fuck or sleep. Now, neither seemed on her to-do list.

"I'm bored. Want to do some yoga?"

"Nah, I have a sore back."

"Meditation?"

"It makes me sleepy."

"Pilates?"

"It makes me jittery."

"A choir?" she asked, as if ordering takeout.

"Bad voice."

"A mummified human bodies exhibition?"

That didn't sound too bad. Walking around is not a hardcore activity and saying yes would get her off my back. Besides, the next suggestion would probably be shopping. Tina was a shopaholic. Better than therapy, she said. She was the type who would shop at Burberry or Harvey Nichols and buy groceries from Waitrose and would rather be shot in the head than be seen in Aldi or H&M.

"We're just connecting buyers and sellers, so what's the problem?" she hissed.

We were at an anatomical exhibition of real human bodies preserved through a process called plastination. The things we'd do if we could get away with it.

An excited man appeared on several screens, explaining the show's history. The original purpose was to train doctors, but it quickly expanded to target "medically interested laymen." The term was malleable enough to mean almost anyone, from coroners to serial killers. They must have calculated that the crowds of visitors would undoubtedly feel superior to their fellow humans on the stands in their permanent death dance.

"We're breaking the law, for starters," I said.

"You mean the law that elites define through education and propaganda? The law that allows the world's top hundred wealthy men to have more money than half the world's population? We're just contributing our one cent to rebalancing the scale."

"Nice talk, but it still feels wrong. Insane, actually."

She listened to her brain, and I listened to my heart. If only we could meet in the middle.

"It's a one-off business transaction. We aren't stealing anything. Besides, what do you prefer—being sane or being happy?" She locked eyes with me. "I need this, Luke. This is the opportunity of my life. *Our* life. If this deal came through, I would stay in the UK with you. No more talk about moving to the US."

I averted my gaze as my heart picked up pace. I would tell my-self later that my decision was rational, that it was the only choice I had. Deep down, though, I knew that when she said she would stay with me in the UK, that was the moment I made up my mind.

A blue-eyed cadaver was holding a violin. A skeleton—all bones except for the eyes and parts of the brain—was holding a pen and staring at an unknown muse beyond our three dimensions, with one of those scary smiles that skeletons have. He had two silver teeth.

"So, what do you think?"

"Fascinating exhibition," I said. For all the wrong reasons. These were the ultimate works of art. God's works of art. Or na-ture's, depending on your side of the fence.

"You know what I mean." She stood in my field of vision, blocking the video on the big screen explaining how the human body is transformed into these grotesquely beautiful figures. Her squint showing the same dark portent that masses of dark clouds indicate to sailors.

"How long have you known that guy?" I asked, trying to bring her mood back ashore.

"Um, around three months."

"And you trust him already?"

"If it puts your mind at ease, the first time we met, his old Jeep broke down on our way back from an art auction in Norwich. We spent three hours in the middle of nowhere waiting for a tow truck. That counts as three years in normal life."

I furrowed my brow but ignored her idiosyncratic take on the theory of relativity. "Where did he say he got it from?"

"Better not to ask, don't you think?" She took a quick drag of her e-cigarette, glancing around for any source of trouble.

"How did they get all these dead bodies?" asked a tourist, in heavily German-accented English. A group was tailing a tour guide.

"Same way they obtain cadavers for medical students' anatomy classes. People who are not collected after a month in mortuaries and the like," the tour guide answered, flashing shiny white teeth with a practiced smile.

"What about consent?" a woman in her fifties asked, with a raised chin.

I imagined her as a schoolteacher with ready-to-use, simple answers that worked for others but never for herself.

"Some of the bodies were donated. As for the rest, well, society has decided they can be used for the greater good. Public interest instead of consent."

Democratic injustice, the major political invention of the twentieth century. And the greater good? How deceptive labels can be. A credit card can put you into debt, whereas a debit card means you have credit. I wondered whether the tour guide would agree to donate his body to this exhibition. Anyway, who was I to judge? I sliced through my fair share of cadavers during med school.

Speaking of which, since being stripped of my white coat, I needed a reason to get up in the morning. If Erkhart's connections could make this transaction go smoothly, I surely wouldn't miss those busy weekends in the ER removing champagne bottles from people's rectums. I could chill and enjoy a mango smoothie on a tropical beach somewhere. And I'd finally be able to stave off the feeling that Tina might one day leave me.

Besides, since my accident, I had already crossed the hardest barrier. I'd killed a human being. Now I could do anything.

"OK," I said, exhaling deeply. "I'll run it by my contact."

I held my hand up in warning when she pumped her fist. "Fingers crossed, he'll agree. He's retired, but I'll convince him."

"Retired? What the hell does that mean? It isn't like he's a bloody heart surgeon, and his hand is starting to shake."

"I'll take care of it. Don't worry."

"Who is he then? Why are you hiding him from me?"

"Better not to ask, don't you think?"

A dead man had been placed atop a horse carcass. He held his heart in one hand and his brain in the other. A group of young hipsters was trying to make sense of the scene by throwing around heavy concepts like emotions, free will, rationality.

I had to admit that from an authenticity angle at least, this beat any other exhibition I had been to. At least here, people wouldn't be raptly admiring a pair of eyeglasses as a work of art before realizing, many days later, that their owner had simply dropped them—true story.

"We need to vet your source first," I said. "What's his name, again?"

"His name is Miller. Gavin Miller. He's solid. Several of my contacts have vouched for him. He sold a Gauguin a few months ago to an art dealer I know in Belgium."

"With all due respect, your contacts couldn't vet Hellen Keller for a driver's test," I said, turning away from the desperate gaze of the man on the horse.

"Well, I can't wait to see your Professor X working his magic," she said.

As we left the exhibition, a man in a Winnie the Pooh costume was standing near the exit. I swear I heard him say, "Hope you enjoyed your tour, you sick fucks." I wondered if I should curse him back, but Tina tugged at my elbow to move as she lit a cigarette.

"How much does he want?"

"Seven figures for sure—oh, stop it," she said, noting my sneer. "You can bargain if you feel so inclined. Shall I set up a meeting next week?"

I extended a hand. "Give me a cigarette, will you."

I hadn't smoked in three years.

CHAPTER 12

"You brought this on all of us, didn't you? Didn't you?" Anne's red face gets dangerously close to mine.

I back away from her spittle and raise placating hands. "Anne, I have nothing to do with—"

"He just blew your cover," she snaps, crossing her arms. "You know these mercenaries. Are you even a doctor? What's your real name?"

I open my mouth, ready to come clean, when suddenly the world goes quiet. Weird how you notice background noise only when it stops. The generator has shut down, along with the lights. I blink away my dark past, focusing on the physical darkness around me.

"W-what's going on? What happened to the generator?" Anne whispers.

"They must be trying to take advantage of their infrared equipment," I say.

I don't think we need to worry about the tunnel. The rebels won't be tempted by that narrow death trap littered with the bodies of their comrades. Besides, when things got quiet, TJ planted some mines there and poured kerosene for good measure. The rebels' best bet is to overrun Piotr's Humvee and storm the main gate.

An explosion in the front yard breaks the earth and throws us to the ground. I wonder how they entered this quickly, but then I realize it must be a grenade or an RPG. The shooting starts with occasional thunderous explosions, the building shaking with each impact.

I set the radio Max left us to the lowest volume to listen in on their comms before climbing over the sandbags to the small, high window facing the front yard. I swipe away the old newspaper covering it and peer through the steel slats, but all I see are occasional flashes of bullets and tracers like fallen stars.

Then the black sky lights up with a constellation of small suns. The rebels are firing some sort of illumination rounds—giant flares that descend very slowly, exposing the entire area. I've never seen anything like it.

The playing field is now level. It seems the rebels have not been watching the same American war flicks as Max and his team.

After a few minutes of gunfire and brief stressful exchanges on the radio, Piotr's voice comes through the static. "We're taking fire from all directions. We can't hold them off any longer."

My heart sinks at another crackle from Piotr, laced with panic, "Echo One, we're being overrun. We need cover fire to retreat."

"Roger that. Don't forget to activate the charges before you pull back." Max replies steadily. "TJ, go get him. Take a medic with you."

Medic? Shit. Michael and Manu study their shoes as if they'd just bought them. Rachel stands up, her eyes on the stretcher.

I exhale. "I'll go."

TJ appears at the basement door. "Who's coming? Hurry."

I grab the stretcher and follow him. We dash through the front yard. Tracers and the falling illumination rounds hover above our heads. I hurt my foot tripping over something, but get back up quickly. It's a matter of seconds before we'll be overrun, and I don't want to be their greeter. We reach the gate.

"In position," TJ radios, aiming his machine gun. We can see Piotr's head inside the Humvee, only six or seven meters away.

"Copy that," Piotr replies. "I'll fire a smoke grenade. *Sadeeq* here will run first. I'll provide cover until he reaches the gate. Then everyone will provide cover for me."

I'd be ready to bet he doesn't know the name of his *sadeeq*—friend in Arabic.

"Ready when you are," TJ says.

About time, because the Humvee looks like it's received half of China's yearly production of ammunition in its frame and spider-webbed windows. The gunfire is constant, and it might as well be inside my head.

Piotr's head pops out of the turret behind the shield, and he fires a smoke grenade from his under-barrel grenade launcher. It sounds like the pop of a freshly opened bottle of champagne. Green smoke blankets the street a hundred meters from the Humvee. At the same time, both parties start another fire orgy, giving it all they have.

The Yemeni soldier opens the Humvee door and runs toward the gate. His eyes are on me until he's shot and falls midway.

Piotr doesn't wait to try his own luck. An RPG hits the Humvee the same moment he leaves it, and the red flower engulfs the vehicle for a second. Piotr grabs his *sadeeq* by the collar and drags him along, but something hits the Yemeni soldier's chest, emitting a torrent of sparks and smoke. Unexploded RPG. Piotr drops the body and staggers the last few steps to the gate.

I catch him as he falls, maneuvering him onto the stretcher.

"Let's go," I shout to TJ.

TJ stops firing and grabs the other end of the stretcher. We run back toward the building, Piotr squealing in pain. "Easy, you *zjopa*."

I assume that is not how you say "saviors" in Russian, but I don't care. All I know is that my back is to the entrance as we retreat. If anyone comes now, the first thing they'll shoot is my ass.

As we enter the building, Max slams the main door shut behind us.

Max extends his hand to Piotr. "Give me the detonator."

"What detonator?" Piotr grunts as he checks his wounds.

"The fuckin' C-4 to blow the fuckin' Humvee that I told you to fuckin' activate."

Piotr's eyes light up with painful realization, then with shame. He closes them and throws his head back with a desperate moan.

In the basement, I leave them to patch Piotr up in the dim torchlight and take a moment to catch my breath. My heart is a hummingbird that is about to leap from my mouth.

Max told us to hide behind the sandbags and shut the door. As if that will delay the inevitable. But I can't resist taking a look.

When I peer through the window, I see ghosts in the darkness. The shadows of the weapons in their hands look like long dicks in their giant frames. One of the rebels raises his assault rifle and fires a burst of bullets that pepper the wall above my head. I duck down.

We get ready to die. I say the "To God we belong and to God we return," prayer in Arabic and feel peaceful. Anne buries her face in Michael's chest. Manu is squeezed between two sandbags in the corner. Rachel is next to me. Our eyes meet. Nothing to be said.

As bullets hit the hospital's main door, Max's voice rasps from the radio. It's in whispers this time, not his usual authoritative tone.

"Now."

The explosion is a solar tornado. The whole building vibrates. The smell of burnt flesh and the sound of agonized screams in the inner circle of hell must be like this. Max and his team let their machine guns rip.

I realize what's happened: they set a boobytrap for the hordes, welcoming them at the door with Claymore mines and IEDs. And what the fire doesn't finish, bullets will.

My ears are ringing, and my head wobbles on a rubber neck. I breathe smoke and dust as hot as the devil's breath. From the window I spot some of the attackers fleeing the scene, one or two with their clothes on fire. The bullets coming from the building don't give them a chance. It's like playing a video game at an amateur level at this point.

When the dust settles, Max comes down to check on us. He's met with stunned faces that are light-years from OK.

I nod to him that no one is hurt, physically at least.

He nods back and lowers his gun. "Hell. What I wouldn't give for a shot of Jameson right now."

Present Day, Friday, 01:07

Studiously ignoring the hungry vultures nibbling on my brain stem, I go to the corridor for a smoke. The smell is there, too. The smell of dread and violent death. Imagine the smell of a damaged electrical circuit multiplied a thousand times.

Michael and Manu are already up there, their mouths and noses wrapped by old T-shirts, surveying the effects of the battle on the hospital door like a couple of meerkats. They pretend they haven't seen me. They no longer know which side I'm on. I'm the Outsider again. That should be my middle name.

"A bomb blasted through the door," Manu narrates while recording a video on his mobile. At his feet is an empty Red Bull. Turns out, Manu has a stash of Red Bulls and Kit Kats that would last a team of astronauts through a round-trip journey to Mars.

"Must be high-caliber shit," Michael muses.

"Shall I tell the Blackwater guys?"

"To do what? Fix the door?"

"Yeah, you're right," Manu says, scratching his head.

Something catches his eye. "Wait. What's that?"

Still recording, he wrestles a metal cylinder out of the corridor wall. Instinctively, I back away.

"Is this … a grenade?" Manu asks.

Michael almost has a fit. Manu quickly shoves it back into the wall. "Oh, shit."

"You imbecile," Michael says, the color draining from his face.

The unexploded ordnance won't stay put in the wall, so Manu keeps it in place with his hand.

"What do we do now?" Manu says, frozen, wide-eyed.

They exchange frantic glances, all civility gone.

"I don't know. Do I look like a Navy SEAL to you?" Michael says.

"Maybe we should throw it in the toilet?"

"What the hell, man. Just ... just go upstairs and hand it to that guy, Max. He'll know what to do with it."

"Why don't you give it to him? You're the team leader," Manu says.

"You asshole." Then Michael looks at me.

"Don't even think about it," I say, preempting him. Tough luck for them that I'm no longer on meds. I would have played catch with it if they'd wanted.

"To hell with both of you. Give it to me." Michael holds it in front of him like a nervous father with a newborn and ascends the stairs in slow motion.

Manu records Michael's heroic ascent on camera, then turns to me. "Listen, Luke. I have an idea."

"Is it better than flushing unexploded ordnance down the toilet?"

"*Ouais, ouais.*" He nods vigorously. "That injured reporter, Karim. He could contact his media buddies and raise awareness and shit, no?" he says, running a hand across his stubble.

I pause. Not a bad idea, for a change.

Present Day, Friday, 01:15

"Hey, Karim," I prod him, grinning. "Wakey, wakey."

"Wha... what?" His pupils are different sizes. Rivers of corrugated blood vessels run through his left eye. His concussion is deteriorating.

"Listen, I've got the next Pulitzer with your name on it."

"Uh-huh."

"You need to call your network and tell them that the hospital is under attack."

"Sure, sure." He dozes off.

"Shit. Get me some epinephrine," I tell Manu, who's capturing all this on camera, "and turn that thing off. I'll sue your ass if my face shows up in any of your stupid videos."

"What are you doing?" Rachel asks. Anne is right behind her.

"I'm trying to get us out of here," I say. I expect Anne to object, but she stays silent.

I inject Karim with the colorless liquid. He opens his eyes wide, his pupils very dilated. I fear he might have a heart attack.

"Hey, welcome back. Listen, how about calling your network? Give them an exclusive from under siege."

"Yes, yes." His eyes swim between the people gathered around him, but the word *exclusive* must've hit some subconscious nerve.

"Great. Here's the sat phone. Take a minute to pull yourself together." I give him a big glass of water. The epinephrine must have left his mouth as dry as Tina's cotton balls.

He holds the phone uncertainly. He nods a couple of times before drinking the water, spilling half of it on his shirt. I thrust his bag at his chest. He reaches unsteadily for his notebook and starts dialing. He misdials a few times, so I take the phone and punch in the number for him and put him on loudspeaker.

"Hello?" A thick voice grunts from the other side.

"Hello. This is Karim Helmy. The reporter in Aden."

"Who?" spits the voice.

Karim starts to focus. "What do you mean who? Put your boss on the line."

"I'm the chief here. Who the hell are you?"

"Oh, Mr. Selim. I'm the freelance reporter in Yemen."

"Do you know a reporter in Yemen called Karim ..." After a muffled side conversation, his voice returns. "Ah. Hi, Karim. What's up?"

Karim is silent, blinking repeatedly. I urge him on.

"We're in a hospital, and I'm injured ... we're surr—"

"Karim, I can transfer you to HR, but I don't think we can cover—"

"No, no, you don't understand. I'm inside a hospital. We're being attacked, and we could die any minute."

"You're in Aden now?"

"YES," Karim says as emphatically as his injured lung can muster.

"Great. Stay on the line. Let me connect you to the news desk. Are you ready to go live?"

"Um ... yes, sure."

Anne turns on the television in the corner and searches frantically for Al Hurreya channel. This news agency is backed by Gulf countries and portrays dim views of the rebels, who I doubt will be happy about us calling them.

The lazy elevator music on the phone drives everyone batshit within a minute. On the television, a shiny anchor is interviewing an author about his book on celebrities' weird baby names—from Frank Zappa calling his daughter Diva Muffin to Ed Sheeran calling his Lyra Antarctica. The elevator music stops before I take my own life with a rusty scalpel. The shiny anchor turns to face the camera.

"Karim. On air in three, two ..." says a whispering female voice before a confident DJ voice booms from the television and the phone with a few seconds lag: "And now, exclusive to Al Hurreya channel, we have on the phone Karim Halim, our reporter in Aden, Yemen. Karim?"

"Um, my name is Karim Helmy."

"Sure, sure, Karim. Please tell us what is happening."

"Um, yes. We're under attack in Aden hospital."

"Who's attacking you?" asks the anchor, wearing his best "I'm all ears" expression.

"The rebels."

"Why are they attacking?"

"Why? What do you mean why? This is war!"

"I mean why are they attacking the hospital?"

"The Golden Belt commander is here, along with some of his men."

"Can you tell us about the war crimes you have witnessed from the insurgent terrorists?"

"What do you mean? We're dying here. Who are you, man?" Karim looks at the phone as if it had personally insulted him. His head wobbles, its weight too much for his neck.

I take the phone from him. "This is Dr. Emmanuel Garnier," I say, turning my back to Manu's double take. "We're going to die here if the international community doesn't intervene. We need an immediate evacuation. There are people from different nationalities here, including Americans."

"Those terrorists are attacking a hospital with injured people. What do you foreign doctors have to say about this?"

"We don't have to say jack sh—" I stop and take a deep breath. In a calmer voice, I continue, "For our own safety, we can't discuss politics. We just want to get out of here."

"I see. Hang in there. Now your voice has reached the world. We will be in touch to get more updates. Good luck."

Good luck? If he were cheering for his favorite football team, he'd say it with more conviction. At least he didn't offer us any bloody "thoughts and prayers."

The line is disconnected. The camera zooms in on the anchor as he continues, "As usual, our news comes to you live from the heart of events everywhere in the world. We will keep you posted on these exclusive updates from Yemen. Now we move on to sports. A special report on the upcoming Champions League quarter-finals."

I'm still holding the beeping phone.

"Well, at least we got our fifteen seconds of fame," Rachel says.

On the roof, TJ seems more exasperated that his Zippo is out of gas than with the war around us. He gets a light from Max before striding off.

"Why do you have a lighter if you don't smoke?" I ask Max.

"It helps me remember why I quit." He bites on one of his baby carrots.

"Listen, I'm sorry I didn't tell you about our plans to escape."

He waves a hand. "Shush. It's fine, your girlfriend was right. I probably would have done the same if I were you. Besides, you have a chance to make up for it."

"She's not my girlfriend."

He shrugs and smiles.

"Does that mean there are no extraction teams on the way?"

"The Emiratis and Saudis aren't even picking up the phone anymore. As for the CIA, they say the insurgents have Strela-2 missiles. These can not only down helicopters, they can also get fixed wing jets. They made it clear they aren't coming without a ceasefire. They hope that peace conference will conclude in a day or two."

Shit. Since *Black Hawk Down*, the Americans have become as wary of aerial extractions as vampires are of the cross.

"There's another problem," Max adds. "We're almost out of ammo. We need to stall as much as we can."

"Wait a second, what did you mean by me making up for it?"

He flashes a wide grin. "That's what I want to talk to you about." I brace for impact.

"We can't last another night." Dramatic pause for effect. "We need someone neutral to negotiate with them."

"I see. And where would you find such a unicorn?"

Max takes another bite and says innocently, "That would be you."

I pause to allow a calming breath. "Let me get this straight. You want me to go out there to those people you just barbecued?"

"Like you say: I killed them, not you. And they don't know of your great escape. They think it was some of my men who killed those guys. You are here against your will."

"Do they understand that?"

"Of course they do. Besides, think of your team and the patients here. You have to protect them. That's what humanitarians do, right?"

"I would do a cactus in the Sonoran Desert rather than go out there with my dick in my hand." I run my hand nervously through my hair. "What do we have that they want, anyway?"

"We're asking for a day-or-two ceasefire. They get their fallen soldiers; we get more time."

"What if they ask for the General's head?"

Max glares at me. "The man is injured. I couldn't deliver him to his death like that. Could you?"

I sigh and break eye contact. "Why me?"

"Why you?" he repeats, as if spitting out rancid orange juice. "Because you fuckin' owe me. And because you're one of them."

I stiffen. "What did you just call me?"

He relaxes and raises his hands. "C'mon now, Luke. You know I didn't mean it like that. Listen, if any of your blue-blooded friends saw the number of beards outside, they would shit their pants before starting to talk. Let's face it—only you can do this.

CHAPTER 13

I have always had voices inside my head. Contradictory messages. Pleas from the past, warnings from the future. They're usually triggered by my real enemy. My real enemy is not poverty or injustice. My real enemy is boredom.

London, August 2014

Nothing in the Mandarin Oriental Hyde Park hotel was oriental, and the nearest Mandarin-speaking country was eight thousand kilometers away. There was surely a metaphor for this, but I couldn't be assed.

The lobby was awash with yuppie clones milling around in canned cool air, smug and scornful. They were probably here for a conference on "Working Together" or "Our 2050 Vision" or any other tick-the-box topic.

The music of somebody's fifth sonata emanated from the walls. An old couple was reading newspapers next to their travel bags; a middle-aged man in shorts dozed spread-eagle on a sofa; and a young couple occupied another sofa, the woman talking on the phone while examining her fingernails, the man endlessly stirring a yellowish drink and staring into emptiness.

We headed toward our meeting at El Barrio restaurant on the ground floor. Tina looked like she'd been born there. She strode by my side, wearing a black suit over a crisp white shirt, heels, long earrings, and blue-lensed sunglasses over her hair because,

"You didn't know that blue decreases the appetite?"

I knew instantly which one was Gavin. He stood up slowly, still chewing. The same way Gregory Peck did in that legendary scene with Sophia Loren in *Arabesque*. He looked like a successful Ponzi-scheme manager. The one who gives the pep talk on the stage in those yearly rallies. Call me insecure or envious, but I didn't like this self-entitled wanker. Besides, he looked at least five years younger than me. Twenty-four, twenty-five maybe.

Tina introduced us, "Gavin, this is Luke. Luke, Gavin."

We shook hands firmly and exchanged greetings. He had a deep voice full of authority and private-school righteousness. I hoped he would prove to be the *shiny but shallow* type. Like an exciting trailer of a boring film.

I didn't like that Tina didn't mention I was her boyfriend, but I swallowed my jealousy. She was probably trying to earn his trust.

The waiter came with a menu that looked more like a magazine. Choice paralysis hit me after page eleven. Even if I knew what I wanted, the different sizes and extras on each order would need a savant to navigate them.

I folded the magazine—sorry, the menu. "I'll take an English breakfast, with beef or chicken sausages, please."

"I'm sorry, Sir, all our sausages are from pork."

"Why? Are you Hindu?" Gavin was getting on my nerves.

"Sir?"

"Never mind, just some chips and a cold brew, please."

After a quick exchange of eye contact with Tina, Gavin asked with a sly smile, "Are you Jewish, Luke?"

"No, I'm the newer villain."

"Aye. I hear you, mate. I'm Irish myself," he said, in an accent thick as Baileys Irish Cream.

My order arrived along with Gavin's omelette and double espresso and Tina's triple shot skimmed iced soy latte with vanilla and hazelnut—this must be one of her "cheat" days.

Gavin raised his eyebrows at me, as if to say, "Let's cut to the chase."

I sipped my coffee, which could have replaced the jet fuel on an F-16s. "So, Tina says you're some sort of art connoisseur," I said, pronouncing it in the French way.

He smiled condescendingly, swirling his double espresso. "Not really. I'm more of a gold rush fixer." He waited for me to bite.

I gave him a flat stare.

He turned to Tina, and his pupils dilated. "In the gold rush era, the ones who got wealthy weren't the ones digging for gold, but the ones who sold them the axes and shovels. So, I'm just balancing supply and demand. I see what people want, and I help them get it."

"So you're more of a shovel connoisseur. A middleman," I said.

"Any different from you, Luke?"

I took the jab. Enough foreplay. "Let's get down to business. Stolen antiquities get sold for five to 10 percent of their open-market value on the black market. The fence takes 50 percent of the cut. The latest open market estimate for your item is twenty million dollars. If you're expecting more than a million, you better say so now so we can drop this and talk about something else. Golf, perhaps?"

"Bejesus. You don't waste time, do you?"

Tina, well-versed in the tension between two rival males, played the bathroom card. "Boys, I'm off to the ladies. Stop dick swinging and play nicely."

He smiled at me mischievously when Tina left. "You don't seem to like me."

"Don't be disappointed, I don't like people I don't know." That was partially true. Most of the time I also didn't like people I knew.

We were playing a game of cat and mouse, except neither of us had figured out who was the mouse and who was the cat.

I said, "Maybe I'll like you better when I see a photo of the item. A proof-of-life kind of thing."

"Sure, that can be arranged." He raised his finger. "But, to be clear ... " He paused for effect. "You see it, you buy it. No turning back. The people I work with are not friendly when they feel somebody is wasting their time."

The Irish finish their sentences with a raised tone that turns statements into questions. Linguists call this "inquisitive inflection," or uptalk. Australians do the same thing. I read once that hostage negotiators are taught to use this tone instead of an assertive one because it makes them sound friendly. All this might be true in general, but I didn't find any hint of friendliness in Gavin's voice that afternoon.

"Who's Mary?" I asked, moving my bishop. Partly to distract him from his next move, but mainly to distract myself from what I really wanted to discuss.

"Pardon?" Erkhart asked, without taking his eyes from the chessboard. His first word since the start of the game half an hour ago.

"When we first met, in your ayahuasca trip, you kept saying, "I see you, Mary." Did you mean ... the Virgin Mary?"

"What on earth are you on about?" he asked, after a few beats, still staring intently at the chess board. "The only Mary I know was my childhood crush. The first girl I kissed."

"I see," I said. I ran my fingertips over the scar on my temple, something I often did when stressed. "I want to show you something."

I had already done my research. The Birch Cent was a prototype for America's first coin. Only ten pieces had been produced, and one of the few which had been accounted for was stolen two years earlier from the mansion of a real-estate magnate in California. I took a photo of the coin out of my pocket and laid it on the table in front of him.

Erkhart looked at the photo for a moment. "And why am I seeing this?"

"It's the Birch Cent," I said.

"The Birch Cent."

"Right, the Birch Cent, yes," I said.

"I see. The Birch Cent." He nodded.

"Exactly." A deep breath. I could do this. "I need your help finding a buyer."

His jaws moved slowly as though he were silently swearing. He closed his eyes and tilted his head back. A minute passed. Was this a scare tactic, or was he trying to control his temper instead of exploding in my face? Even with his eyes closed, this was more intimidating than any stare contest I'd ever had.

When he came back to earth, he flicked the photo away with the tip of his index finger. "Not going to happen," he said.

You had to give it to him. The guy had class.

"Why not?"

He gave me a frosty look. Rather than meet his gaze, I focused on a couple of overgrown white hairs in his thick eyebrows.

"Listen, it's a one-off," I said, sweating. "Nobody will get hurt."

"No."

I remembered what he once said about donating his collection to charity in his will. "I'll even give a percentage to charity. I promise."

He flicked his eyes at me, not sure if I was joking, before shaking his head in disbelief. "This is the second most vile rationale humans use to justify doing evil things."

"Listen, pragmatically speaking, if I don't do it, someone else will."

He shook his head again, this time in resignation. "And there you have the first."

My blood boiled. "You're very good at talking without actually saying anything. Just because you have silver hair doesn't mean you can sit there spouting this *Reader's Digest* psychology at me."

"I can give you money, if you need it."

My face reddened. "It's not about the money. Well, it's not *only* about the money. I have to do this, not take charity from you."

"Do you eat chocolate?" he asked.

"What?" I said, startled.

"I've not eaten chocolate in ten years. Instead, I tolerate Bonne Maman jam in silence."

"What are you—"

"Come with me. I want to show you something." His eyes were on the small room in the corner. The only room in the house I had never entered.

Bluebeard's room.

The room smelled of ink, coffee, and time. It had no windows, and the big mahogany desk to the right was full of letters, pens, stamps, and postcards.

"Have you ever wondered why countries like Switzerland and Belgium are the top chocolate producers in the world?" he asked, standing in the middle of the room.

"I don't know. Farmer subsidies?" I say, shifting my weight, waiting for him to get to the point.

He gave me a scornful look. "Which farmers? They don't have a single cacao tree."

I shrugged, confident in my ignorance.

"It's tariffs. They've zero percent for cacao beans but three hundred percent on the final product. So poor countries have to sell the cacao beans for pennies per pound. They've no chance of developing them into a product and having a share of the pie. My first million came from investing in chocolate companies. These days, I dedicate most of my time to this," he said, pointing to the stacks of handwritten letters on the desk.

"I write over five hundred letters every month to lobbyists, policymakers, and their constituents in the developed world, urging them to abolish tariffs on poor countries."

I rifled through some of the letters. His handwriting was elegant. Handwriting that didn't care about time, deadlines, or goals. What a waste. He still believed in democracy.

"You think anyone cares?"

"I don't know. But I know that I'll keep sending these letters until I die."

I didn't doubt that he was regretting his youthful actions, but maybe that was because he was no longer young. Time was no longer on his side. Time—the block of dry ice we think we have plenty of until it evaporates into thin air.

"Why are you telling me all this, Erkhart?" I asked, wearily.

He faced me. "Chocolate was my sin. Don't make this cent yours."

I stood erect and said, "All this is a little deep for me. Are you going to help me or not?"

"Your life is ahead of you, Luke. Don't piss it away on greed."

I said the words I'd memorized, in anticipation of rejection: "If you don't help me, I'll go all the way on my own. I'm not turning back."

He winced as if he'd bitten into a lemon. The silence stretched out uncomfortably between us. "I'll put you in touch with Max Gorsky," he finally said.

"Red Sox," Max grumbled, his gaze fixed on the road.

I glanced at my gray socks, then peered toward his but couldn't make them out between his blue jeans and brown leather boots. "Excuse me?"

"Nothing people of the Old World would understand. I'm missing the Red Sox game for this."

I had nothing remotely helpful to add.

"No matter where I am or what do I do, pure love for the Red Sox will always be my benign addiction."

"Riiight ..."

"You?"

"Me?"

"What's your addiction?"

Compared with of all my malignant addictions, American football—or was it baseball?—didn't seem that bad—but only for a second.

"None that I can think of," I said. "Do you want me to drive so you can cry it out?"

He glared at me. I was about to remind him to keep his eyes on the road when he said, "You're a smart one, aren't ya? My advice: avoid being a smart-ass while we work together, and I'll guarantee you don't get a bloody nose at the end of all this, OK?"

Great. It seemed we would fit together as seamlessly as a green-on-blue ensemble.

Max turned on the radio. A husky voice I would do anything to have crooned about a tall man, a dusty coat, and a red right hand. Max, apparently less impressed, turned the radio off. He took a quick glance at his watch. "So, have you done any of this before?"

"What part, exactly?"

He sighed deeply in an "it's going to be a long day" kind of way. "This!" he said, pointing to the steering wheel of the Range Rover he was driving on the M40 on our way to Oxfordshire.

I assumed he wasn't referring to operating a car, which was good because I hadn't driven since my accident.

He continued, "Going to buy illegal tracking devices from a bunch of tossers ..."

"Whoa!"

"What? Did you expect me to sugarcoat it? Didn't your father-in-law tell you how these things go down?"

"First of all, Erkhart is not my father-in-law. Second, I know exactly how these things go down. So you do your job and I'll do mine."

"Do *my job*? My job is to make sure nobody fucks you up. What's yours again?"

True. He was basically babysitting me. We remained silent for a while, but I couldn't keep my mouth shut for long. At that time, and like for most people, silence made me anxious.

"Are you carrying?" I asked.

"What? A gun? What the hell do you think this is, a bank robbery in the Wild West? Of course not." After a moment, he said, "Carrying a gun doesn't make people fear you. In the end, it's the heart that pulls the trigger, not the hand."

"You don't say," I said, yawning.

"Speaking of hearts, how close are you and your girlfriend? What's her name again? Tanya?"

"Tina. I've been asking myself this question for some time now."

He nodded and took a baby carrot from a plastic bag next to him. I watched him eat it.

"Are you going to say something witty now?" he asked, still chewing.

I rolled my eyes. "Have you always been like this?"

"Like what?"

"This macho Billy Big Bollocks."

"No, smart-ass. I'm not your typical alpha male. My pistol of choice is even a Glock 43."

"So what?"

"They say it's a women's pistol because it's small and easy to use. Men like pistols because they remind them of their dicks. Think about it: the balls are full of bullets that are ejected through a barrel once the trigger's pulled. The only difference is what each type of projectile does: one gives life, the other brings death."

He plowed on, clearly enjoying himself, waving another carrot. "Whoever invented pistols probably had penis discontent. An ancestor of those who go for the Magnum and Desert Eagle shit. Contented people with no Freudian chips on their shoulder—they go for the more practical stuff. The Glock 43 is reliable and easy to conceal."

Meet Max Gorsky. Erkhart's favorite fixer. Ex-military with the flavor of PTSD. When he wasn't fighting as a security contractor in some lucrative shithole, he passed the time working in a private military firm in London and doing some PI work on the side for friends. There was something different about him, though. In a world where everyone had to look and act the same, Max stood out. He was the type of man who would leave the cinema after five minutes if he didn't like what he saw and wouldn't care what others thought of him.

I had met him a couple of days earlier, at Erkhart's, where I had never seen any visitors before. When I arrived, Max was busy explaining how a client had recently sought his help. The client had slept with a woman on a boozy night out and had failed to notice, during his heroic quest, that the sheath of his sword was torn. So, he'd knocked her up and now wanted Max to "take care of the baby." Instead, Max broke his jaw, as a friendly reminder to never consider such a thing ever again.

When we shook hands, I noticed Max's tired eyes as if he was about to fall asleep. Blue eyes that had seen it all. I wondered if Max had allowed Erkhart to read his palm.

Max had already done his homework. "Gavin is connected to the Irish mob in Limerick. Their main specialty is drugs and organized crime. But they also like dabbling in stolen antiquities because they're small and easy to smuggle. They probably got this coin from their American cousins, and now they're stuck with it. This is both good news and bad news. Because it means they're clean—but dangerous."

"Anything else on Gavin?" Erkhart asked.

"He's the numbers geek," Max said. "College degree, no priors. His father was an accountant for the mob boss. Guess it runs in the family."

"We need to be one step ahead at all times," Erkhart told me. "Max will tell you how. Meanwhile, I need your word that you won't act on your own without consulting with us."

"Scout's honor," I say, raising my hand in a Scout salute.

So we hit the road.

As the car swung past the steel gates and into a vast estate, I noticed the intercom was heavily coated in dust. We cruised through the unkempt grounds and up to a grand beige-colored estate. Hell, this place was at least three times bigger than Erkhart's villa. Max parked next to a beat-up Peugeot that stood in contrast with the ornate white windows and doors behind it.

"OK, buckaroo, listen up," Max said. "The guys we're about to meet are anarchist kids who call themselves Wealth Sharers or some shit like that. Basically, postmodernist squatters who stake out fancy properties that their foreign owners rarely use. The kids squat or rent out these places most of the year, thanks to a tracking system on the owners' phones that monitors their movement."

He unbuckled his seat belt and grinned at my awestruck expression. "Bet you've never been inside a manor house before."

Chief Hobo looked me up and down warily. "So, who's your friend again, blud?" he asked Max.

He was tiny compared to the massive leather armchair he was sitting in. A chair worthy of a Rockefeller.

We had to take off our shoes upon entering the enormous mansion. Max's socks were new, and multi-colored. The hole in mine didn't help to boost my confidence. The carpet was a treat for the feet. A blood-red, soft, thick Persian rug.

We sat in a circle with four youths who looked like high school dropouts, OD'ing on crisps, video games, and weed, next to a fireplace with a deer head on its mantelpiece. Half a dozen other kids lounged around with headphones and computers, oblivious to our presence. I could hear the song "Numb/Encore" emanating from the nearest headset.

"He's my accountant," Max said in a guttural tone, exhaling a cloud of marijuana smoke worthy of Vesuvius.

A burst of laughter, amplified by the weed buzz, erupted from the circle. The joint was passed to me. I had to take a couple of tokes or risk more laughter. In such settings, someone is usually identified as the outcast.

My sight wandered to the dark green drapes on the wall, and I wondered for a second if they were full of arsenic.[7] I also wondered if I had déjà vu. If I had already sat with these people before. In a different age with different names.

"Why don't you want to join us, blud?" Chief Hobo asked Max. "We're practically a charity. Just the other day, we housed three homeless nitties in a banging place on Mayfair that belongs to the Gaddafi family, free of charge. Now tell me, where's the harm in that? True social distribution of wealth."

"Forgive me, but the first words that come to mind before 'social distribution of wealth' are 'breaking and entering.'" Max's eyes twinkled.

I passed the joint without puffing this time. The room was beginning to feel unpleasantly warm. As my heart rate increased, the scar on my temple started pulsating, and I braced myself for an oncoming headache. That's the thing about early life trauma. It's like etchings on wet cement. It scars your soul, wiring you to see every situation through its lens, keeping you on your toes for life. This time, the sting in my head passed.

"I mean, let's be honest, bruv. These rich toffs buy the best gaffs to launder their money, yet they stand empty most of the year. If they ever actually visit them, they show up with their Lamborghinis and Hummers to spike up the prices, and then drive their fat asses back to their corrupt lives. Where's the fairness in that?"

....

7   In the Victorian era, many fancy houses featured green curtains whose pigments were produced from arsenic. One of the side effects of arsenic poisoning is pale skin, a trait that was prized by bourgeoise classes at that time.

The logs in the fire crackled.

One of them asked me, "You ain't one of them, are you, fam? I mean, rich daddy financing your stay in the West?" He said it with the kind of smile that would allow him, based on my reaction, to say he was just kidding.

I had this Egyptian/English barber who cut my hair when I was a teenager. He went by Cockney Pharaoh. He was called that because he spoke cockney like the best of them, but with a pure Egyptian accent. He would say things like, "I was pulling on a snout as I charvered that bloody slag while she was sniffing a line of zip." All with the accent of a grade-seven Egyptian public-school student who learned English from a replacement philosophy teacher. Neither Egyptians nor Brits grasped what he was on about most of the time. But they never failed to be amused by the funny combination. Early in life, I wished that, whatever I did, I wouldn't end up like Cockney Pharaoh.

"Hardly. I was born in London, and I live in a shoe box," I said.

"You look Indian though."

"I'm not Indian. My parents are from Egypt."

"See, I knew it, toff guy." He pointed at me as if he'd just solved the riddle of the Sphinx.

"Mate, Egypt doesn't have a Prius tank worth of petrol in its belly, alright? It's not Saudi."

"Why not? They both have deserts."

Max, who had never experienced the joy of such questioning, interrupted Culture 101. "With all this stoner talk, I'm surprised you haven't been caught by now."

"They don't even know we exist, thanks to the dark web," Chief Hobo chuckled. "We're even expanding to Dubai, Sydney, Singapore. We have a 4.8 rating, mate."

It took my stoned brain the time it takes a two-year-old Samsung mobile to turn on before I managed to respond, "Wait, you have ratings?"

"Of course. Exactly like Amazon or eBay, only everyone's anonymous. It's amazing what people can do with an invisibility cloak. We began this idea of wealth sharing as a social protest, but we don't mind a bit of profit while we're at it."

"If it's anonymous, then how do people pay you?"

"Bitcoin, of course."

"How do you even access the dark web?" I asked.

"You mean you've never been on it? What year were you born, mate?"

Snickers from the comrades. I was back in Dennis's basement. Some things never change.

"Enough of the hacking crash course," Max cuts in. "Do you have our stuff?"

"Ready since a long time, fam." He pointed to a nearby tote bag.

Max went through it quickly with an expert eye before handing it over to me. It was full of rectangular black gadgets and a couple of innocent-looking USBs. Max nodded, and I handed Chief Hobo a fat wad of cash.

"Sure you don't want the Saudis' Brighton beach house for a weekend with your girlfriend, or perhaps one of the Mubarak family's houses in Chelsea? Free of charge for our loyal customers," he said, counting the money.

"Yeah, but nah. I don't want to be in the middle of the act when the owner pops up," Max said.

He looked at Max incredulously. "We ain't amateurs. Even if their hacked mobiles didn't tell us where they are, we get immigration alerts as soon they set foot in the country." He relaxed in his chair and pointed to the bag he just gave us. "That's what you just bought. Big Brother technology. The ability to play God."

Max and I looked at him blankly. He flushed. "What? I'm majoring in philosophy."

"Alright, Master Yoda," Max said, rising to his feet. "Speaking of philosophy, you're fighting social hierarchies that have survived evolution and repeated themselves for millennia. For inspiration, google the Liberian American slaves. Once they were freed, they made it back to Liberia only to enslave their own people on their massive farms."

CHAPTER 14

I return to the basement. Upon seeing my face, Rachel asks, "Is everything OK?"

"He wants me to negotiate with the rebels."

"What did you tell him?"

Is this worry in her eyes? I shrug. "I guess I'll do it."

"Luke, are you sure this is a—"

"Great idea," Manu interrupts. "You need to explain to them the consequences of their actions."

"I'll merely beg them not to kill us, Manu."

"No, man, no. That's the wrong way to do it."

I fold my arms. "Well, what would you advise, then?"

"Tell them if they don't leave us alone, NATO will nuke the shit out of them."

"Wouldn't that just confirm their belief that we're their enemies?"

"Man, you need to have balls of steel. That's the only thing those people appreciate."

"I tell you what, Iron Man, why don't you go instead of me then?"

"Ahem. But you are the best intermediary." His tone loses its steam.

I cock my head. "How come?"

Manu shrugs and changes the subject. "Hey, can I make a video interview with you before you go?"

"Eat shit, Manu."

A sickly silence engulfs us as we are lost in our thoughts. Nobody speaks when I go to the crash trolley and rummage through it. I find my emergency stash and put two Vicodins in my pocket.

I also take a Red Bull from Manu's corner, pretending not to notice the stack of Ambien strips in a rubber band beneath it, and down half of it right in front of him. Dare to say a word, you selfish twat. If this is my last night on earth, I surely don't care what anyone thinks of me.

Manu gets his oud from behind a sandbag and plays "The Sound of Silence" on a loop. A song I once liked, but not any longer.

He stretches his mobile out to Anne. "Hey Anne. Can you record me while I play?"

She looks through him with glassy eyes.

"Give it here. I'll do it," Rachel says impatiently.

He plays, ignoring the camera, as though Rachel were a secret fan, stealthily recording him.

I run a finger across my scar and exhale. I need to control the flashing red lights of my headache. With all this smoke, chainsaw roar, and bad reception inside my head, I fear an episode is coming. I want to hit something.

Manu hits a high note and throws his head back. I can't take it anymore. "Shut up, man!"

His fingers freeze and he looks at me with Bambi eyes.

I hold up my hands in apology. "Sorry, Manu, I just need some air."

I bolt out of the basement up to the ground floor. A few minutes later, I hear footsteps. The last thing I want is Michael checking on my mental health from an HQ-approved checklist. Please, God. No.

"Are you OK?" It was a typical checklist question, but coming from Rachel, it doesn't feel that bad.

"I lied to you. I know Max from before. But I had no idea he was in Yemen when I came here."

"It doesn't matter. You don't have to do this."

"I know, but I want to."

"Well, it's true that the potential rewards are huge. Imagine, you could get a conference room named after you at HQ. The brave doctor who saved the day."

"You mean reckless idiot."

"I guess we need to increase the odds of you coming back alive then," Michael says.

We turn to face him.

"How's the General?" he asks.

"I don't know," I say. "I haven't checked on him for a while."

"The mercenaries are giving him up in exchange for a way out, right?" Michael asks.

"No, they're not."

"What? Are they nuts? Why not?"

"Good question, Michael. Go ask them why they're not giving up an injured man to be summarily executed."

"This doesn't make any sense. They're fucking mercenaries." He shakes his head and blinks. Twice. "What if he's dead?"

"What are you on about?"

He raises his hands. "Nothing. I'm just exploring … scenarios."

Michael and I lock eyes for a moment before he looks away.

Rachel cuts in. "We're still responsible for the General's health. That's what *the book* says, Michael."

Michael nods vigorously. "Of course!"

"I was keeping this for a special occasion. Preparing for death seems as good as any other," Rachel says, taking a massive spliff from her bag.

I can't help but smile. This girl isn't going to stop surprising me any time soon. I find her intriguing. She has the eyes of a nun who loves hard rock.

We are in the abandoned nurses' room on the first floor, where I had chosen to keep my meager valuables. It has a bed, a desk, a cracked mirror, and a dart board. I planned to sleep here tonight, seeking refuge from the basement crowd. But I didn't mind when she offered to keep me company for a while.

She put some soft music on her mobile, and I hear the laugh again. Every time I listen to music, I hear Tina's laugh for a fraction of a second between the tunes. I used to turn the volume up to prove myself wrong, but I would still hear for a blink of an eye her laughter. That intense, white-crystal definition of joy. I no longer listen to music. But tonight, there's nowhere to go.

This will only be the third time I've ever smoked weed. I find it overrated—a celebration of red-eyed sluggishness. Yet maybe that is exactly what I need tonight. To shut my brain down and enjoy life without it. Maybe that is why the pharaohs scooped the brains of the dead out of the nose during mummification. They must have been the first to discover the concept of "no brain, no pain."

The immaculately tight, cone-shaped wrapping shows that she's a pro. We sit on the blood-stained mattress, which I made sure to gallantly cover with an extra blanket. I fling my boots under the bed.

"How come you wear boots in summer?"

"They're my lucky shoes," I say, easing back against the wall beside her.

She gives me the honor of sparking the joint. I inhale deeply, rest my head against the sticky wall, close my eyes, and breathe out a cloud of smoke.

I hand her the joint. My blood vibrates, and an air of stillness turns off most of the lights in my frontal cortex.

After two more rounds, clouds fill my brain and only one thought emerges. I say, "Now I know who you remind me of—that girl who sang 'White Rabbit.' Without the sixties fringe, of course. She was gorgeous."

"A compliment, finally!"

I'm surprised, too. Since I left the UK, my eagerness to please stemming from the need to conform in my early years bounced me toward the opposite extreme of anti-social behavior. The scales that balance my life exchange movement like a crazy metronome that refuses to settle for the middle. Like sublimation where solids turn to gases without becoming liquids. If only I could find the sweet spot of the middle.

The weed is making me thirsty. I gulp some water from a bottle on the bedside table. It tastes of heavy metals and humility. For two weeks before this lockdown, ground water had been distributed for drinking through sewage trucks, if you were lucky enough to get it. I study the bottle under the fluorescent light. Say what you will, but you bond more with people over rusty water than over Evian.

We smoke in good silence that I learned the hard way to appreciate. On her last puff, she stands and stretches before casually opening the desk drawer. Dirty Harry's pistol winks at her from inside. She picks it up cautiously, expressionless.

"Can you teach me how to shoot?" she asks, her eyes fixed on the gun.

"I'm no expert, but someone once told me that you pull the trigger with your heart, not your finger."

She purses her lips, still weighing the piece of hard metal in her hand before putting it back in the drawer. "It's not for me then."

"You think you're too righteous to get corrupted?"

"No, not righteous. Just a coward." She smiles and stares into space. "When I was young, my mom told me the story of Cain and Abel, and I cried so much that she added her own twist to make things easier. She told me that Cain had died on the inside long before he killed Abel. And that the worst type of death is to die while you're still alive. I prefer her version."

She faces me. "You know, he was shaking."

"Who? Cain?"

She rolls her eyes. "The guy who was holding me. His whole body was shaking."

"If it's any consolation to him, I was shaking all the way until we were back in the basement." I chase the memory out of my head. "Anyway, now you know where the gun is. There's a small box with my passport and some money inside the hollow shaft of the curtain in the foreigners' room. I need you to take it if I don't come back. Would you do that?" I feel like I'm writing my will.

She nods, avoiding my eyes.

"So, what's your strategy for tomorrow?" she says after some moments of stillness.

"Not to get killed. Maybe it would be karma, but dying for something that isn't your fault is a shitty way to go."

"Drop the act. I knew your type the moment I met you."

"Yeah? What type is that?"

"I don't know why some people are ashamed of being good. They try to hide their warmth under a mask of cynicism."

"Is this where you tell me I'm meant for bigger things in life?"

"No. It's where I tell you not to be ashamed of who you are."

"What about you then? What makes an only child like you go to the end of the world looking for herself?"

"How did you know that I'm an only child?" she asks playfully.

"Takes one to know one, I guess."

"You're right. I'm an only child. My parents are successful doctors, but retired parents."

She talks about her life. How she ran away from the chilly weather and cold existence with her estranged German dad and the loveless marriage of her Swiss mother and Portuguese stepfather. Her first lifeline was a scholarship to study international relations in London. From there, she did anything to stay away from her small village, where life felt like a pressure cooker, people marinating while waiting for their turn in the slaughterhouse. She thought city life was what she needed, until she saw how lonely everyone was. Everyone desperately busying themselves, to avoid looking in the mirror. The colorless cycles of working, drinking, and fucking.

"Same thing we're doing here, no?" I say.

"True, except war surgeries don't give you shitty hangovers."

She jumped at the first opportunity to leave the old, cold continent and work in the aid sector. Same as her ancestors escaped their problems by traveling to the colonies, searching for adventure.

"Why did you come here, Rachel?" I find myself asking, after a few minutes of silence.

"I told you. I needed to change myself by changing my environment. It's all about what you're connected to, and how. Ash and diamonds are both made of carbon atoms, only arranged differently."

"Blimey, that's deep. Except I meant why did you come to this room?"

She punches me playfully in the shoulder. "I don't know. I thought you needed some ... emotional support."

"Did you know that the word 'emotions' comes from the word 'to disturb' in Latin?"

"Here comes the existentialist."

Her smile is contagious. Our eyes hold for a moment too long. That's all it takes sometimes.

Rachel leans in closer. My lips mold into her velvety, silken ones.

We ended up spending the whole night together. I hold her, and we talk as if there's no tomorrow. I have no worries. No fears. When you're inside Jonah's whale, you don't need to worry about rent.

I tell her stories of my rejections and my attempts to fit in. My teenage accident and my parents' deaths. How I met Max and the coin job disaster. How I became distant from everyone, including myself, after that. How I feel bad for letting everyone down. How I need to find Erkhart to tell him I'm sorry. How I'm searching for something I've lost.

A few hours later, we're lying naked under separate sheets. She reaches out and caresses my face, first stopping short of the slightly elevated scar tissue, then touching it extra softly. We had taken off the masks of our clothes and enjoyed being in each other's presence. We didn't have sex. Our intimacy wasn't that selfish.

Rachel is the first woman I've been with since Tina. And for few hours, life doesn't seem so distant anymore. Ironic, given there's a fifty-fifty chance that this life will be snatched away from me very soon.

It feels completely different from being with Tina. There's no dopamine rush. Dopamine is the anticipation-of-reward hormone. The thrill of the chase. The feeling you get smelling a new book. If dopamine had a smell, it would be Tina's.

Serotonin, on the other hand, is the contentedness hormone. When you stop chasing and settle in peace with what you have. The smell of childhood summer holidays. Both Rachel and I are naked under separate sheets, but somehow this is enough physical contact for me. If serotonin had a smell, it would be Rachel's.

Present Day, Friday, 06:34

I wake. Darkness and light are still fighting in the sky, but I know I can't sleep again. I have a magnificent morning glory like a tent wedge. Rachel is sleeping with her hand under her head, and I wonder if she has auburn hair all over.

I leave the bed, feeling the freedom of Adam and Eve in heaven. Before consciousness and obligations. I'm holding the sun.

But perfection lasts for only the briefest of moments before the sun melts the wings of Icarus. My brain catches up and says, "Now pop your pills for the last time before you get shot, errand boy."

The weed buzz is flushed away, revealing the naked rocks of my addiction, with its ragged edges like predator teeth. Some things are never meant to be uncovered. Rachel's presence helps me relax. But until she can go inside my blender of a head and caress my mangled electrical wires, I'll always be alone.

Waves of resistance course through my body. I can do this without drugs. Hell, I *should* do this without drugs. I need clear skies inside my brain for once. Clouds don't help when the difference between life and death could be a single word. Clouds may even welcome death—since being high is being complete and being complete is the end.

I stand paralyzed in the middle of the room. To score or not to score. My face is split by the crack in the mirror, and I hope it's not a sign of what's to come. I catch sight of the dartboard and decide that I'll throw a dart, eyes closed. If it hits the bull's-eye, I'll swallow these small fruits of heaven. If not, I'll face life sober.

I tie Rachel's blood-red scarf around my forehead like Robert De Niro in *The Deer Hunter*'s Russian-roulette scene. I take hold of a dart, pull the scarf down over my eyes to make it a blindfold, and feign a few practice shots to get the feel for the right direction to the center of the circle. The epitome of human perfection. Da Vinci's *Vitruvian Man*. The mandala. The samadhi, the ...

"What are you doing?" Rachel's voice interrupts my spiritual drift.

I stand stock-still, poised for my throw. The dart is next to my temple, my left leg ahead of my right, air held tight in my lungs.

"Have you gone mad? Do you realize you're still naked?"

I throw the dart.

Tack! It hits the board. I bow to the imaginary cheers of a crowd. The task is done, regardless of the result. Now it is decided. *Que sera, sera.*

"Luke, do you hear me?" Her voice comes from the world of sanity, the world of statistics, mortgages, prenups, childhood trauma, nine-to-five working hours, pain and suffering.

I take off the blindfold and glance at the dartboard and then at Rachel. She's staring at me. Sitting on the bed, covering up under the sheet.

I fill my lungs with the air coming from the window, shimmering with smoke and regret, and say, "I love the smell of insanity in the morning."

I throw the pills from the window.

I go to the bathroom, squeeze out some Colgate from a tube left by God knows who, and brush with my finger, unwilling to go search for my toothbrush.

My expression in the mirror is of someone on a bus trip who's just realized he left his wallet at home. My stomach is somersaulting. I turn to the toilet and throw up.

I feel slightly better. I yank the handle when I'm done, but no water comes. I stare at the vile contents of my stomach and reflect upon the art of plumbing. Where does all the shit and vomit go? Who literally takes the piss? How is it that the West's greatest achievement was to separate people from their internal realities?

I take my memory stick from my pocket and throw it in the toilet. It sinks into the excrement and vomit. Right where it belongs.

The team is having breakfast, but the thought of eating tickles my gag reflex. Manu waves me over, but Michael elbows him to let me be. Anne is staring into oblivion, carving circles in a plate of hummus.

I pray, then sit far from them and turn the old television on. No news about the conference. Instead, Orson Welles is explaining to a mate of his in a black-and-white film: "In Italy for thirty years under the Borges, they had warfare, terror, murder, and bloodshed, but they produced Michelangelo, Leonardo Da Vinci, and the Renaissance. In Switzerland, they had brotherly love. They had five hundred years of democracy and peace, and what did that produce? The cuckoo clock!"

I take a Red Bull from Manu's stash. The hum of the generator and a slow drip of water from God-knows-where is driving me nuts. I long for the pills I threw away.

Michael looks anxiously at Anne, who is still in her contemplative drift. "Do you need bread with that hummus, Anne?"

Anne stops her fork movement. "I need a divorce, Michael."

Everyone freezes. Even Yehia stops eating.

Michael's eyes dart in all directions. He hisses, "Hon! What are you—"

She finally looks at him. "Don't 'hon' me, Michael. Our marriage ended when you slept with that Dutch nurse in Malakal. I'll file for divorce if we ever get out of here. I want you to know now."

The General's cousin sheepishly enters the basement and asks if we can talk outside. I'm happy to escape the toxic air and still have time to kill, as I've decided to go after Friday's prayer. I've gone to the mosque every Friday since I arrived, much to the puzzlement of my team and the Yemeni staff. I'm sure Max and Manu have overestimated how much the rebels consider me "one of us."

In the hallway, the General's cousin and the General's nephew are waiting.

"So, you're going to meet Akrami?" Nephew asks in Arabic.

"Yeah."

"Why?" asks Cousin.

I shrug. "You know. Negotiate surrender. See if we can have some peace around here."

"Peace?" spits Nephew. "Those *dihbashis* are the cause of all these wars. You can't have peace with them."

"Why not?"

"We need to free Palestine," says Cousin matter-of-factly.

"Ah, OK, yes?"

"To do that, we first need to have our independent South and eliminate the near enemy: the Shiite."

"OK. But why not have peace with them? You all have the same cause, no?"

"We can't have peace with those hypocrite *rawafed*. They are either at your feet or your throat," Cousin says. He wears the expression of a true believer. The most dangerous lies are the ones we tell ourselves.

"Do you know who first said that?"

"Yes, my grandfather."

No point telling him it was probably Churchill describing the Huns way back when. I do believe, though, that he probably heard it from his grandfather, not through the BBC. Humans perpetuate the same ideas through space and time.

"Why are you defending the Sunni so much?" I ask. "I haven't even seen you pray."

"I don't pray. But Sunnis are the true Muslims."

"By the way, how come we see *you* pray?" asks Nephew.

"Because I'm Muslim."

They exchange a confused look.

"You have a Christian name," he says.

"I have a foreign name. That doesn't mean I'm Christian."

They exchange a dumb look.

I'm not surprised. Yehia told me shortly after our arrival that national staff don't like me because of my Western name, which made them assume that I'd converted to Christianity.

"Are you Sunni or Shiite?" Cousin asks.

I shrug. "I'm Muslim."

They exchange a knowing look.

Enough of this. I feel jittery from the lack of cocktails. I want to leave before they enlighten me with a theory on how Shiites are the ones responsible for the Spanish flu.

"So, if Akrami agrees to our surrender, shall I tell him you prefer to die?" I ask.

"No, no," Nephew hastens. "I mean, we just want you to be careful. Tactical retreats are halal, after all."

"One last thing. Can you please stop justifying all your hatred and fear with Islam?"

"Why?"

"Because the more you do, the more ignorant and pathetic you sound."

I turn to leave. Cousin stops me. "Just don't let them mess with your mind. I was captured by Akrami's militia in Sanaa and held for two weeks. Every day, they would haul one of us out of the cell. They'd later return with bloodied knives, announcing that the man had been beheaded. When my turn came, I almost shat myself. But they just transferred me to another cell, laughing. That's where I found all the men they'd told us had been beheaded."

"But why the mock executions? Did they need to extract information from you?"

"Not at all. There were no interrogations. Maybe their TV was down or something."

I leave the room. In all these long years, nobody has ever managed to conquer Yemen. Except the Yemenis themselves.

On my way to the roof to meet Max, I remember something. I slip to the canteen. The lights are out and no one is there. I approach the body on the trolley in the corner, my heart pounding. What was the right answer for the trolley dilemma again?

General Rahimi's lips are dry and parted. His eyes are rolled upward in their sockets and one of his arms dangles off the trolley, turning blue, his hand clenched like a claw.

There's no way to know the exact nature of his death, let alone who did it. I try to convince myself it could have been natural, but the timing is uncanny. My bet is on succinylcholine, a potent muscle relaxant that can cause paralysis. Forty milligrams of SUX are enough to convince the diaphragm to stop working, which means you stop breathing.

One thing I know for sure—I'm not going to be the one telling Max about this. He wouldn't believe me.

I instinctively close his eyes, but then realize what I'm doing and open them again, trying not to squirm. The left one is fine, but the right one only opens halfway. I can't remember if the General had a wonky eye. I decide to leave it like that and sneak out of the room.

I go to the roof, hoping that no one has seen my little detour. I resist the urge to wash my hands.

"You look ready," Max says, with a proud expression. "Especially after last night." He winks.

I give him a stony look. "I got lucky, but not in the way you think. These days, it's easier to find someone to fuck than someone to hug."

"Are you sure you're not gay? That Swiss girl is as hot as white chocolate. Lift up those long exotic legs and the sky will never fall to earth."

A surge of annoyance rises with my bile. "How about Akrami, is he exotic, too?"

"Akrami?' Max sucks his teeth. 'He's a trigger-happy fanatic with a trail of blood behind him. They call him the brother of the martyr—his brother hugged fifty kilos of RDX and went all fuckin' Samson at the city gates a few weeks ago."

Ah, shit. What a family. "What else do you know about him?"

He shrugs. "Fuck would I know? We met in a battlefield, Luke, not in one of your team-building workshops in Geneva."

I close my eyes. I need an ice pack or a cold drink for my throbbing temple.

"So, you don't even know what he looks like?"

"No offense, but they all look alike." He raises his finger, remembering something. "One way you can recognize him is from his pistol. He carries a Luger."

I bite my lower lip, hard. "Yes, Max?"

Seeing I'm about to explode, he says quickly, "Ah, OK. It's an ancient pistol. It has a leather grip and two screws at the top and bottom of the handle. You'll recognize it immediately, trust me."

"Let's see how far trusting you will get me."

"Speaking of trust, about my mom ..."

"Yes, I put her inside the hollow handle of the toilet paper roll in the second-floor bathroom."

"You put my mom in the toilet?" he hisses from between his teeth.

"I put her there for now. I'll find her a much better place when I can. Anyway, if I don't come back, feel free to book her a suite at the Sabaa hotel."

"Fine. Just make sure to come and take her back."

I smile bitterly. "I'll sure as hell do my best."

CHAPTER 15

London, September 2014

I used Erkhart's platinum membership to invite Gavin to play squash at the members-only Hurlington Club in Mayfair, with its BBC-accented staff and four underground squash courts.

The game was full of sweat and grunts. We were evenly matched. Yet I'd already won before we began. I chose to play there because I knew there was no mobile signal in the underground facilities. In the changing rooms, Gavin asked for the Wi-Fi log-in, and I gave him the credentials of a dummy network I'd created using Chief Hobo spyware. I was inside his phone.

After the game, Gavin handed me a photo. Lousy quality, from a lousy angle, with a lousy striped-bed-linen background. The coin itself was the lousiest thing of all. A rusty, miserable piece of gray metal. It lay on a black velvet bag with "Sotheby's" stitched in gold lettering. Next to the bag was yesterday's *Daily Telegraph*.

Nice touch with the bag. The last time the coin had been legally sold was at a Sotheby's auction, for over twenty million dollars.

In return, I showed him a bank draft of one million dollars to confirm the funds had been secured. He emphasized the transaction had to be in cash, and we agreed to discuss the meeting point as soon as I had all the queen's heads in my possession.

A week later, my doorbell rang unexpectedly at 9 PM while I was contemplating the philosophical dilemma of to eat or not to eat. Staying hungry versus the agony of preparing dinner.

"Gavin?"

He stood there, all shiny and tanned. A royal blue wool jacket over a starchy white shirt open to reveal half his chest. Hollywood chic, Hollywood fake.

"Alright, Luke? Thought of popping round your gaff for a wee bit," he said, stepping inside.

"Do you enjoy showing up in people's homes uninvited, like in a cheap film? Or is this the Irish mob's MO?"

He chuckled. "I knew you'd do your homework. Who I work for isn't a secret anyway." He looked around like a seasoned real estate agent. "Very small place you have here. Lacks a woman's touch. I guess Tina doesn't come around very often."

I faced him. "What do you want, Gavin?"

"I wanted to tell you that I'm ready. What about you? We good?"

"Yeah. I have the cash."

"The whole mil?"

"Yes. A drink?" I asked, giving up on him leaving anytime soon.

"Aye, grand." He grinned.

"I only have coke and orange juice," I said, realizing that he probably expected a Jameson, or at the very least, a Guinness.

"Coke, then," he said, relaxing on the couch, smile fading as he looked at the television. "What's the craic?"

"Documentary about the CIA's role in the coup against Mosaddegh in Iran."

"Wars in the Middle East? Is this harking back to your roots? Not sure that's a good idea."

I rolled my eyes. "Why is that?"

"Makes you feel that you don't belong anywhere."

"Not sure if that would be a blessing or a curse."

He pursed his lips and shook his head. "Nah, you're better off with who you are now. At least you have the choice on how to fuck up your life without having to blame society or religion."

I handed him his drink without a word. After a pause, I asked,

"How much does Tina know about our deal?"

"Only what she needs to know."

"Which is what exactly?"

"Nothing. A woman's involvement in a pissing contest can make things messy."

"A mobster and a philosopher. Always an interesting combination."

"I'm not a mobster. I only work with them. My da was the accountant for Jimmy Levine, the head of the Limerick mob," he said. "He was killed in an accident when I was young. Jimmy gave me my dad's job when I grew up. I didn't have a choice. My da wouldn't have wanted that for me, but his death made it inevitable. I'm sure you can relate."

"Why do you think that?"

"Yours was killed too, right? I mean your real old fella."

"Yes," I said, feeling a lump in my throat.

"What did you feel when his killers got away with reduced charges?"

"OK, Gavin. You did your homework, too. Don't overplay it."

"OK, Luke. I won't. Anyway, after a while, I found myself deep in it. Nurturing asset funds, creating shell companies, setting up foreign corporations in the Virgin Islands, Monaco, Dubai."

"So you don't mind working for drug dealers and murderers."

"It's only temporary. One day, I'll be free to do my own thing. For now, I'm following the natural order of life. You know the prisoner's dilemma, Luke?"

"The one where two gang members are arrested and held separately, and each has to either stay silent or betray the other without knowing what the other will do?"

"That's the one. It's not only a model for game theory, it's a model of life. You know what's the best option if you're not sure what the other person will do?"

I shrugged. "Stay silent?"

"Wrong. Always betray."

I was about to tell him that his mobster friends might not agree when he continued, "You're Muslim, right?"

I stiffened. "Yes."

"I guess you know the story of the Prophet's granddaughter, when people killed her father and entered her house. Some poor sod was crying when he came and took her gold ankle bracelets. She asked him, 'Why are you crying, enemy of God?' He replied, 'How could I not—I'm stealing from the Prophet's granddaughter.' She said: 'Don't steal from me, then!' He said, 'I'm afraid that if I don't, someone else will come and steal from you.'"

I felt a bit ashamed that he knew this story and I didn't. I wondered if that was his intention.

He continued, "From the Akkadians to the British Empire, if you didn't grab your chance, the next in line would. If I didn't get the job with the mob, or you didn't buy your mobile made by slave workers in China, someone else would step in, and you and I end up at the bottom of the food chain."

The problem with Gavin, I decided, was that he had a lot of self-portraits in the dark areas of his subconscious. I decided a little sabotage was in order. "Enough of situational ethics, Gavin. Do you have this chip on your shoulder only with me, or is it with everyone?"

"What's that again?"

"On the surface, you seem to have everything, but the more you try to show how much better you are than everyone else, the more your insecurities shine through."

For a second, black shadows flashed in his dark pupils, but then he remembered he was supposed to be Gregory Peck. He chuckled and straightened the collar of his crisp shirt in a way that I suspected was unconscious, a nervous tic. He looked at his watch and stood.

"I have better places to be on a Saturday night." He added coldly,

"Our transaction must take place within the next three days. I'll send you the details soon. Be ready to move within a few hours' notice."

"I'm not sure that's—"

"That's the way it is, Luke. That's how it is to work with mobsters, in case you're still wondering."

He opened the door. "Run it by Daddy Erkhart. He'll tell you the mob's MO in such transactions is not very different from his own."

I managed to keep my face blank until the door shut, then I grabbed my mobile. I had told neither Max nor *Daddy* Erkhart about my updated plans for Gavin. I dialed a number from memory.

"He just left. He doesn't suspect anything. Will tell you where and when very soon."

I woke up groping at a string leading back to the dark corners of my memories, but all that was left of my dream was gray clouds and a feeling of dread.

The clouds faded. Tina was awake, watching me. Her eyes were the deep blue of a faraway ocean. This could have been a romantic moment, but instead my stomach clenched. Maybe it was the look on her face, or maybe it was my upcoming rendezvous with Gavin.

"Hey," she said softly.

"Hey."

"Have you ever thought of us taking the coin and the money and splitting to Thailand or Latin America?"

I stared at her, not sure if she was serious.

She laughed. "Don't worry, Luke. I know you're too decent for that."

She stood from the bed, put on her silk robe, and left the room, returning with her mysterious green morning juice in one hand and my double espresso in the other. She handed me the coffee and stood gazing out the window.

"You alright, love?" I asked, sipping the bitter liquid.

"All good," she said, without looking back.

The weather was cloudy and windy. The kind where you wished you had the luxury to stay in bed all day. A luxury I didn't have. I finished my coffee, took a quick shower, and went back into the room. She had changed into an elegant black dress and was facing the mirror.

"I had a weird dream last night," she said. Her tone was flat, as though she were hypnotized.

"Yeah? How so?"

"I don't remember all of it. Only fragments," she said, finishing her makeup. "In one of them, I was reading Satan's mission statement, according to the University of Cambridge dictionary. It read, 'And the devil confined me; behold, I am here for the ruins of men.'"

I caught her reflection in the mirror. I needed to say something. "Hmm. I wonder what that's all about."

"Are you going to be OK?" she said, turning to me, looking immortal as usual.

"Of course. Everything's going as planned," I said, buttoning up my shirt.

She came over and helped me with the top button before placing her warm hands on my cheeks.

"I love you," she said. Then she kissed me and left the room.

That was the first time I'd heard these words from Tina. And the last time I ever saw her.

CHAPTER 16

Present Day, Friday, 13:47

I read about a revenge tradition in the south of Egypt where tribes take matters into their own hands: an eye for an eye when someone kills one of your own. The vicious cycle of violence can be broken only if the member of the tribe with the mark on his head goes to the rival tribe with white burial shrouds in his hand. He's ready to die and give them his life, trusting they will give it back.

Sun rays burn my skin when I step outside. The world is sharp and clear, without my usual high clouding my awareness. Too many stimuli bombard my brain. I feel everything intensely, from the rumble of my stomach to the insects crawling beneath my skin, and I want to sit on the nearest rock and weep. I decide that, if I come back alive, I'll tell Rachel I like her.

The hospital yard looks like a herd of baby dragons had a birthday party and disagreed on who would light the candles. Smoke is still rising from charred cars and the smell of cordite fills the air. The spot with the remnants of the near-miss rockets is so different now with all the destruction around it. Almost cartoonish.

I make sure I'm not walking into any unexploded ordnance. One of the countless sad facts of war is that, on average, one in seven bombs, rockets, or projectiles won't explode upon impact. They will lie dormant for days or decades until they give a kiss of death to descendants of the sins of the past.

I avoid looking at the bodies with flies circling them like

pilgrims. Red flesh, white bones, empty eyes glimpsing a realm beyond thought. If I don't see them, I don't feel guilty for leaving them as they are. And if there's a message here, I don't want to hear it. Ahead of me, the Humvee, or what's left of it, smells of defeat. I look away from Piotr's *sadeeq,* the charred body with the unexploded RPG still sticking from it.

Friday prayers finished half an hour ago. As in previous weeks, months, and years, many of the prayers went unanswered, such as, "Please God, help me kill the others."

I'm wearing my white coat, which in a hospital is the Superman costume to my Clark Kent, but now feels like the shroud of my own grave. I walk slowly out of the main gate, hands in the air, expecting to face dozens of guns attached to khat-buzzed fingers, ready to shoot at any miscalculated move.

Instead, there are only two men standing twenty meters to my left, one leaning on a tree peppered with bullets, eating an apple. Their Klashes dangle from their shoulders. Relaxed and chilled, like the banana-curved clips of their weapons, as opposed to the hard-angled, disciplined M16 clips of Max and his team. But that's not what stops me in my tracks. What stops me is that they don't look remotely Yemeni or even Arab. They are extremely tall Black men.

"Why so slow? We don't have all day, man," the apple soldier says in English, before adding with a grin, "We have a hospital to destroy."

I wonder if I've stepped into a space-time warp before I hurry across to them, and we disappear together, I assume, out of the bull's-eye of Ray's sniper rifle.

The second soldier stops, as if he's forgotten something. "Do you have any *Abu Helalin?*"

The guy with two crescents—*Abu Helalin* in Arabic—is the nickname of Captagon, one of the Middle East's widely used illegal stimulants. Fighters love Captagon, not only because its billion-dollar trade makes many of them filthy rich, but also because, like all amphetamines, it numbs pain and hunger, and suppresses fear, empathy and the need for sleep. Pop a couple and you'll fight for hours like Popeye on spinach, more aggressive and braver than if you'd trained for years. Unless, of course, you catch a heart attack and die biting your tongue.

"What? No."

"Tramadol?" the one with the apple asks.

"No, I ... I ..."

"OK, OK. Keep moving."

The setting in the makeshift camp is different from what I expected. The rebels are scattered in groups that total at least seventy men. Some are eating, others cleaning their weapons, but the majority are asleep. Foreign soldiers are mixed in with the Yemeni ones, probably Somalis or Eritreans, maybe even Ethiopians.

Huh. It's not only government forces who use mercenaries. Second-oldest profession, indeed.

They have no uniform. Some wear the traditional *thob* and suit jacket; others wear military khakis. Some are wearing jeans, and some are in black training suits. Some are bearded, some are clean shaven. Some cover their faces, some don't. Hell, some have weapons, and some have none. Some look like they haven't even had their first kiss, while others look like they'll never live to have another one. Their motives are probably just as varied, from thrills to vengeance to lack of other options. They have only one thing in common. The way they look at me now. Predators assessing their prey. Several start to follow us.

This is what can happen when citizenship of a failed state means penalties, not benefits. Demand is much higher than supply, and scarcity switches people to a gold rush mentality, snatching for themselves what will never be given.

We reach a small, shaded area where five or six rebels are sitting and chewing khat, their weapons lying at their feet. I expect them to wave off the crowd following me with military discipline, but they don't seem to object. Hardly an ideal situation for the private proposal I have in mind, which I didn't share with Max. The air becomes heavy—sweet and sticky.

A bulky bearded man in his late thirties with a beige keffiyeh wrapped around his forehead, assesses me. He's wearing khaki pants and what used to be a sky blue T-shirt, now gray from wear. His Klash lies faithfully between his legs, old, robust, and with a foldable stock. Probably an original Russian model, not one of the new Chinese models saturating today's market.

This must be Akrami.

He says, in Arabic, "So you're the most expendable of the lot, huh?" He points at my crotch. "Elephant balls."

"Why would I be afraid? I'm a civilian coming in peace." My voice comes out higher than intended.

He chuckles, or coughs. A gurgling sound of lungs slushy from chronic smoking. "You don't know what they did last time they wanted to *negotiate*?"

My extremities go cold. Apart from putting my life in danger, not knowing is making me look stupid.

His eyes narrow. "You're not Yemeni?"

I swallow hard. "No. I'm Egyptian."

"Egyptian? We were told the doctors inside are foreigners."

I know what he means. For better or worse, Arabs are not considered "foreigners" to each other. "Yes, we have foreign medical staff inside."

"Do you work with General Rahimi?" asks a thin man in his mid-twenties with restless eyes. He's wearing an ancient Harley Davidson T-shirt.

"No, we're volunteer doctors from an independent organization. We came here to help—"

"Which organization?" calls out a bearded man with his arm in a sling.

"International Aid. It's based in—"

"What about General Rahimi and his mercenaries?" says Sling Man, pulling at the back of his dark baggy pants, which are two sizes too big.

"What *about* them? They broke into our hospital and threatened us with guns. You expected us to fight them with syringes?"

The faces around me are hostile, fueled by uppers and cigarettes. Their wires are crossed with excess energy that needs release. Otherwise, they would short circuit and bloody implode or something. I doubt that any of them have prayed the Friday prayer, but I don't doubt they're ready to become "martyrs." God only knows which martyrdom is selfless sacrifice and which is selfish investment.

Murmurs rise. Some of them think I'm a spy, others mock my chef costume, and others want to shoot me on the spot—to send a message to the "pig Rahimi." Like he bloody cares.

The bulky man raises his hand. "One moment, brothers."

Silence falls. Finally, a sane man.

He chases something in his mouth with his tongue before he spits. "So, you surrender?"

Bloody hell. "It isn't me you should worry about. We're not part of this fight."

I step forward. Harley-Davidson flinches, his hand moving instinctively to his Klash. Shit. These guys need to try downers for a change. The bulky man keeps his bloodshot eyes aimed at me while he cleans his teeth with a toothpick.

I say to him, "I need to discuss something with you in private," and an angry roar comes from the crowd behind me as though I had cursed all of their mothers' reproductive organs. One of them shoves me in the back. I keep my eyes on the bulky man. He waves a fly from his face, stands slowly, dusts himself off, and puts his arm around me like we were old mates. Then he starts walking me toward an empty place. The man has a flair for drama. In another life, I can see him playing King Lear in Shakespeare's Globe.

I smell stale sweat. His dark brown skin is wrinkled like leather.

"Nice Klash you have there," I say as we walk. "I can differentiate it from a dozen M16s firing at the same time."

"Did you come here to talk about the supremacy of Soviet guns?"

So much for my ice breaker. Fuck you, Dale Carnegie.

We stop by the shade of a palm tree. He fiddles casually with the belt undergirding his sizeable belly. That's when I notice the antique pistol in his waistband.

"You must be Akrami."

"I didn't know I'd become international."

We sit casually on the ground, like two hitchhikers trying their luck on a desert road.

"What's your name?" he asks. His pupils, dilated from khat and God knows what else, are holes to his soul.

"Adam."

"Adam what?"

"Adam Elraey."

"Adam Elraey what?"

"Oh, I see. Adam *Mohamed* Elraey."

"Hmm. Do you have your passport?"

Shit, my passport says "Luke Archer." Interesting that no one even bothered to search me. No wonder Max's team has managed to hold them off so far. "No, they took it from me inside."

"No problem. I already know who you are."

"But we just met."

"I've seen you all my life. You are one of the Western puppets. One of those who sit on the fence, waiting for the wind to push them to one side or the other."

"I'm Muslim just like you. I just happened to be born in the West. That doesn't—"

"How many of the foreign fighters are there?"

His question startles me. "I'm no longer sure. Many came after the General arrived, and we're not allowed out of the basement."

"Want to be my man on the inside? I'll give you a phone."

"I can't," I say before I give myself the time to think twice.

"Why? You think they're accepting you as one of them?"

"I'm not one of them and I'm not one of you. Besides, you'd never respect me if I did this. And I wouldn't respect myself."

He waves me off dismissively, his slack expression clearly indicating that he couldn't care less. "OK, what do you want then, Adam *Mohamed* Elraey?"

"The foreign fighters inside are ready to consider the option of surrendering and giving you the General if you provide them with a safe way out." I hide the fact that the General is dead because I hope this will make the bargain more worthwhile.

He chuckles, which baffles me. He's not even considering it. I feel like a rookie lawyer in a trial that's already lost.

"Why would we do that? We're going to get all of you in the next few hours," he says, in a light-hearted tone that only makes things worse.

"To save the lives of your men, and to spare the lives of the medical team and patients inside." I avoid waxing lyrical about the rights of prisoners and of the wounded. Talking about international humanitarian law in a situation like this is like having a Narcotics Anonymous meeting in a poppy field.

"You know, that's the difference between people from the West and us. They've so many options that they don't know what to do with them. In this part of the world, we don't have *options*. Only necessities and sacrifices. My brother sacrificed his life at the gates of this city. He had no other option but to go forward. Same as me here." He smiles. "Now they're giving me an *option*? Do the Yemenis killed by American drones every day get options? Your friends have finally met rivals who can shoot back. I'll be damned if I don't give them a taste of what it means to be the underdog."

I want to interject emphatically that they are not my friends, but he continues, "A lot of good men died yesterday." He removes his keffiyeh and scratches his head freely. His hair is more rebellious than he is—he must have killed his barber. "If your friends had surrendered earlier, those men would still be alive, their wives would not be widows, and their children would not be orphans."

I feel I should say something, but my mind is a blank.

He nods toward the hospital. "We're going to take this hospital. We're going to take this city, and we're going to take the whole country, whether it costs us one life or a thousand. Our deaths are fuel for our cause. But your people's deaths are just a waste of the other options they could have chosen."

He wraps his keffiyeh back around his head. "Take Bakr, for example—the guy with the sling who was asking you all those stupid questions back there."

"Well, they weren't all stupid, to be—"

"Bakr was one of the leaders of the protests that started months ago. Bakr met with Rahimi's security forces to *negotiate*. Rahimi's men told them they would let the rebels pass, but to identify the leaders and give them safe passage, they had to raise their hands as they passed. You know what happened?"

I shake my head no, and he smiles again.

"They sniped everyone who put up a hand."

The coldness rushes through my extremities again. I think of little bunnies dying in forest fires. Koalas unable to outrun their fate.

He continues in a rusty tone, "That's how the men who sent you negotiate."

My hopes of changing his mind are evaporating. We're separated by a dam of life experiences. I try to change the subject. "So, you would execute them without trial?"

A black cloud passes behind his eyes. "Trial? If people used laws to kill your family and take your home, what would you do to them? Prosecute them using the same laws they made?" He shakes his head in disbelief. "Over here, we make our own laws. Your

Egyptian President Nasser once said, 'What has been taken by force can only be returned by force.'"

I'm about to point out that this came from a leader who lost all his wars, when he faces me. "So, you listen to me. You tell those mercenaries that the time for negotiations has passed." His pupils have almost swallowed their entire irises. In them, I can see the ruins of a great civilization. "We're patient. We will finish this our way."

I don't doubt the patience part. They've been waiting for their promised imam for over a thousand years.

"I'll give you a six-hour ceasefire," Akrami says. "In return, I want the bodies of my martyred soldiers for proper burial."

"Yes. I can facilitate that. Send your men to retrieve the bodies after *Asr* prayer."

I stand to leave but he stops me with a raised finger. "One more thing. My men might not have caught on yet, but I know that it was civilians who killed two of my men the other night. Simply because they were killed with their own guns."

He spits the remains of his toothpick out with conviction and looks toward the hospital again. "You go back now and wait for this land's justice. We're all guilty, in our own way."

I make my way to the roof and fill Max in on what Akrami said. He doesn't seem particularly surprised by my report. "Did you kill him?" is all he asks.

"Akrami?"

"The General," he says forcefully.

"As I just told you twice, he was already dead when I checked on him. It could've been one of your men for all I know."

"You know damn well it wasn't one of us. That needed a special level of medical knowledge and cowardice."

"Max, I wouldn't—"

"Why not? Don't tell me it's against your hypocrite oath."

"Hippocratic."

"Whatever. Now Akrami will think we have no honor to offer giving him up alive. You should've told him he was dead."

"We talked about more important things, like how he's going to fuck us all up regardless, six hours from now." I feel a pang of guilt. "You think it would have made a difference?"

He sighs. "Not really. Those fanatics would never let American soldiers walk away."

"They don't seem that radical."

"I'm not in the mood for psychological profiling, Luke." He grabs the immortal communal pack of Camel and taps out a cigarette, studying it for a while. "My mom is where you left her. Make sure to move her in a more decent place."

I nod.

He lights a cigarette. Mid-way through, he asks, "Do you believe in hell?"

I don't know what to tell him. All I have are a few beliefs and many questions. Most of our lives consist of things we can't see. We can't access the thoughts of our loved ones, but we can hear their words. We can't see the light, only what the light reflects. Each cell of our body dies and is replaced, some faster than others, and we almost have a new body every seven years. Who are we then? Maybe dying is a tragedy only if we think we have separate selves.

"I believe in a higher order," I finally say.

"And do you believe this *higher order* created hell for those who lost their souls?"

"I see people who've lost their souls every time I walk in the street, Max. You don't need hell for that."

I tap out a cigarette for myself. "Heaven and hell are incentives for people who believe in the illusion of having separate souls, while actually there's only one. I believe that the body dies but the soul is indestructible because it's from God. The only source of life."

"Goodness me, T. S. Eliot. Try some of this on Akrami when he storms in and maybe we can all have a group hug."

"Hey, you asked."

I light the cigarette. I want to smoke the whole thing in a single drag. Our smoke mixes together, curls upward, and vanishes into the eternal pale blue sky. We don't speak for a few minutes, smoking being the modern-day equivalent of a meditation exercise.

Part of me doesn't care what Akrami will do to us. I think of parallel universes where infinite numbers of our selves exist, of universes inside universes. A universe for sperm, where they have their own lives. A universe for fetuses where wombs are skies. An indifferent universe where self-aware humans kill each other.

As though reading my mind, he asks, "So you think all of this is meaningless?"

"I don't think anything. I'm in awe of people who claim to know the purpose of the universe when I still don't know why we close our eyes when we sneeze."

I read a book in Erkhart's library once, in which two yeast cells were discussing the purpose of their lives while eating sugar and drowning in their own shit. They never guessed they were making champagne.

I hardly ever share my religious views with anyone, as the discussion usually comes with side orders of condescension and self-righteousness. In the end, both God lovers and God haters pray when the plane starts to fall. I'm what you call a reluctant mystic.

Max stamps out his cigarette and rises to his feet. "Whatever happens, I hope I'm not reincarnated back into this shithole of a universe. I'm tired of mortgages."

Piotr slaps his neck loudly as Max and I enter the canteen. He examines the crushed mosquito as he yawns and claws at his neck like a leper. "Our bloody health insurance better cover fucking filariasis."

Taking off his armor plates, Max responds, "There's no health insurance in the first place. Welcome to the American dream, *tovarish*."

"Fuck your American dream," sneers Piotr. "I was better off with Wagner."

Ray, already out of combat gear since the news of the ceasefire, says, "If we were with those nutter nationals of yours, they would've solved this pickle by dropping a seventy-year-old ugly-ass Soviet bomb on the neighborhood, to get rid of both us and the rebels."

Piotr grunts, "Better than leaving us behind to get bayonetted up our asses like Gaddafi."

CHAPTER 17

London, October 2014

I arrived forty minutes early for our 9 pm meeting, at Hopwood Park service station on the M40 south of Birmingham, in a black SUV. This was the first time I'd driven since my accident, ten years ago that month. I had no choice. It wasn't like I could show up in a black cab.

I had kept Max in the dark about what I was doing, so I was on my own. My hope was that a fair number of people would be around, but only a handful of commuters were present, and most were inside the building. I parked the car, got out, and breathed air pregnant with rain.

My "high" cloud was thick around my brain that night. I saw myself from above, as though I were in a video game. As though I had died and been given another chance to make things right. I pressed the joystick from my hiding place in the clouds and my feet moved.

I passed a frowning woman pushing a stroller next to a man biting into a McDonald's apple pie. Her forearm was tattooed with the word "Smile" in black lettering. A couple took photos in an endless number of poses near a tree. My phone buzzed. Gavin.

"Head to the furthest picnic table, toward the exit of the rest area. You'll find the words "Drive Safely" carved into the table."

"Why the change?" I asked, as my knuckles turned white around the phone.

"You didn't think we would do a million-dollar transaction

surrounded by fat kids armed with Big Macs, did you?"

"Is that supposed to be funny?"

"Just do it." He hung up.

I got some coffee from Starbucks and walked to an empty cluster of picnic tables. The table in question was around a hundred meters from the rest house. "Drive Safely" had been recently carved into its wooden bench. If it were still raining, would we do the deal in the rain like in gangster films?

I sat there swirling my cold brew, wondering about the game Gavin was playing. He wouldn't want to double-cross me. The word would spread, and they wouldn't be able to work in this racket for a long time. But what if they weren't playing the long game? What if this was a one-off? It didn't matter; I was playing a game of my own.

A red four-wheel-drive stopped twenty meters away from me. Three men got out. The last one was Gavin. I could see the shape of a fourth, the driver, behind the wheel. Bloody hell!

"We agreed it's only me and you?" The part of me in the dark, inside my skin, shuddered, but the part in the light held its ground.

"Oh, don't fret. The lads wanted to make sure I didn't get lost."

The smallest of the *lads* was the kind of beast who would hand you your teeth if you said the wrong thing.

"Have you got the money?" Gavin asked.

"Have you got the cent?"

He produced a velvet bag from his pocket and flashed a coin from it. I moved toward it, extending my hand, but he gestured for me to stop. He studied me for a long moment. Nothing in his gaze suggested he would buy me a drink and invite me to his hometown when all this was over.

"Where's the money, Luke?"

"It's in the trunk of my car, Gavin."

"Would you mind getting it out?"

I cast a nervous glance at his companions before heading to the car to retrieve a gray gym bag. A five-hundred-pound

Porsche-design Adidas bag that Tina had bought me on one of her shopping crusades. This was the only time it had carried more than its worth. I hoped I could have it back.

I placed the bag on the "Drive Safely" table. Gavin took his time making his way over. He actually seemed to be enjoying this. He opened the bag and quickly flicked through the notes, then zipped it up and inhaled sharply, looking up at the black heavens.

"Do you know why I chose this place, Luke?"

"Let's see, is it where you first had car sex? How the bloody hell would I know, Gavin?"

"Nice one. No, I wanted you to drive here. How was it to drive again, Luke?"

My heart took a free fall down a dark well. A thought flashed in my mind. *RUN.*

"I was sure I could play you like a pawn," he said. "Your carelessness and impulsive behavior make you an open book." His condescending tone was full of rust and bile. His words had a smell of their own.

"Don't pretend you know me."

"Aye, I know you too well," he said, smiling but not really. "Adam Elraey, the geeky kid with a motorbike."

I furrowed my brow. I was missing something here. My heart was pumping so hard I could feel it in my ears. I was sweating but my spine had turned to ice.

"You still don't know who I am? I see you didn't even recognize the car."

The red Cherokee was suddenly too familiar. Right out of my worst nightmares.

He continued, "You probably never looked back on that night, but karma has kept a receipt."

I was paralyzed. For a second, I didn't know whether to scream or laugh. The smell of fresh-cut grass and the prickling sound of shy spits of rain were replaced by the stench of diesel fumes and the roar of motorcycle engines. My accident flashed through my head. The flash of white light on impact. I never did follow up on what happened to the kid in that Jeep.

"How come you're here?" I managed to say.

"Do you know where the term 'red herring' came from?'"

I nod. Through the haze in my mind floated stories of peasants in medieval England who would throw red herrings to drive the noblemen's dogs off the scent of the fox.

"Alright. Good. In this case, the coin was the red herring. I had you under the microscope for months. I knew about your connection to Erkhart. And I knew Tina could lure you into doing this job."

This wasn't a business transaction. It was personal.

"I never forgot that accident, Gavin. I didn't want it to happen."

He shrugged. "Except it did."

"So, what now?"

"Now, justice. You're coming with us. Nice and easy."

His goons advanced slowly, like vultures encircling a wounded animal.

I took a cautious step back. "Well, Gavin. I admit that I didn't know who you were. But in the story of the red herring, I think you're mistaken about the dog."

This was personal for me, too. But for a completely different reason.

He tensed. I moved my hands up in front of me, palms facing outwards, and pointed my middle fingers downward. The Arab way of giving the finger.

"What are you doing, you gobshite? Move," one of the goons said.

Gavin froze. A deer in headlights.

Men ran toward us from all directions, guns drawn, shouting "Freeze!" and "Get down on the ground!" Two contradictory orders that only added to the confusion.

It was hard to get DI Thompson to agree to my secret signal. She insisted it had to be something I didn't usually do.

One of the goons tried to run to the Jeep, but shots were fired and he froze.

The Jeep screeched to life, but the flashlights of three police cars coming from the opposite direction convinced the driver to cut his great escape short. He got out of the car, raising his hands, flashlights gleaming on his shiny bald skull.

Cops pinned Gavin and his companions to the ground, two officers each. I crouched next to him and cocked my head to one side. I could smell the scent of the freshly cut grass again. I didn't know whether to laugh or cry.

He smiled acidly. "This ain't over yet."

I shrugged. "Except it is."

I moved away from him while DI Sarah Thompson, the National Crime Agency liaison officer, approached. "What is all this Hollywood shit about? You knew this man from before?"

"He was in a car accident I had long time ago."

A woman in plainclothes came and removed the wire from under my shirt without even looking at me. I grunted as the plaster ripped off a few of my chest hairs.

"Easy, love," I said.

She glared at me and walked away. She could probably kick my ass without breaking a sweat, but I was euphoric.

It was true that I hadn't known Gavin's real identity. But I knew all along he was trying to screw me. God bless Chief Hobo and his gadgets.

"Why were you so late? He almost killed me."

"An attempted murder is a good way to seal the case. Could you not get him to say how he stole the coin, to make the case more airtight?"

I shook my head in disbelief. "What else did you want me to do, cuff him for you?"

She tilted her head and waved a hand placatingly. "Come, now!"

"And Erkhart?"

"As agreed, surveillance in front of his villa in case of mob retaliation."

At least he would be safe. Still, I felt sorry for causing him trouble. I bet he hadn't seen this coming when he read my palm.

"Can I leave now?"

"We're good here. Just make sure you don't leave the country."

"Of course," I said, thinking of my midnight flight.

"Do you need a ride?"

"No, I'm fine." I started walking.

"Luke."

I stopped and turned. "Yeah?"

"Your car is over there." Pointing to the opposite direction of where I was walking.

I headed back to the car, exhausting all my brain capacity to think of nothing, and sat in the driver's seat, the adrenaline rush ebbing. I took my mobile from the glove compartment, sent a message to an international phone number, snapped the phone chip in half, and put the phone under the car's front wheel. I popped two pills and put the plane ticket to Geneva in my jeans pocket.

I started the engine and gripped the steering wheel with both hands. In awe. The back of that Cherokee was racing toward me, and I clamped my eyes shut, but the car was still there. I switched gears, and my insensitive foot pressed the accelerator a bit too hard. The car jolted into motion with a screech, kicking back gravel and dust, crushing the mobile.

Shit, I forgot the Adidas bag.

The resurrected past had awakened all the hungry ghosts inside my throbbing head. I stood at the door to my flat for the last time. I couldn't take my meager valuables with me to the meeting point, and it wasn't like I had Jason Bourne stashes all over the city. I opened the door and turned on the lights. A waft of an unfamiliar stale smell tickled my nose.

"Oh. You made it!" The voice sounded as if its owner had just woken up from a power nap.

A jolt of surprise surged through my body.

"Have a seat." The intruder pointed a black pistol with an unusually long barrel toward the chair opposite him.

I couldn't move. "This ain't over yet." I didn't expect Gavin's move to be *that* quick.

"You won't sit? OK, I'll stand." He leveled the gun toward my head. He wasn't tall, but he had a wrestler's compact body and thick neck. A professional assassin with a gun facing an unarmed amateur. I was fucked. Please, God, make this quick.

The phone rang. The assassin looked instinctively toward it for a fraction of a second. I switched off the light and leapt forward. A bullet grazed my left side. I stumbled into him in the dark. Long live small flats. My left hand blindly seized his right wrist, but then a heavy head butt smashed my nose, and I breathed copper and rust.

Years of training, and I still lacked a fighter's instinct. I had gym muscles, not street reflexes. I had to consciously choose my next move.

I used my body weight to carry and drop him to the ground with a judo move. While in the air, I twisted his wrist and heard the gun thud on the floor a moment before his body followed, ass first.

A hide-and-seek with the gun would determine someone's life in the next few seconds. The phone kept ringing. Someone was desperate to reach me by phone. Tina?

I kicked as hard as I could where I expected his head to be, but I missed, and my leg landed on his ribs. He kicked the side of my knee from his grounded position. I screamed. He rugby tackled me, and I fell to the ground. In the faint glow of streetlights coming from the window, I glimpsed a silver blade heading for my jugular and caught his wrist with my left hand.

I tried to flip the blade toward him like I'd practiced hundreds of times in my martial arts classes, but the guy was a pro. The long pointy edge kept heading toward my neck. I was breathing blood through my nose. He was close enough that I could smell the alcohol and cigarettes on his breath. Without thinking, I spat in his face, put my legs around his waist and flipped our positions. Now I was on top, but he was still holding the blade. He pulled me toward him, slammed my head to the floor, and slipped from underneath me. He stuck the stiletto up to the handle into my back.

A laser-focused line of fire dove inside my body and deflated me in a second. He picked up the gun.

From behind the fog of pain, the doorbell rang. "Dr. Archer? Can you turn down the noise please? People are trying to sleep here." My grumpy middle-aged neighbor. A Serbian spinster who thought I was a secret bin Laden fan and who I thought was a Milosevic cheerleader.

"Sure, Ms. Petrovic, you'll never have to worry about me again." I croaked, biting my lower lip.

The assassin's head tilted between me and the door. He seemed surprised I had the guts to say anything—or maybe he thought it was a secret code between me and the old hag.

The next three seconds passed very quickly. The narrow ray of corridor light seeping from beneath my front door went off, followed by a cry from Ms. Petrovic. The door opened after two quick thuds.

The assassin turned to face the door and fired at the two dark silhouettes kneeling outside. He shot the first shadow, but the second muzzle flash came from the other one.

The assassin fell to the ground. An uncontrolled fall of utter surrender. I thought of crawling to disarm him, or search for his knife, not comprehending that it was planted in my back. But I was too feeble.

The lights came back on. Max was dressed all in black and holding his pistol. He didn't bother kneeling and checking for a pulse, but rather shot the assassin in the head, point blank. Only then did he look back to see Ms. Petrovic lying in the corridor, blood seeping from her skull.

He gritted his teeth and turned to me. "I hope I'm not disturbing, Mr. Archer. Erkhart wanted to check on you."

I gurgled blood from my open chest and mouth.

"Is it too late to ask why you involved the police in a deal you begged for?"

I gurgled again. "Amb … ambulance."

He dropped the phone and it landed next to my head. "Have it your way, James Bond. I hope you can at least manage to dial 999 on your own." And he left.

I inched my way toward the phone, but the world darkened. I paused, waiting for my sight to adjust. Instead, I passed out clutching the handset.

The wax melted and, surrendering to gravity, Icarus plummeted into the ocean.

It would have been fittingly ironic if I'd bled to death right there on the ground. Max was like a chef who'd made a banquet but was too lazy to add the salt. I got lucky because some other noise-sensitive soul, God bless them, called the police, who came to find three bodies marinating in blood instead of a loud neighbor.

One centimeter. The difference between death and life was one centimeter. If the blade had been one centimeter to the right, it would have hit my heart. Instant death.

One centimeter would probably have made all the difference for Gavin's father, too. If he'd been one centimeter shorter, I might have only grazed the top of his head when I flew into his car on that moonless Wednesday night. I might even have become a family friend who would go crimson every time the accident was mentioned, apologizing profusely. And Gavin's dad would pat my shoulder and say, "These things happen, lad. Just be careful next time."

A one-centimeter cut in the brake cable is all it takes to transform a car with a clean safety record into a killing machine.

One centimeter is the difference between winning a gold medal at the Olympics or ending up as a bus driver in a world that has one winner and too many losers.

One cubic centimeter of any living matter has more than ten billion cells, each with its own factory for DNA and its own chance to mutate into cancer.

One cubic centimeter of anthrax spores is enough to kill the entire population of Cambridge.

The nurse put one cubic centimeter of fentanyl into my IV drip.

I drifted away again.

CHAPTER 18

Present Day, Friday, 18:27

After dinner, TJ is explaining to Yehia how sex is the solution to all the problems of the Middle East. How people in Yemen will stop fighting once teenagers have access to pussy, not guns.

Yehia patiently retorts that he knows how to put an end to the Americans' thirst for violence, whether in warzones or in modern-day gladiator sports like WWE or American football. The solution is to wash their assholes with water instead of using toilet paper when they take a shit, hence stopping everyone from going to war because of the itchy bottoms.

Everyone else in the basement is gathered around the television for the final day of the Stockholm conference, anxious for any news on the ceasefire. A white middle-aged man in a suit preaches to other white middle-aged men in suits, stating that four of every five Yemenis need urgent assistance.

For the zillionth time, the white man is shouldering the burden of saving the savages from themselves. A white priest performs an exorcism till death using the holy water of democracy and the unyielding cross of capitalism. If only he'd become an atheist.

Rachel heaves a sigh and asks Nephew, "Do you think this crazy war will ever end?"

He smiles. "There will always be someone to fight. But we're the good guys. Even the angels are fighting with us."

"Really? What do angels look like?"

"I don't know, but the enemy saw them."

Rachel just stares at him.

He continues, "A month ago, a friend of mine asked people to say *takbeer* and went up a building where one of the insurgent snipers was stationed. And he overpowered the sniper and brought him down. When people asked the sniper how a man with no gun overcame him, the sniper said, 'It wasn't only one man. There were many!'"

Rachel nods slowly. "Very interesting."

With the number of drugs fighters take, I would not be surprised if he saw Achilles riding the Trojan Horse coming for him. I don't blame them, though. Wars and drugs have always been a good match. From the Carthaginians, to Viking elite troops, to kamikaze pilots. Hell, even Achilles himself was on drugs. Not to mention large sections of the British and American armies in World War II, who munched on Dexedrine like M&M's.

"God is on our side to free our home country," Nephew says, trying to regain her interest.

"Good luck finding anything in the rubble to call home," Rachel says.

"Isn't it weird that there isn't a single Yemeni at this conference?" Michael says to no one, eyes fixed on the screen.

"Yemen is not one of the players. It's the playground," Manu says.

"Thanks to the abundance of soldiers of fortune," Anne mutters.

Max cocks his head. "Did you know that a Hollywood actress hired Blackwater to be peacekeepers in Darfur? Their deployment was prevented by the US government. In this case, the US government allowed the massacre in Darfur that mercs could have prevented."

"You can't compare mercenaries to soldiers," Anne says.

"You say tomato. You know what, this is part of what I hate

about the so-called *civilized* world. The ones who make the rules design them so they stay on top." He points to the television. "This is all a charade to give the ones who don't make the rules the illusion that they have a say. It's all just words."

He pauses for a moment. "I was a Navy SEAL for eight years. This one time, we were in Fallujah's second siege, in 2004. You have any idea what happened there?"

"Of course," Manu chimes in, seizing the chance for one of his stories. "It reminds me of another siege when I was in—"

"Spare me," says Max. "With your security constraints, I bet you knew more about duty-free French wine than about local culture." He waves a dismissive hand. "I was there with my team hunting down Zarqawi when we caught another target instead. A former Egyptian intelligence officer who'd joined the resistance. He had been working with us to monitor an asset in Afghanistan. This asset was forced to cooperate because the authorities in Cairo were holding his family. So the intelligence officer believed what they told him in school about justice being a good thing and helped the innocent family of his asset out of Egypt. Long story short, we caught wind of his betrayal and before you could say "original sin," he was on the run. The only shelter he found was with the resistance in Iraq."

"Did you manage to speak to him?" asks Michael.

"Yeah. Everyone thought he was lying about his motives, but I believed him. If he'd said that the asset threatened him, or that he was a double agent for the fuckin' Panamanians, they would have believed him. But no. It was too naive a reason to believe. I didn't know what to say when he asked me, 'What would you have done if you were me?'"

"What happened next?" Michael asks.

"I got a medal for my killing sprees. The next year, I decided to be a pragmatic instead of a fanatic."

"Impressive how you took the high road and became a

mercenary," Rachel says.

Max flicks his eyes at her and a ghost of a smile hovers over his face. He says, "The whole world is on the low road, doctor. At least I'm walking my own."

"And the Egyptian officer?" Michael asks.

"He was supposed to be transferred to Gitmo, or worse, back to the Egyptians. I have no idea where he is now."

I'm in no mood for these discussions. I see parts of me in everyone here. Long gone are the days of black and white. Angels and demons. Humanitarians and mercenaries. Even in Hollywood, Big Brother's massive nudging machine, Superman is fighting Batman, and the Joker is the hero now.

I wonder whether Michael did kill the General. How did he justify it to himself? Or was it Manu? Maybe both of them shared in digesting the sour justification. No way it was Rachel, and Anne wouldn't have it in her to do it.

My thoughts are interrupted when I hear Yehia asking TJ, "So which state are you from?"

"Texas, man. Strong horses and real men. You must have heard of us."

"Sure, my favorite porn star is from Texas."

Anne raises the volume on the television, as the "Breaking News" logo flashes across the screen. "Quiet, quiet, *quiet*," she hisses.

We hold our breath. Even TJ and Yehia come closer to hear the conclusion. Yet another middle-aged white man in a suit takes the podium and starts talking. He brags about how the international community managed to reach understanding but not agreement, then expresses optimism for the next round of negotiations, which will resume next week in Antalya.

On the screen, everyone is smiling and shaking hands and patting each other on the back of their bespoke suits.

I don't want to meet any of the panicked eyes around me. We

can't last another night, let alone another week.

"What does this mean? Is there a ceasefire or not?" Anne asks.

On his way out, Max says to Anne, "Like I said, it's all just words."

Present Day, Friday 19:34

"They are indeed receiving reinforcements," I say, peering west through the scope that Ray detached from his sniper rifle.

The rebels have finished collecting their fallen men, and Cousin and Nephew have collected *sadeeq*'s remains—thankfully, without the unexploded ordnance that was attached to it. Pickup trucks full of more men and supplies keep arriving at the spot where I met Akrami.

The six-hour ceasefire is due to finish in less than thirty minutes. Max is getting some shut-eye in the canteen, while Yehia, Manu and I are lingering on the roof with TJ and Ray after helping them carry up some spare sandbags to reinforce the parapets. Piotr is on guard duty at the far corner of the roof.

"Show me." Manu plucks the scope from my hand.

"You look like you have urine retention. Let's bond over some Dutch courage," Ray says with a wink, heating up his crystal meth glass pipe. He has no interest in our rookie sitrep as he already received the update from Piotr.

I should have guessed from their eyes, which burned with an endless supply of fire. Tired around the edges, yet screaming for action at the center. He and TJ are definitely on uppers—not my particular escape remedy, but everyone has their own Dorian Gray picture to transfer guilt to. Drugs help this transfer. That's probably why the word "pharmacology" comes from the Greek *pharmacos*: "scapegoat."

The breeze is refreshing. Ray says Piotr doesn't like talking with civilians much. "They're too complicated for his taste. Besides, he prefers crack."

"Nah, that's not it." TJ smirks. "He's just pissed that I won the kill-count bet we wagered the day we arrived."

"Hasn't Max told you this is a train-and-advise, not a combat mission?" Ray says with a laugh.

"Max is a fucking closet idealist. He probably still believes the shit about how force-feeding democracy down people's throats is good for them. Piotr and I knew the day we arrived we would *get some*."

Ray contentedly exhales a faint blue wisp from the meth pipe. His eyes sparkle and the bags beneath them shrink. A smile of excitement invades his face, replete with immaculate white teeth. For a brief moment, as the smell of ammonia tickles my nostrils, I see Ray the child, before life happened.

Waiting for his turn, TJ looks at the pipe in Ray's hand as though it contains eternal youth.

"So, Ray," says Yehia, "you didn't get in on their bet?"

"No, mate. I thought it would be some easy Gulf money. Last mission before I settle down and open a pub back home."

"Now look at us," TJ says. "Turned out to be a fucking suicide mission. And if that wasn't enough, we're locked down with a bunch of whiny tree huggers."

Ray purses his lips, then takes another hit from the pipe and muses, "You can't beat following this up with chasing deer after sneaking into Richmond Park before dawn. My favorite thing to do between tours. You're all invited if we ever got out of here."

"You know what I'd do if I get out of here alive?" Manu asks. "I would marry Clara and settle down in Colombia. No more missions."

Ha. I knew there was a Clara somewhere.

"Were you in the Army?" Yehia asks Ray.

"Army, no way, mate!" Ray says indignantly, buzzing with energy as though he'd swallowed a beehive. "British Royal Navy. *Si vis pacem, para bellum*. If you wish for peace, prepare for war."

"How did you join?" Yehia asks.

"It's a long story." Ray hesitates for a second. "It all began with Arsenal, the football club. Do you know it?"

"Who do you think I am, a Maasai shaman? Of course I know the Gunners," Yehia says.

"Well, yeah, alright. I wanted to catch their Spurs game in Highbury with my *boyfriend*." He emphasizes the last word as he looks at TJ, who accordions his forehead and then nods twice, as if saying "I should've guessed."

"On that night, we got ambushed in South Kilburn by a gang of white ass homophobic shit cunts with shanks and baseball bats. I decided to blame it on Arsenal, so I wouldn't go mad."

My heart skips a beat, wondering whether it was the same gang that killed my dad.

Yehia and I mumble some condolences and Ray nods, as if he'd heard them a thousand times before.

"So you joined the navy because some scum beat you and your boyfriend up?' TJ asks.

Ray sighs. "Now we're all going to fuckin' die, I guess that getting my girlfriend knocked up at the same time didn't help much."

TJ shakes his head. "You *think* you know a guy ..."

Ray extends the pipe in my direction, but I wave it away. My brain is in overdrive already.

I swear I can see Manu's head tiny movement from side to side, as if he were on a wavelength of his own. The two Ambien he downed an hour ago with half pint of Jack Daniel's were mellowing him out. Seems I'm the only one not on drugs these days. But even though my headaches gave me good reason, I did it in hiding. These people are different. They have no shame in openly consuming hard drugs. Or killing for money. They are either the most honest people I have seen or the most disillusioned. That's where we are heading, I guess. Lines keep blurring between right and wrong. Between good and evil. Between legal and illegal. Until our need for more eats us from the inside out.

The uncomfortable silence must have compelled Manu to ask TJ, "How does it feel to kill someone?"

"What's this? A group therapy session? Shall we bet on who will cry first?" TJ rolls his eyes at Ray, who smiles and shrugs while handing him the pipe. "Allow it, bruv."

"Killing is like fucking," TJ says, exhaling a long hit. "The first time, you feel you did something wrong. The second time is experimental. By the third time, you feel larger than life. It doesn't matter if you've killed a raghead or nuked Nagasaki." He takes another hit of the bond-building fumes. "Thank God most people deserve to die, eh?"

"Wow, *génial*," slurs Manu, as he scrambles for his phone. "Can I have that on tape?"

"Once we're out of here, you can have my ass on video if you want," TJ grunts.

Manu nods as if it's a done deal.

TJ reluctantly offers the pipe to Yehia. "You want some?"

Yehia looks at me. He hasn't chewed khat in a while. Funny how Yeminis can stand starvation for months but a couple of days without khat can break them.

"Khat's big brother," I say, reassuringly.

Yehia takes the pipe.

"I'm thirty-four. I'm not dying young, am I?" Manu says, talking to no one in particular as he rests his head on the parapet.

"Well, Manu. You're definitely dying older than Amy Winehouse and Jesus Christ," I say.

That doesn't seem to help him much. The pipe finally reaches him. Manu takes a hit. Immediately, the methamphetamine fucks with his brain and his eyes open wide.

Ray says, "How about you, Yehia, how did you become a nurse?"

"I always wanted to be a doctor. But here, you rarely get a chance to be who you want," Yehia says.

"Yeah? How come?"

"Supply and demand. That's the main difference between our world and yours." Yehia continues, "Here's an example. I was studying for a diploma in the UK a few years ago. I was impressed with how people stand in queues, greet each other while opening doors, and stop their cars for pedestrians in the street. One day, I visited my uncle in Sheffield, and I had to take the last train back to London. The weather was bad and the two previous trains were canceled. And then I saw it: when the last train arrived, everyone dropped their civilized masks and fought to board the train. They knew their civilities wouldn't get them anywhere because there wasn't enough for everyone this time. This last train, my friend, is the only train in Yemen. Here, if you don't fight, you'll stay on that cold Sheffield platform forever."

"Why didn't you stay in the UK then?" Ray asks.

"I ran out of money. Or rather, my dad did. He was a wealthy merchant, but he wasted his money digging for mystical treasures from the time of Sheba."

Ray chuckles.

"I'm serious. Searching for buried treasures of the past is a popular business here."

Ray purses his lips. "That's like buying very expensive lotto tickets. Spending money like that is like choking a goose. In the long run, the goose will die."

"My friend," Yehia says, smiling wryly, "in the long run, we *all* die."

The sky is black and blue, shades of sadness. The horizon is occasionally pierced by flashes of shelling. A little kid throwing arrows haphazardly. A cupid—but this one is for hatred. Every time the crimson flower blooms in the distance, you know that humans are being killed, houses destroyed, and families torn apart at this very second. I turn my gaze upward to the stars and the black holes that have been witnessing us for millions of years and sigh.

"I'm popping to the loo," Ray announces, standing. "I piss like a camel these days."

Has he not figured yet that meth is a diuretic?

When Ray leaves, TJ cracks the joints of his thick neck and asks me, "What's your story with Max?"

His direct question catches me off guard. I try not to glance at Manu. "We met through mutual friends in London. Nothing serious."

He scratches his stubble. "So, you're Arab, huh?"

"British. I'm British."

"Yeah, of course! You know, I've always wondered. If Arabs hate us so much, why do they keep coming to the West?"

"Come on now, TJ. This isn't the time to debate politics," I say quickly. I try to gauge his pupil size in the dim light. The shit he's smoked seems to have made him more edgy than alert.

"I don't mean *you*, man. I'm just wondering why Muslims hate us so much?

Shit, when is Ray coming back?

"I think the problem is in politics, TJ, not cultures. Politicians only understand power. They've reduced us to apes fighting each other."

"I won't go down quietly then. I'll land apeshit on those assholes. You know, two of my uncles died in the Oklahoma City bombing, so it's not only them who have a score to settle."

Yehia and I exchange a glance and stand up, deciding it is time to leave. I resist the urge to say that it was highly unlikely that a white supremacist like Timothy McVeigh had shouted *Allahu Akbar* right before he blew up the Oklahoma City building. But I decide to save both of us the trouble and keep treating prejudices like another force of nature that's out of my hands. Like summer heat or a midnight urge to piss.

"Whoa ... what's going on here, bruv?" Ray comes hurrying in, still zipping his fly.

"Nothing, Ray. It's time for us to go back down to the basement," I say.

I help Manu to his feet. He stands between me and the half-moon, still lost between the yin and yang of the uppers and downers fighting over his mind.

And then I feel this warm wetness on my face. For a moment I suspect that TJ has spat on me, and I'm disgusted at how copious and rusty his phlegm is, but then Manu collapses. A millisecond later, I hear the sound of the bullet that smashed into his head.

I look down and my hands are full of blood. Dark blood flicked with shiny bone fragments and soft-brain matter.

Time dilates. Everyone but me drops flat to the ground. Ray and TJ are reaching for their guns and shouting, but their voices are a million miles away. Piotr is running toward me, and I tilt my head, watching him move in slow motion until he smashes into me, and we both fall as a second gunshot rings out.

Piotr looks at his bloodied shoulder and grunts, "I fucking hate civilians."

A side view of Manu's face is in front of me. His eyes are rolled back in his head, but his lips are moving. No words come out. A part of his skull is missing, and his brain pulsates with blood as an air bubble forms at the edge of the hole in his brain. His lips are still moving, and I wish they would stop.

And just like that, Emmanuel Garnier's countdown reaches zero.

Present Day, Saturday, 05:56

The sun rises, burning away the wispy clouds of the night. The sky is gray, and the air is pregnant with dread. Inhale too much of it and your body shivers.

The images of last night flash through my head. Being rushed back to the basement, Anne screaming, Michael patching up Piotr's shoulder.

Rachel is cocooned next to me in her sleeping bag. Her honey-colored eyes keeping watch on me, and I recall an eventful day back in London that changed my life forever.

The sight of Manu's body wrapped in bloodied white sheets a few meters from me convinces me I won't be able to sleep again. Next to us, Anne and Michael are pretending to be asleep, but I can see Anne's body shaking as she cries silently under her covers.

Rachel's breakfast consists of cigarettes chain smoked through the cracks in the metal sheets on the ground-floor window. Rays of sunlight filter through the same cracks, thin shafts of light revealing a hidden world of flying particles floating aimlessly in the air like snow dust.

She extends her pack to me. Green Marlboro. I hate menthol, but beggars can't be choosers. I light one and take in a perfumed breath, fighting not to wrinkle my face in disgust.

She hands me a bar of chocolate. I take a bite, and remember Erkhart. The chocolate turns sour in my mouth, the taste of a rusty coin. A two-hundred-year-old coin that's worth everything. Or nothing. I almost gag on the molten mud in my mouth and give the bar back to Rachel. I know now that I can survive without chocolate.

I search my mind for something to talk about that is not worse than silence. Something not full of existentialism. The silence continues.

She lights another cigarette. Her smoke rings are impressive. I light one too, in solidarity.

"I'm Jewish," she says softly.

I think for a moment, then shrug. "If you don't tell, no one will ask."

"It's not fair. To carry who you are like a sin you haven't committed," she says.

I smile weakly. "Welcome to my life."

I place my fingers on my temples and clench my eyes shut,

hoping the drilling inside might stop for a second. Instead, the ringing in my ears gets worse.

"Luke?" she says, concerned.

I exhale audibly. "Prasher."

"What?"

"In 2008, the Nobel Prize in Chemistry was awarded to three people for some gene discovery. But it was actually another guy, called Prasher, who made that discovery many years before. The moment the winners were collecting the prize in Sweden, Prasher was working as a bus driver in Alabama."

She draws half a smile and shakes her head. "Tough luck? Human error?"

"I think it's more than that. Do you watch football?"

"Not really."

"Me neither, but get this: Denmark didn't qualify for Euro 92 and yet still won it. Yugoslavia was disqualified because of the war, so Denmark took their place and went on to take the title."

There's something wrong with me, and for once I can't stop talking. It's like, if I stopped talking, she would cease to exist.

"Okaay…"

"We were just talking about fairness. Thought these stories would be relevant."

She arches her thick eyebrows, and I feel like a total idiot. But then her smile begins to rise, like the sun. "You're cute," she says. She's about to flick away her cigarette butt, but she stops suddenly and whispers, "Did you hear that?"

A mortar lands next to the window she's leaning against.

Black powder was invented in the tenth century, nine centuries before bullets. Maybe that says enough about why explosives are abundant in low-budget modern warfare. Mortars are a classic siege weapon and infantry's best friend. The basic but effective design of mortars has not changed much since the 1860s. The mortar shell is lobbed from a short tube that can be launched from anywhere, from rooftops to trenches. Its range depends on the rings around the shell, which act as fuel charges. Varying the number of these rings allows for a range as short as two hundred meters or as long as five kilometers. Other than the explosive charge, its casing is designed to fragment and spray shrapnel for twenty-five meters in all directions.

Rachel's hit. I scoop her up, tumble back to the basement, and frantically check her for wounds as the salvo of mortars shakes the whole hospital. She has a piece of metal lodged in her right side along with many small shrapnel cuts. I take the shard out and start cleaning the wound, which is ten centimeters long but superficial. No arterial damage; the blood oozes out instead of spurting.

A couple of mortars hit the yard, and the walls shudder amid dust and smoke. Anne is covering her ears and emitting short bursts of screams that make the hair stand up on the back of my neck.

"Cover your sectors!" From the roof, Max's voice booms over the radio. "Check for spotters. Get the spotters."

Machine guns roar to life above us. But bullets are no match for bombs. I can picture Akrami's men honing their coordinates with each round by communicating with forward observers—or spotters—who could be hiding in any window with a line of sight to the hospital and a telephone, telling them how far off the last round landed so they can adjust their aim to pinpoint the rooftop.

I hear Ray shout, "I think I got one!"

Rachel is starting to regain consciousness, and I tell her, "It's OK, honey, it's OK. Everything is under control."

"What's happening?" she says, after a few experimental breaths.

"Just stay still. I'm almost finished."

Max shouts again, "Abandon post! Regroup in the canteen!"

I shrink inside myself as I hear the whistle of approaching doom. My teeth chatter from the shockwave or from fear—or both—as a round hits the roof like a hammer to the head. Pieces of the ceiling fall and the walls tremble.

The shooting stops.

"I'm hit! I'm hit!" The shout comes through the soundtrack of war. I don't recognize the voice. With its shriek of universal agony, it could be anyone's.

Yehia leaps to his feet. "I'll go get the injured."

I don't even look up as I close Rachel's wound with butterfly bandages.

Yehia is midway up the stairs when there's a second direct hit to the roof. Max and TJ are coming down the other way, dragging Ray and Piotr with them. TJ looks in decent shape, but Max has blood on his head and all over his right side.

Yehia swiftly clears a table and he and TJ roll Piotr onto it. Michael starts cutting off Piotr's clothes with shears. He's unconscious, and his injuries are serious. Yehia keeps pressure on the main wounds in his chest and right leg while Michael checks for other wounds.

I turn to the basement's entrance to assess Ray. His body is like a doll's torn by an angry child. Shoulders splayed against the wall, legs spread. His face is too peaceful to be alive. His gaze is something out of this world, as if he's seeing things I can't, unknowns finally becoming knowns. One hand is missing, and the other one is palm up, as if in surrender. His blood is a bright, deep red. His stomach is open, and his intestines look like gray snakes. The fava beans we shared last night are seeping from them. Beans from the same can fill my throat. I swallow hard and look away.

A third direct hit to the roof, and then everything goes quiet except for water pouring down the wall and the metal sheets on the windows. A mortar must have hit the water tank. The basement is now full of diluted blood and chaos. Juices of life drip slowly and steadily to the floor and meet the water coming from the walls.

Nephew and Cousin aren't hurt, as they had been guarding the entrance as usual, but one look at them says that they're losing their shit. I hold Rachel's hand and shut my eyes. I need a moment where I don't see red.

The color fades before I open my eyes again. "Max, are you hit?" I ask in a voice I don't recognize.

Blood is coming from his ear. The blood on the side of his head is black, and I doubt any amount of water would clean it. I repeat my question.

"I'm fine," he says sullenly. He unstraps the small medical kit from his combat vest and throws it to me. It has a tourniquet, Kerlix gauze, dressings, and an airway tube.

What worries me more than his injuries is that the big sign on his wide forehead saying, "Trust me, I know what I'm doing" is gone, replaced by a pulsating blue vein in his temple that betrays how much he's struggling to look composed. It doesn't take a military tactician to know what he's thinking. Now that their vantage point is gone, it's time for the full-on assault. The moment that any soldier dreads, when they finally admit that they're in a fight they can't win.

CHAPTER 19

Present Day, Saturday, 08:17

My peripheral vision is out of focus, and my jaw is clenched. The headache is firing electric sparks across my brain. I guess this is as far as my resistance can take me. I need to pop some pills very soon.

It's only a matter of time before our Jenga tower collapses. I double check for any ventilation shafts that I can squeeze into, Bruce Willis style, but no such luck.

Max and TJ are in their Alamo position, in the canteen. Ray's body is in a corner next to Manu's, covered by an old blanket. A blanket that once held the warmth of bodies huddled together for safety and the coldness of bodies shivering from illness. A blanket with stains of blood and wet dreams. I'm sure Ray doesn't mind.

Michael sits with his back to a wall, eyes closed and an endless silent prayer on his lips. He's clutching his lab coat to his chest as though it were a bulletproof vest.

Anne is sitting next to Manu's body. She seems intensely focused. I shift to look at what's grabbed her attention. Maggots swarm at the bottom of the wall, gathering around something. It's the carcass of the rat that Jamal killed three days ago. Another lifetime ago seems more accurate. The swarm of maggots almost covers the rat. Its intestines, full of the excretions of anaerobic bacteria, bloat its stomach like a balloon about to burst. Until then, they're working their way from inside its mouth and around its crushed skull, reducing it to the primary components of life. At least maggots aren't starving in Yemen.

I change the bandages on Rachel's wound. "Are you OK?" I ask.

"Yes, I'm fine. It's nothing. In comparison."

Thinking of the promise I made when I went out to meet Akrami, I say, "Will you still hang out with me when all of this is over?"

This is probably inappropriate, considering we just lost one of our team members. I feel like tears should be shed, but what good would that do? Besides, I don't feel like crying. Does this make me a bad person?

"Why not?"

I gaze intently into her eyes.

"What are you doing?"

"Just checking that your pupils are the same size," I say, snapping out of it.

She smiles despite herself. "I don't have a concussion. And I seem to remember that you called me *honey* when I got hit."

"I thought you needed some ... emotional support."

She averts her gaze, only to have it land on Piotr's body on the ad hoc operating table. Her smile fades along with her blush.

He's still alive, but his soul is trickling out of his wounds. A sizable tattoo covers the left side of his chest, a circle of crosses with bent ends. It's a Kolovrat—an ancient Slavic religious symbol for forces of life or something, the symbol Hitler stole for his swastika. I probably won't get the chance any time soon to ask Piotr about which of these two ideologies inspired his body art, though, because under the tattoo his inferior vena cava is ruptured. His liver is also a mess, and he has three deep shrapnel wounds in his chest.

People don't die on the spot like in the movies. Even lethal wounds don't kill immediately. I've seen my fair share of gurgling gasps, rolling eyes inside fractured skulls, and exposed, still-pulsating brains.

I check the crash trolley for my stash, hoping to pop a few, then mix the rest for a makeshift anesthetic for Piotr. Nothing. Twenty potent opiate pills are missing. Where are they?

My headache intensifies, as if having this stash on the ready kept it in check. A crazy thought crosses my mind, and I look back at Anne. She smiles weakly at me. Her pupils are pinpoints in the wild whites of her eyes. Bugger. She's not in shock, as I thought earlier. She's intoxicated.

I rush to her. Her head is wobbling and a thin line of drool has reached her chin. I put my fingers inside her throat to make her vomit, but she bites my hand. I do the only thing that comes to mind; I punch her as hard as I can in the stomach. Michael flinches, watching from afar. Maybe he's the one in shock. Anne clutches her stomach and I reach for her mouth again. With Rachel's help, I get my fingers inside and this time she pukes.

"Breathe, Anne, breathe," I say.

Her eyes open and close and she keeps looking around as if seeing us for the first time.

"Keep breathing, Anne. Are you breathing?"

She gives me a confused look and says, "*I am* breathing."

Good. Nothing to be done now except keep an eye on her. This task we give to Michael.

I find three pills on the ground, next to Anne's water bottle, which must have fallen in her attempt to take the express train to Valhalla. I grit my teeth. I don't want my last action to be depriving a severely injured patient of pain killers. I bloody hate moral dilemmas.

Before I change my mind, I crush the pills to dissolve them and inject Piotr with them. Then a thought hits me. I remember someone saying something about Piotr's drug of choice. I go down on all fours and start searching through his bloodied pants.

"What the hell are you doing?" Rachel asks.

"Just a second."

Yes! There's a little baggie with what remains of Piotr's crack in a side pocket. Two tiny rocks inside the blood-smeared pouch, but they'll do. Crack is made of cocaine and baking soda. And cocaine is an excellent regional anesthetic, but not a central one. This means Piotr could wake up at any moment while we're operating, but he's a big boy. He can handle it.

I crush the rocks and mix them in a somewhat clean glass with half a vitamin C tablet from the near-expired piles of useless donated meds. Cocaine needs an acid to be water soluble. I add water and mix as I apply heat from Piotr's lighter. I suck up the mixture with a hypodermic syringe and jab Piotr with it.

I'm not a vascular surgeon, but Piotr's only chance is that I pretend to be one. I reach my hand inside him until I feel his aorta and keep squeezing it to improve his blood pressure, while Rachel tries to suture the leakage of his internal plumbing. Major blood vessels are elastic, and when they're severed, they retract. Trying to pull the shortened two ends back, if you can find them, is like trying to plug your computer cord into a socket that's too far away.

This is when superficial veins come in handy, as cord extensions. But only if you can find the retracted severed vein and clamp it until you get the superficial one from the leg, all the while pumping endless IVs into the leaking body. Then comes the real trick: stitching these delicate blood hoses together. This is a completely different league from stitching skin. Perhaps that's why vascular surgeons are the most arrogant in the field.

Rachel's body shakes with each shot outside. I can't blame her, especially when each one sounds closer. As for me, I'm resisting every urge to ditch the scalpel and run for my life.

To make matters worse, the muscles in my right forearm and my right eye twitch, their nerves fried by storms of electrical impulses. Another warning sign that my headache is getting out of control. I squeeze my eyes shut and clench my fist. The sweat on my forehead feels like the moment you open an oven and hot steam engulfs your face. The fun will start when the trembles reach my fingers or when I fall headfirst into Piotr's open ribs.

I manage to take the saphenous vein from his ankle to use as a vein graft. As if this weren't hard enough, we have only 4.0 sutures, which are thick enough to hang yourself with. Rachel and I get started, slowly and meticulously stitching his blood vessels together.

I'm blinking sweat off my eye when the basement door slams open, making my hand jump involuntarily, slicing the piece I just spent half an hour tying. Piotr's blood spurts from within him like a fountain of protest.

Nephew and Cousin enter, hands in the air, followed by three rebels. I don't know how they crossed the yard with Max and TJ firing from the canteen, but it seems the Arab saying "numbers beat courage" comes from real experience. I move to stem the bleeding, but a voice orders us to stop.

I take off my surgical mask. Michael's hands are up in the air, his face pale as a sheet. One of the rebels approaches, hitching up his baggy pants and looking at Piotr's body. He's the arm slinger I met yesterday. What was his name again? My mouth is so dry you could light a match on my tongue.

A rebel with a goatee says, "We got you now, *motherfucker*." He says "motherfucker" in English and then laughs.

Arm Slinger glares at him, and Goatee shuts his mouth.

My sight wanders. Two cockroaches snuggle near the corpses of Ray and Manu. I'm going insane. I blink twice. The cockroaches are still at it.

"Hello, Dr. Adam. You really are a doctor after all! Where are the mercenaries?" Arm Slinger speaks. His English is not too bad.

"Upstairs. The General is dead. His body's on the second floor," I say in disgust.

Let him burn in hell. He's the reason we're in this mess.

Arm Slinger gestures to the third gunman to tie up Nephew and Cousin. A fourth is behind the door, watching the corridor.

They are only reconnaissance. Goatee is fascinated by the insides of Piotr's body, peering down intently as if surveying the Grand Canyon.

"We have to finish this operation here," I say. "We only need fifteen—"

"No, Doctor. You're done here. Hands up—both of you." Arm Slinger points his gun at Rachel.

Michael stretches his hands up even further, if that's physically possible.

"No," Rachel says firmly.

Silence. Even I look at her as if I misheard.

"What?" Arm Slinger asks stupidly, looking at me as though he doesn't understand what "no" means.

"I can't. If I let go of his vein, I'll need another ten minutes to find it." She's beginning to lose her temper.

"But I'll kill you if you don't!" he says, waving his weapon.

"I'll kill him if I do."

He hesitates, looking at Goatee. Goatee scratches his chin and then shrugs. "Shoot her," he says in Arabic, his tone casual as if they were discussing what to have for dinner.

"Shut up," says Arm Slinger, glowering at Rachel, his eyes darting back and forth between Piotr's body and her.

He finally says, "How about now?" and shoots the prone body point-blank.

The bullet goes through Piotr's head, ricochets somewhere in his skull and emerges from his right ear, chunks of brain splatting against the metal table. The echo tolls like a church bell. I wince and step back. Rachel recoils. Even Goatee clears his ear.

The ringing in my ears is like a giant vibrating fork trembling inside my head. My eyes water from the acrid smell of cordite, and I gag at the sight of Piotr's head, smashed like a bad egg. My face and hair are flecked with bits of his brain. I feel dizzy with hypotension from the stimulation of my vagus nerve, and I try to steady myself.

"Operation successful," says Arm Slinger. He smirks at Goatee as if to say, "See? I know how to deal with this shit." He then cocks his Klash dramatically.

Click, clack!

He actually seems to be reveling in the moment. Sadistic fuck. Only a few weeks ago, he was the oppressed only because he couldn't be the oppressor. My mistrust in human nature has been restored.

He says, "Your turn, Doc." And points the gun at me.

I feel the sweat evaporating from my body. I open my eyes as wide as possible. My surroundings have never looked so colorful. The air has never felt so warm. Rachel, frozen where she stands, has never been more beautiful. I hold all this inside me, along with my breath, thinking that life is worth living after all.

"Wait," Goatee says. "Ask them if they've got any food first."

"*Man*, we'll search for food later."

"But—we're hungry!"

I point to the mini fridge, trying to gain time. Arm Slinger nods toward it impatiently. Goatee goes to check its contents.

"Nothing much here," he says, his head inside the fridge. "They do have some milk though." He opens the bottle and drinks before quickly spitting his mouthful on the floor. "Shit. It went bad long ago."

I don't tell him the milk hasn't expired. It's Anne's almond milk. For a moment, I'm not sure whether to laugh or cry.

The commotion outside increases. About twenty gunmen enter, strolling in with Akrami as though they're on a walking tour. Akrami wears the same stoic smile as yesterday.

Arm Slinger briefs him in Arabic about the General and the remaining mercenaries upstairs.

"Did you know?" Akrami asks me.

"Know what?" I say, looking around; Michael still has his hands up.

"That the General was dead."

"Yes, I did. It wouldn't have changed anything, you said so."

"No, it wouldn't. It's just a matter of knowing who to trust. Although it may seem trivial to you, honor matters here."

"Matters how exactly? To determine whether you can catch your *fajr* prayer before or after you kill an unarmed doctor?" I point to Manu's body. Although I'm no longer sure which of the two bodies under the white shrouds is his.

He shakes his head and shrugs at the same time. "That was his destiny."

"Fuck off."

He thrusts out his bottom lip, as if he's disappointed in me.

"Can I kill him now?" Arm Slinger asks.

He reminds me of my bullies in school. Not the apex predators like Dave, but the hyena packs behind them. The bystanders who do the real damage. The ones who laugh along.

One of the younger rebels steps up and says, "Don't kill that one, uncle. This man saved my life. I would have bled to death if it weren't for him."

I have no idea what he's talking about, until I recognize him as the kid I tried to deter from going back to the frontline by telling the white lie about his femoral artery.

"Enough," Akrami says. "Both of you. We still have a fight here. We'll deal with them later. You two stay here." He points to Arm Slinger and Femoral Kid. "The rest go upstairs to finish this. Call me when it's over." He then strolls outside with his lieutenants.

The rebels who went up are greeted by a series of booby traps, sending body parts flying left and right. Less than a minute after their departure, they bring five bodies down but Arm Slinger orders them to take the injured out of the hospital to their own medical staff.

When they leave, Arm Slinger points his gun at me. "You convert infidel. You knew this would happen."

"Listen, my friend. Either use your gun or shut up."

His nostrils flare, but he doesn't respond. Femoral Kid takes him aside before he has a stroke. If he hadn't done it at that exact second, he wouldn't have seen TJ coming.

They both whirl around as TJ hurtles through the door, knife in hand. He plants the blade inside Arm Slinger's neck, and Femoral Kid yelps and leaps backward. TJ swings at him, but the Kid opens fire. TJ is hit, but he still has the reach to jab the Kid in the heart. The burst of ammo coincides with another detonation from the second floor, probably from the rebels this time, as no casualties come down for treatment.

TJ is on the floor, taking his last breaths, an unforgiving crescent of bullets stapled across his body. I don't know how he's still alive.

Not knowing what to say to him, I take his radio and only manage a clumsy, "Thank you."

His eyes are on me. He blinks no more.

So much for the military clearing tactics we see on the television. It seems TJ didn't have the same plans as Max. He wasn't bunkering on the second floor with him. He must have been hiding somewhere, waiting for the right moment to slip out with the least resistance and noise. Hence, the knife.

So here I am, standing over the corpses of three people who were alive less than a minute ago, radio in hand. The noise of chainsaw on metal fills my brain, covering the sounds of bullets. I take a breath and press the call button.

"Max, you there? Max, pick up, it's Luke."

A few seconds pass.

"Max, are you still there?"

I hear the crackle. "Hey Luke, I thought you hated goodbyes," he says, as the line cuts in and out.

"Listen, there's no point in fighting. Surrender and let me do the talking. I'll get us out of here."

"No, Luke. I'm about to find out if your version of justice exists elsewhere. I won't be paraded around this city."

"You don't understand. Listen to me."

"I can't hear you, Luke. I have to go. Don't forget to deliver my mom home." He shuts off his radio.

One full minute later, Rachel takes the radio from me and pushes me to sit.

We hear movement on the second floor. Doors being kicked in, but no shooting yet. An expectant silence.

Then, Max's loud shout rings out, "Long live the Red Sox."

An explosion shakes the whole building, with clouds of smoke, dust, and debris pouring everywhere.

So, that was it: his last stand. He must have strapped himself in explosives and detonated once they entered. I feel a chill up my spine despite the burning smoke. The drilling in my head reaches a critical level, and my brain is covered in red alarm lights. Rachel leads us out of the building, but I want to lie down. Maybe I'm lying down already? I no longer know if I'm standing or sitting, awake or dreaming. Finally, colors and sounds mercifully fade.

CHAPTER 20

My first thought is, "I'm dreaming." My second is, "I have slept half the dream and now I have lost the plot." My third thought is, "Tina is back and she's holding me."

"Everything's OK, Luke." The voice comes from nowhere and everywhere in between the noise in my head. Why is the voice telling me everything's OK? That means something is *not* OK! Shouldn't I sleep more then?

God knows how long I've been awake, thinking I was dreaming, mistaking the dirty gray ceiling above me for the insides of my brain. Until Rachel's face comes into view.

"Super Mario is finally awake? Too much blood for his taste, I'm sure." Arabic words, followed by the familiar hyena snickers.

I sit up, holding my head. Michael, Anne, Rachel, Yehia and I are sitting in the triage tent surrounded by armed men.

Akrami is sitting cross-legged on a wooden chair, a toothpick in his mouth. He spits it out and says, "I'm glad you're back. We don't have all day. Your friend killed seven of my men and injured twenty in his suicide attack." He stresses the word suicide. "What a coward," he murmurs.

"I didn't know anything about that."

"Same as you didn't know the General was dead?"

"I want to call my embassy," Rachel says, managing to keep her voice from shaking.

The hyenas smirk.

I look around for Femoral Kid to defend me, but then I

remember that TJ killed him. We have no friends left.

Akrami uncrosses his legs and leans forward. "You can call your embassy. Don't forget to ask them how much they're willing to pay for your release. You better hope it's more than Al Qaeda will pay."

"This patient's health is deteriorating, and he needs urgent medical attention. Otherwise, he will die." She points at a sleeping Karim, blissfully unaware of what's going on.

He shrugs and points a finger to the sky. "Life and death are in God's hands."

Rachel shakes her head. "And here the people thought you were coming to rescue them. You're no different from General Rahimi."

"Same way the people thought you were here to help, but you are only spies." He regards me for a moment. "Egyptians won't be paying much money, if any. So maybe I should just kill you right here."

Suddenly I'm up close and personal with Akrami's Luger. Of all the people who have pointed guns at me in the last few days, Akrami is the scariest. Not for the antique Luger but for his eyes. They are not trigger happy, revengeful or even calculating, but cold, lifeless ones, full of indifference.

He finally smiles. "Maybe not! I'll spare you for what you did for my nephew, God rest his soul. You can go ask for the ransom. Tell them what you saw here. Maybe then, people will realize that there's a war going on here. On their screens, it is evening news. It only becomes a problem when the flames of war reach their blue blood." He addresses his men. "Take the foreigners away and leave the Arab."

"As for this Yemeni traitor," he says, turning to Yehia, "deciding his fate is going to be easier."

Yehia is standing very still, his face ashen.

The men walk toward Rachel, Anne, and Michael. It's clear from the state of Rachel's bandage that her wound is bleeding again. Anne and Michael are huddled together, wide-eyed.

My mind screams that the wisest thing to do is stay silent. Then, for a split second, my mind travels, and I see the strangest of things. Not Akrami and his guns. Not Rachel and her shadow of fear. I see myself dead on the dirty floor, from above. I ascend and I see the tent and the hospital. The torn city. The ravaged country. The destroyed horizon. Then the stars. And more stars. And a peace I have never felt in my life saturates my soul. Just for this second.

I take a deep breath. I feel something bitter in my throat, and I try to swallow. I manage to speak, "I'm not going anywhere without them. I'll give you ransom money if you let us out safely, in a boat."

Silence.

Akrami looms above me and says in Arabic, "Say that again."

I realize I had spoken in English. I switch to Arabic. "How much money do you want?"

A few whistles and some laughs from his men. "Millions for sure," he says.

"I can give you the General's wealth if you get us out of here." I point to Yehia. "Including him."

"Luke, what are—"

"It's OK, Rachel. I can deliver," I say, my eyes locked on Akrami.

"Listen to her Luca, or Adam, or whatever your name is. If you are taking us for fools, we will not be laughing." His voice and eyes are different now. His mood swings from relaxed friendliness to fierce antagonism, and it's both confusing and dangerous. Akrami continues, "I offer you a way out, and you bluff to save your friends. You think you can talk your way out of this?"

"I'm a man of my word. Get us on a boat and the money is yours."

His men stir.

"He's lying."

"How would he know where the General hid his money?"

"This girl would sleep with all of us just to live one extra day."

Akrami raises his hand, his gaze still on me, and silence falls again. "Do you even know how to sail a boat?"

I look at Michael, who is overcome with fear and has no idea what we're saying. "He can sail a boat," I say in English.

Michael nods vigorously.

Akrami draws a tight-lipped smile. "I like this game." He rubs his palms. "So, where is the money?"

"Where is the boat?"

His smile widens and he looks at his feet for a moment. "Let's take our angels of mercy here to the port," he finally says.

The sun peers from behind an overcast sky sticky with humidity and desperation. A strong wind hisses over the unpaved streets, and the resulting sandstorms color everything in sepia tone.

We are on the way to the harbor in three cars. The main street is empty except for gunmen at random checkpoints. Most side streets are barricaded with rubble or scorched cars. We pass by a huge Spider-Man graffitied on a building on a street filled with garbage and liquid sewage. The fresh colors feel out of place. If only I could be as optimistic as whoever painted it. A dirty white cat runs through a puddle of sewage with a dead rat in its mouth.

"Is that Mezcal?" I ask Rachel.

Rachel looks from the window then at me, her eyes narrowing, not sure if I was trying to send her a coded message.

"Never mind," I say, trying to relax in my seat.

"Rain is coming," Akrami says from the passenger seat. He looks back at Rachel. "You should see my country after rain cleans everything."

"Until the next sandstorm," Rachel says, gazing out the window.

The car hits a pothole. As Akrami fixes the keffiyeh on his head, he says, "Have you seen the real Yemen before?"

"What do you mean by the real Yemen?" she asks, facing him.

"The Yemen where families take turns for meals. Where children who die before they're born are spared. And in the meantime, the West sends us—what do you call them—hillbillies with rockets and liberals with Band-Aids. I don't think people like you can even understand what I'm talking about."

"So, you admit that we're doctors, not spies?"

He grins at her in the mirror as we pass by a beautiful white mosque. Its minaret is askew due to a direct shell strike to its base.

The smell of salt and freedom fills the air. Empty fishing boats appear, cradled by the blue of the sea. The convoy stops in front of the marina, and we get out of the car. The sandstorm has eased.

Two guards at the gate salute Akrami. Time is not on his side. He's in charge now, but soon government forces and other rebel groups will battle for control over the city. War has a way of reinventing itself, Russian-nesting-dolls style.

He orders everyone to stay at the entrance. There are mumbles of disagreement, but all comply. He takes only three of his men with him: two of them carry a stretcher with Karim, still dozing on and off. The other carries Manu's body in its white shroud.

The docks are empty except for one old man who seems to be living there. He's heating some tea on a bed of fire and wood. It wouldn't surprise me if he was sitting in a spot where Marco Polo or Ibn Battuta set foot when they visited this port centuries ago, when it was the center of international trade, or where Al Qaeda operatives walked in their final preparations to attack the U.S.S. *Cole*, some years ago. The old man studies us for a moment before deciding it's none of his business. In front of us is a decent-looking tugboat. It should be enough to get us out of here.

"Here is your boat," Akrami says. "Now, where is my money?"

All the eyes are on me. I take off my right boot. I rotate the heel slowly. It opens to reveal two things inside. One is Max's ring. The other is the Birch Cent.

There's a saying in Egypt: "Life is like a cucumber—one day in your hand, one day in your ass."

The spyware Max and I took from Chief Hobo wasn't that so-phisticated. Actually, it turned out that Max wasn't very tech-savvy at all. I found the same software on bloody eBay. Regardless, I didn't only use the tracking devices to follow Gavin's movements, but also Tina's.

The insecure internet network I managed to lure Gavin to sign up for at the underground squash game allowed me access to his phone. And there it was—the message history of their betrayal. I should have guessed. Tina was the kind of person whose true nature could be seen only in hindsight, like Napoleon, Nasser, or your first love. She was my vision of euphoria—until the hangover kicked in.

I managed to get access to her phone while she was taking one of her two-hour baths, and I put a camera inside her bedroom smoke detector. That was how I recorded the sex tape that Manu saw by mistake.

It was also how I saw that she kept the key for a Network Rail storage unit near Heathrow—which she had thankfully paid for online—in a hidden space under the wooden floorboards below her bed, sitting atop two whiskey-flavored condoms. Next to it was a snub-nose Smith & Wesson .38 with a magenta grip. Say what you will about Tina, the girl had taste. The last time I saw her, I took the key and, after a moment's hesitation, put the box of bullets in my pocket, making sure there weren't any in the cylinder.

The storage unit had only one object in it: a two-hundred-year-old rusty coin known as the Birch Cent.

Less than an hour before I'd gone to meet Gavin, I replaced the coin with a memory stick that contained a copy of her sex tape. At that moment, the cucumber was definitely in my hand.

Safekeeping the coin was Tina's insurance policy, so she could be sure her gangster prince wouldn't run away without her. He didn't seem afraid of the reverse. A mobster like him could get a posh civilian girl like her anytime.

Gavin's intention to double-cross me was the only reason that he got out on bail until his trial, as the absence of the coin at the meet-up strengthened his case. He was free, but not for long. The number I contacted the night of his arrest belonged to his boss—the man Gavin had arrogantly mentioned to me: Jimmy Levine. I sent him recordings of Gavin and Tina's conversations plotting to run away. This was less for revenge and more because I had to choose who the mob's hammer of revenge would fall on: Gavin and Tina or Erkhart. And, well, the sex video I included as a bonus was maybe just for revenge.

Anyway, DI Thompson told me that Tina disappeared without a trace while I was in the hospital. As for Gavin, according to Europol, two weeks after his release on bail he was found on a backstreet in Milan with two bullets in the back of his head. I tried not to feel guilty, but I failed.

I also felt guilty when it came to Erkhart—another one to disappear during my hospital stay. I had no idea where he'd gone, and I wasn't sure I could face him, even if I found him. The man had done nothing but help me, and all I did was give him trouble in return. In this regard, he was my fifth parent.

I offer the coin to Akrami, but he's still focused on the shoe I'm holding. I rotate the heel shut and say, "This coin is—"

"Give me that ring."

"It's not real. It's ... it's ... "

"Don't bother, I know a real diamond when I see it."

I take a step backward. "You don't understand. This ring is—"

I'm stopped by the muzzle of a Klash held by one of his men, pointing at me. Akrami snatches the shoe, rotates the heel, and takes the ring.

He lifts it up to the sun. "But this is not worth millions as you claim. A couple of hundred thousand, tops!" His face is made of stone, but a muscle twitches below his right eye.

"It's the coin," I say. "This cent is worth twenty million dollars. If you sell it for 10 percent of this price, you'll have two million."

His bemusement turns to rage. "Who do you think we are, huh?" he shouts. "You think we're savages who care about an old shilling your grandpa gave you that's worth the price of my Klash?"

"No, I can help you sell it if—"

I see the butt of his Klash coming. I almost dodge it, but he's too quick. It meets my jaw and my knees buckle. He swings another shot at my ear. I fall.

The sky turns red and speeds to fall on me. I shut my eyes.

He keeps hitting me, and his hyenas join in, their shoes sailing into my body. Rachel screams from a faraway place. Surrender comes with the taste of rusty coins in my mouth. When they finally stop, I slowly open my eyes. The sky is still high above, but now it's almost black.

"You half-breed son of a dog. You think you're smart, huh? Here is your rotten shilling." Akrami throws the coin into the ocean with all his might. I try to follow its path, part of me not believing he threw it.

"We don't need your lies. And the joke's on you," he says, waving the diamond ring at me. "I was never going to kill you anyway. We're the new legitimate power here and we are not so savage that we would kill foreigners in our first week in power, even if they are piece-of-shit liars like you."

His fists clench and he paces back and forth like a caged wolf. I remember what Cousin told me about their mock executions.

A couple of seagulls fly away from the fishing boat they were chilling on nearby, preferring to keep their distance from us, this anxious mutant species.

Akrami looks at the ring in his palm and then to me. I'm spent on the ground, so he turns to Rachel. "All you bring us is poverty and violence. But when we have the choice, we choose to let you go. Remember to tell that to your ambassador."

"Go!" He waves his hand toward the boat. "There are no bullets with your names on them today."

Ian Fleming once said that you only live twice: once when you are born and once when you look death in the face. If that's true, then I'm probably more alive than most people on the planet.

The rebels decrease in size, slowly merging back into their world of chaos with their guns and cars. The clouds have dispersed, and the promise of rain is postponed. Only the sun remains the same, promising to light all the roads man dares to walk. Its rays reflect the glint of Max's ring winking at me from Akrami's finger.

Anne and Michael are maneuvering the boat. Possibly the last thing they'll ever do together. Michael is steering, while Anne is next to him, trying to get a signal from the radio. Yehia crouches on his heels next to Karim's stretcher and Manu's body.

Rachel is pressing some tissues to my nose to stem the flow of blood spilling down my face and shirt. Her auburn hair is untidy, and her face is pale, framed by the yellow sun and the blue horizon.

"Did you know that mixing yellow and blue rays makes white?"

"Shut up," she says. "You're bleeding all over yourself."

"Speaking of which, next time I put my life on the line for anyone, remind me that I only have one nose. And one chance to be a millionaire, for that matter."

Yehia comes closer. "What a stroke of luck. Was that true? What you said about that shilling?"

I say nothing. Anne and Michael are managing well. They pull us out to the vast sea. The still water is thick and creased, like it's covered in plastic. Seagulls fly above us, chirping, and I wonder if they are angels in disguise.

I shut my eyes, determined not to look back to the shore. I draw fresh breaths, full of sea salt and blood. The taste of rust lingers on my tongue. I have transcended my physical pain into the peace of numbness. I wish to never leave this boat. Never see land again. This is my liminal space. In between worlds of opposite extremes. In between me and myself.

Rachel hands me more tissues. "Keep pressure on your nose with these. Luke. Do you hear me?"

I take the tissues. I consider asking her to show me the heart line on her palm, to see if it matches mine, but instead I simply smile at her.

"Call me Adam."

THANKS

To Marcia Lynx Qualey for being the most experienced and the kindest person I have met in this cut-throat business.

To Michel Moushabeck for believing in *Guns and Almond Milk*.

To David Klein, Richard Thomas, Awais Khan, Rob Hart, Clare Coombes, Scott Pack, Howard Norman, Sophie Goodfellow, Craig Clevenger, and Dr. Shahed Yousaf, for your support and guidance.

To Livia Brown, Andrea Drury, Francesca Capoluongo and Pamela Paterson, for reading early versions and your encouragements in a time I really needed it.

To my Mom, my Dad and my siblings for all the love, support, and companionship.

Most of all, to my amazing wife, Tanya Brown. This book, and its author, would be pale versions of themselves without you.

ABOUT THE AUTHOR

Mustafa is an Egyptian aid worker, trainer and writer. He studied pharmacy, public health, and management.

Mustafa has over a decade of humanitarian experience in more than a dozen conflict zones around the world—including most Arab Spring countries at the highs, and lows, of their uprisings.